Northern Wake Library
Wake Tech Comm. College
6600 Louisburg Road
Raleigh, NC 27616

NELSON MANDELA

Other titles in the People Who Made History series:

Susan B. Anthony
Napoléon Bonaparte
George W. Bush
Julius Caesar
Cesar Chavez
Cleopatra
Charles Darwin
Charles Dickens
Frederick Douglass
Thomas Edison
Albert Einstein
Anne Frank
Benjamin Franklin
Galileo
Mikhail Gorbachev
Adolf Hitler
John F. Kennedy
Martin Luther King Jr.
Malcolm X
Mao Zedong
Elvis Presley
Oskar Schindler
William Shakespeare
Mark Twain
George Washington

PEOPLE WHO MADE HISTORY

NELSON MANDELA

Leora Maltz, *Book Editor*

Daniel Leone, *President*
Bonnie Szumski, *Publisher*
Scott Barbour, *Managing Editor*
David M. Haugen, *Series Editor*

Wake Tech. Libraries
9101 Fayetteville Road
Raleigh, North Carolina 27603-5696

GREENHAVEN PRESS®

San Diego • Detroit • New York • San Francisco • Cleveland
New Haven, Conn. • Waterville, Maine • London • Munich

© 2004 by Greenhaven Press. Greenhaven Press is an imprint of The Gale Group, Inc., a division of Thomson Learning, Inc.

Greenhaven® and Thomson Learning™ are trademarks used herein under license.

For more information, contact
Greenhaven Press
27500 Drake Rd.
Farmington Hills, MI 48331-3535
Or you can visit our Internet site at http://www.gale.com

ALL RIGHTS RESERVED.
No part of this work covered by the copyright hereon may be reproduced or used in any form or by any means—graphic, electronic, or mechanical, including photocopying, recording, taping, Web distribution or information storage retrieval systems—without the written permission of the publisher.

Every effort has been made to trace the owners of copyrighted material.

Cover credit: © Landov

LIBRARY OF CONGRESS CATALOGING-IN-PUBLICATION DATA

Nelson Mandela / Leora Maltz, book editor.
   p. cm. — (People who made history)
   Includes bibliographical references and index.
   ISBN 0-7377-1603-7 (lib. bdg. : alk. paper) —
   ISBN 0-7377-1604-5 (pbk. : alk. paper)
     1. Mandela, Nelson, 1918– . 2. Presidents—South Africa—Biography. I. Maltz, Leora. II. Series.
DT1974.N44 2004
968.06'5'092—dc21   2003051615
[B]

Printed in the United States of America

Contents

Foreword   8

Nelson Mandela: A Philosophy of Forgiveness   10

Chapter 1: Growing Up in South Africa

1. **A Country Childhood** *by Martin Meredith*   24
   Nelson Mandela spent his childhood in the farmlands of the Transkei, the home of the Xhosa people. There, he grew up listening to stories of his Xhosa ancestors and their resistance to British colonialism in Africa.

2. **Mandela's Education** *by Virginia Curtin Knight*   34
   Nelson Mandela was educated in the royal Thembu court and at a series of British missionary schools. Both his formal and informal education would profoundly influence him throughout his life.

3. **Johannesburg** *by Fatima Meer*   39
   Drawing on Mandela's reminiscences in letters to his family from prison, longtime friend and Mandela biographer Fatima Meer describes the youthful Mandela's arrival in the thriving, enormous city of Johannesburg.

Chapter 2: Mandela the Activist

1. **1948: The Nationalists' Victory and the ANC Response** *by Sheridan Johns and R. Hunt Davis Jr.*   45
   The Nationalist Party won the 1948 elections and proceeded to create the system of racial segregation known as apartheid. Sheridan Johns and R. Hunt Davis Jr. examine the ANC's response to the Nationalists' victory.

2. **The ANC's New Activist Agenda and Mandela's "M-Plan"** *by Stephen M. Davis*   63
   When the apartheid government came into power, Mandela led the African National Congress in a campaign known as the "M-Plan," a strategy to keep the movement alive by moving it underground.

3. **An Emerging Leader** *by Anthony R. DeLuca*   68
   Using the interplay between personality and politics as his focal point, historian Anthony R. DeLuca gives a broad overview of Mandela's life in the years between the landmark Freedom Charter and his final imprisonment.

4. **Life with Him Was Always a Life Without Him**
   by Winnie Mandela   81
   In this account, Winnie Mandela describes meeting Nelson and the tumultuous years leading up to the Treason Trial.

Chapter 3: Trial and Prison

1. **Remembering Rivonia** *by Nelson Mandela*   87
   Mandela describes his arrest and imprisonment for illegally leaving South Africa. Not long into his sentence, police discovered the Umkhonto headquarters at Rivonia, and Mandela was retried in the Rivonia Trial.

2. **The Defense Strategy** *by Joel Joffe*   99
   One of the attorneys who defended Mandela at the Rivonia Trial describes the first day of the case. According to an agreed-upon strategy, the defense opened with Mandela's powerful statement from the prisoners' dock.

3. **Life on Robben Island** *by Mac Maharaj*   110
   In this interview Robben Island prisoner Mac Maharaj, who completed his twelve-year sentence in 1978, described conditions on the island along with Mandela's views on various issues.

4. **Mandela Was an Inspirational Prisoner**
   by Eddie Daniels   121
   Eddie Daniels, who was a prisoner on Robben Island with Mandela for fifteen years, describes how Mandela provided inspiration for him and the other prisoners on many occasions.

5. **A Warden Remembers Robben Island**
   by James Gregory with Bob Graham   126
   In a controversial autobiography by Mandela's jailer on Robben Island, James Gregory shares his perspective on his most famous inmate.

Chapter 4: Leading the Rainbow Nation

1. **Mandela Is Released from Prison**
   by René du Preez   136
   In this eyewitness account of Mandela's release from the Victor Verster prison on February 11, 1990, René du Preez describes how South Africans greeted their long-jailed leader with joy and great excitement.

2. **Mandela's Philosophy of Post-Apartheid Forgiveness** *by Don Boroughs*   141
   After the end of apartheid, Nelson Mandela pressed for all individuals and parties in the new South Africa to forgive one another and move beyond the painful past.

3. Mandela and the AIDS Crisis in South Africa
   by The Economist   147
   Spurred on by President Thabo Mbeki's controversial AIDS
   policies and his general lassitude on the issue, former
   President Nelson Mandela takes on AIDS, the most urgent
   concern of South Africa in the 1990s.

Appendix of Documents	154
Discussion Questions	176
Chronology	179
For Further Research	184
Index	187

Foreword

In the vast and colorful pageant of human history, a handful of individuals stand out. They are the men and women who have come variously to be called "great," "leading," "brilliant," "pivotal," or "infamous" because they and their deeds forever changed their own society or the world as a whole. Some were political or military leaders—kings, queens, presidents, generals, and the like—whose policies, conquests, or innovations reshaped the maps and futures of countries and entire continents. Among those falling into this category were the formidable Roman statesman/general Julius Caesar, who extended Rome's power into Gaul (what is now France); Caesar's lover and ally, the notorious Egyptian queen Cleopatra, who challenged the strongest male rulers of her day; and England's stalwart Queen Elizabeth I, whose defeat of the mighty Spanish Armada saved England from subjugation.

Some of history's other movers and shakers were scientists or other thinkers whose ideas and discoveries altered the way people conduct their everyday lives or view themselves and their place in nature. The electric light and other remarkable inventions of Thomas Edison, for example, revolutionized almost every aspect of home-life and the workplace; and the theories of naturalist Charles Darwin lit the way for biologists and other scientists in their ongoing efforts to understand the origins of living things, including human beings.

Still other people who made history were religious leaders and social reformers. The struggles of the Arabic prophet Muhammad more than a thousand years ago led to the establishment of one of the world's great religions—Islam; and the efforts and personal sacrifices of an American reverend named Martin Luther King Jr. brought about major improvements in race relations and the justice system in the United States.

Each anthology in the People Who Made History series begins with an introductory essay that provides a general overview of the individual's life, times, and contributions. The group of essays that follow are chosen for their accessibility to a young adult audience and carefully edited in consideration of the reading and comprehension levels of that audience. Some of the essays are by noted historians, professors, and other experts. Others are excerpts from contemporary writings by or about the pivotal individual in question. To aid the reader in choosing the material of immediate interest or need, an annotated table of contents summarizes the article's main themes and insights.

Each volume also contains extensive research tools, including a collection of excerpts from primary source documents pertaining to the individual under discussion. The volumes are rounded out with an extensive bibliography and a comprehensive index.

Plutarch, the renowned first-century Greek biographer and moralist, crystallized the idea behind Greenhaven's People Who Made History when he said, "To be ignorant of the lives of the most celebrated men of past ages is to continue in a state of childhood all our days." Indeed, since it is people who make history, every modern nation, organization, institution, invention, artifact, and idea is the result of the diligent efforts of one or more individuals, living or dead; and it is therefore impossible to understand how the world we live in came to be without examining the contributions of these individuals.

NELSON MANDELA: A PHILOSOPHY OF FORGIVENESS

When Nelson Mandela was released from prison in 1990, he immediately spoke of his desire for peace in South Africa and emphasized the need for reconciliation among all racial and cultural groups. Imprisoned in 1962 for five years, and then resentenced in 1964 to a life term after being convicted of sabotage, Mandela had spent most of his adult life on Robben Island, confined under appalling conditions and forced to do mindless and backbreaking labor. Like his fellow inmates Walter Sisulu, Mac Maharaj, and others convicted of crimes against the apartheid government of South Africa, Mandela's eyesight had been irreparably damaged by the blinding sunlight that reflected off the chalky white faces of the limestone quarry where he broke rocks by day. At times Mandela and his fellow prisoners were made to stand knee-deep in seawater in midwinter collecting seaweed from the shore. Mandela had to beg for years for a decent blanket to offer some protection against the cold Atlantic winter, and his diet consisted of an unending stream of corn porridge. These hardships and deprivations probably contributed to the high blood pressure and tuberculosis he suffered in his sixties.

Mandela's long and arduous imprisonment included intellectual and emotional deprivation as well. He was denied newspapers and books and was allowed to exchange only a few letters per year with loved ones. When his mother died, Mandela was refused permission to return home to bury her, though security arrangements could easily have been made. When his twenty-five-year-old son Thembi was tragically killed in a car accident in the Transkei region in July 1969, emergency leave was likewise denied. Imprisoned when his daughters Zenani and Zindzi were infants, he did not see Zindzi until she was fifteen and had a contact visit with Zenani only after her marriage in the late 1970s. He and his wife Winnie were allowed only two half-hour visits per year during which they were monitored and separated by glass. Only in 1981 were they allowed a contact visit. Winnie also suffered her own trials of police harassment: She was repeatedly banned from political events, exiled from her home, placed under house arrest, and intermittently jailed over several decades.

THERE WAS A MIDDLE GROUND

Even those who were ignorant of the conditions of his imprisonment expected the seventy-one-year-old man who walked through the prison gates to be aged and bitter, beaten and broken. White South Africans in particular were concerned that this man, whom the South African government had for decades described as a dangerous terrorist, would incite retribution for banning the African National Congress (ANC) and imprisoning himself and many others. They were shocked when, in the first speech Mandela made on the evening of his release from prison, he immediately sought to assuage white fears by speaking of the need to forgive past wrongs. South Africans could barely believe Mandela's almost saintly ability to forgive his enemies and to rise above his personal grievances. Speaking to the international press the day following his release, Mandela stated that there was a middle ground between white fears and black hopes and that the ANC would find it. He reached out to his former captors with conciliatory words: "Whites are fellow South Africans and we want them to feel safe and to know that we appreciate the contribution that they have made towards the development of this country," adding that "any man or woman who abandons apartheid will be embraced in our struggle for a democratic, non-racial South Africa."[1]

The virtues of forgiveness, tolerance, and reconciliation that Mandela became famous for espousing after his release in 1990 were in fact attributes that Mandela had possessed throughout his political career. Although the South African government had painted him as a violent terrorist, and cited his 1961 conviction for sabotage as proof, Mandela's advocacy of armed struggle was a position he resorted to only in the face of the appalling racism, brutal violence, and stolid intractability of the apartheid regime.

If Mandela had been the world's most famous prisoner before 1990, after his release he became one of its most important and respected leaders. Feted across continents, he was awarded numerous honorary degrees from various universities, and shared the Nobel Peace Prize with South African president F.W. de Klerk in 1993. In addresses to international audiences on every such occasion, as in his speeches to the South African people, Mandela insistently called for tolerance and reconciliation, for the renunciation of violence by all parties, and for forgiveness of the evils of apartheid. What seemed to truly capture people's admiration was his optimism for future cooperation unfettered by the sins of the past. Rory Steyn, a white South African former member of the apartheid-era police force before serving as Mandela's presidential bodyguard, explained how he came to change his position from that of an apartheid supporter to a loyal Mandela devotee. Listening to Mandela's speeches time and again as he accompanied him on his hectic schedule through the country, Steyn commented: "Relentlessly, Mandela would repeat his offer of reconciliation: 'Let's forget the past and together create a better future for all South Africans.'"[2] Through his unflagging personal example of humility and respect, Mandela not only represented the triumph of the human spirit over adversity, but many believed that through his philosophy of forgiveness and peace, he also miraculously saved South Africa from the bloody revolution that most had thought would inevitably accompany the rise of a new government.

For black South Africans, of course, Mandela's release symbolized the apex of their long struggle against the separatist apartheid government, as well as a sign of their own impending liberation. But for black South Africans who had considered Mandela their leader for decades, Mandela's tolerance and forgiveness were elements of his personality they knew well already. These moderate ideals were not a result of mellow old age, but merely a continuation of the same philosophy of pragmatism and coexistence that Mandela had fought for from the mid-1940s up until the time of his imprisonment in the early 1960s. Indeed, Mandela had long embodied ideals of nonracialism and coexistence: It had been the abject refusal of the Nationalist South African government to even entertain Mandela's vision, or to engage in any sort of dialogue, that had finally forced Mandela and the ANC to advocate armed struggle.

Why, then, if Mandela was such a moderate and wise

leader, did the South African government imprison him in the first place, and why was world outrage not brought to bear against his imprisonment? In Mandela's view, black liberation—the claim to the basic human rights to vote, to live where one pleased, to own land in the country of one's birth, to earn a decent wage, and to be protected from indefinite imprisonment without a trial—had never been incompatible with the continued freedoms and security of the white population. The ANC had long embraced a policy of nonracialism, so many of its top leaders were of Indian and white descent, and the organization counted Jews, Muslims, Christians, and Hindus among its members. While some black political organizations sought to drive the whites into the sea, Mandela and the ANC proclaimed, "South Africa belongs to all who live in it, black and white."[3] These words formed the opening phrase of the Freedom Charter that Mandela and other members of the ANC Youth League drafted and adopted in 1955. This phrase was repeated nearly forty years later as the opening line of the new South African transitional constitution drafted by the ANC in 1993.

THE AFRICAN NATIONAL CONGRESS

Soon after arriving in Johannesburg in 1941 from the Eastern Cape where he had grown up, Mandela became involved in the African National Congress (ANC), which had been founded in 1912 to fight for the declining rights of black South Africans. Led mainly by intellectuals, the ANC focused on legal and constitutional change as a means of obtaining greater liberties for blacks. At the time, few white South Africans—especially in official capacities—paid attention to ANC demands. Mandela quickly became a key member of the ANC and was instrumental in founding a new, more activist wing of the group, known as the ANC Youth League, in 1944. In his autobiography, Mandela wrote of this time:

> I cannot pinpoint a moment when I became politicized, when I knew that I would spend my life in the liberation struggle. To be an African in South Africa means that one is politicized from the moment of one's birth, whether one acknowledges it or not. An African child is born in an Africans Only hospital, taken home in an Africans Only bus, lives in an Africans Only area, and attends Africans Only school, if he attends school at all.
>
> When he grows up, he can hold Africans Only jobs, rent a house in an Africans Only township, ride Africans Only

trains, and be stopped at any time of day or night to produce a pass, failing which he will be arrested and thrown in jail. His life is circumscribed by racist laws and regulations that cripple his growth, dim his potential, and stunt his life. . . .

I had no epiphany, no singular revelation, no moment of truth, but a steady accumulation of a thousand slights, a thousand indignities, a thousand unremembered moments, produced in me an anger, a rebelliousness, a desire to fight the system that imprisoned my people. There was no particular day on which I said, From henceforth I will devote myself to the liberation of my people; instead, I simply found myself doing so, and could not do otherwise.[4]

Historian Stephen Davis has argued that a new generation of leaders such as Nelson Mandela, Walter Sisulu, and others not only instituted fundamental changes in the ANC, but were also responsible for the seminal shifts in ANC policies during the 1940s and early 1950s. For it was in these years that the ANC was transformed from a small, largely ineffectual organization into a massive, popular resistance movement. The ANC dramatically expanded its membership, changed its tactics from striving for constitutional change to working closely with trade unions, and began to support dramatic and widespread strikes.

Passive Resistance

These policy shifts within the ANC took place against the turbulent backdrop of World War II (in which South Africa fought on the Allied side) and the economic instability that followed. As did African Americans in the United States, black South Africans who had fought for their country had hoped to be rewarded with a minimum of legal rights after the war, but the more liberal white political forces in South Africa were narrowly defeated in the 1948 election by the Afrikaans-dominated National Party (known as the Nats). Unlike in the United States, where the postwar era of the 1950s ushered in a series of important reforms, in South Africa precisely the opposite happened: The Nats (who would rule without interruption until 1994) began to implement their segregationist policies of apartheid soon after coming to power. The postwar political climate in South Africa rapidly declined after 1948 as the Nats promulgated a series of wide-ranging and restrictive laws, including the Group Areas Act, which restricted different races to separate settlement areas; the Immorality Act, which prohibited sexual relations between

races; and the Population Registration Act, which classified all South Africans by race, making race the most important single determinant of identity. The deterioration of the political climate only strengthened ANC resistance to apartheid, and along with a new generation of ANC leaders, led to important grassroots growth of the ANC after 1948.

An additional important influence on ANC tactics in the late 1940s and early 1950s was Mohandas Gandhi's philosophy of nonviolent protest, known as satyagraha (from *satya*, meaning love, and *agraha*, meaning firmness). In 1913 Gandhi (then living in Durban, Natal) had led a legendary march of Indians from Natal to the Transvaal to protest the treatment of Indians in South Africa. Continuing this legacy of resistance, in 1946 the Indian Congress had implemented a massive two-year protest in Natal to oppose new, repressive laws. People from all walks of life suspended their livelihoods to participate in rallies, protests, and picketing. Two thousand citizens were jailed, and the protest established a model of widespread, "applied" politics over and above the intellectual resistance effected by speeches and meetings.

THE DEFIANCE CAMPAIGN OF 1952

Inspired by this recent demonstration of satyagraha in Natal, Mandela, with Yusuf Cachalia as his deputy, organized a massive campaign of peaceful resistance against the unjust treatment of blacks. Launched on June 26, 1952, the so-called Defiance Campaign involved a nonviolent refusal to comply with various apartheid laws, which resulted in the arrest and jailing of eighty-four hundred volunteers who took part.

The government reacted to this protest by clamping down even more harshly on political dissidents (notably Mandela and Sisulu), banning the Communist Party, breaking up resistance meetings, and arresting hundreds of civilians. Fearing that it would only be a matter of time before the ANC, like the Communist Party, was declared illegal, Mandela sought to devise a scheme for the survival of the ANC as an underground organization. The "Mandela-Plan," or "M-Plan" as it came to be known, called for the division of the national organization into a network of small units, or cells, that could operate independently on the local level to keep resistance alive within the black communities. ANC member Govan Mbeki, reflecting on the implementation of the M-Plan, comments: "The government, by its repressive laws, kept pushing us deeper and deeper underground, honing our recruitment and actions, making us better and better."[5]

Throughout the 1950s, apartheid became more and more entrenched, and the South African government less and less tolerant of any sort of political opposition. In 1956 over a hundred "dissidents," including Mandela, were arrested and tried for treason in a long and drawn-out trial that continued until 1961, at which time all were acquitted for lack of evidence.

THE QUEST FOR POLITICAL DIALOGUE

Soon after his acquittal in the Treason Trial on March 29, 1961, Mandela stepped up his requests to speak with the various ruling political parties. In April 1961 he wrote to Prime Minister H.F. Verwoerd and stated his desire for a national convention of all South African political parties. He received no reply. In a subsequent letter, this time to the leader of the United Party (the official opposition to the Nationalists) in early May of that year, Mandela again stressed the need for a convention of all South African political parties. Biographer Mary Benson reports Mandela's blunt terms: "Talk it out or shoot it out. . . . It is still not too late. . . . A call for a National Convention from you could well be the turning point in our country's history."[6] But the United Party leader also did not respond.

Mandela's next move was to throw his energy into planning a large workers strike that would begin May 29, 1961, and last for three days. Just prior to the strike date, police raids intensified and ANC leaders and organizers, along with ten thousand African civilians were arrested. At the same time, the government-controlled newspapers reported the discovery of a "plot" by all nonwhites to "invade" the white cities on May 29, while failing to report Mandela's repeated denials of this absurd plan. On the day of the strike, the army, bolstered by hundreds of white civilians enlisted to deal with this "emergency," was present in the black townships in full force: Armored cars patrolled the streets, helicopters circled overhead, and police vans drove through the black neighborhoods broadcasting warnings that all who heeded the stay-away-from-work mandate would be fired from their jobs and expelled from their homes.

The strike was not a complete success. Although hundreds of thousands of township residents supported the strike at great personal risk, more were terrified into submission by the government's scare tactics. Mandela, meeting with journalists in secret, commented, "If the government reaction is to crush by naked force our non-violent struggle, we will have to reconsider our tactics. In my mind we are closing a chapter on this question of a non-violent policy."[7]

ABANDONING PASSIVE RESISTANCE

In June 1961 as secretary of the National Action Council of South Africa, and speaking in the wake of the general strike, Mandela asked, "Is it politically correct to continue preaching peace and non-violence when dealing with a government whose barbaric practices have brought so much suffering and misery to Africans?"[8] Increasingly, Mandela and his comrades were forced to conclude that their tactics of nonviolence were patently ineffective. Biographer Charlene Smith comments, "While satyagraha may have been effective against a government with a conscience, such as the British Empire, which could be moved by the suffering of those who protested injustice, it was ineffective against the barbarity of apartheid's governors."[9] This sad realization finally provoked Mandela to reject the Gandhian policies of nonviolent resistance to which he had adhered for nearly twenty years. After nearly two decades, these tactics seemed to have made no dent in apartheid's armor, and instead of improving conditions for the black man in South Africa, if anything, the condition and prospects of the black South African had only further declined.

In 1961 Mandela reached the decision to shift ANC policy from that of pacifism to one of limited violence. He founded a branch of the ANC called Umkhonto we Sizwe, or Spear of the Nation, to carry out what it considered necessary attacks. From the outset, and throughout its tenure, Umkhonto (often abbreviated MK) targeted not individuals but rather government installations such as power plants and railroad lines in order to disrupt the daily functioning of the country. The strategy was to try to force the government into dialogue with the ANC. If Umkhonto could undermine the economic stability of the country, foreign investors would be scared off, resulting in foreign disinvestment, loss of business, and a devaluation of the currency. That, the ANC assumed, would hit the white man where it hurt—in his pocketbook.

That December, after self-taught crash courses in explosives, Umkhonto members struck, destroying targets in Johannesburg, Port Elizabeth, and Durban. The targets were symbolic, and as planned, there was no civilian loss of life. The only fatality was a member of the MK explosives team. The leadership chose December 16, which had traditionally been the date of the annual ANC conference, as the day upon which to launch its new policy, highlighting its dramatic shift from talk to action. For the Nationalist government, December 16 had further significance. It was the date on which black armies were defeated by the white Afrikaner invaders during the "Great Trek" of the mid-nineteenth century. The Great Trek was a mass migration of Afrikaners (farmers of Dutch and German descent known as Boers) into the interior of South Africa between the 1840s and the 1860s. Seeking to remove themselves from the control of the British, who were ruling the southern area of the Cape, the Boers departed for the interior, waging war and eventually destroying whatever indigenous African cultures they encountered in their quest for land. December 16 had thus been commemorated annually since that time as the anniversary of Afrikaner victory.

Immediately following the first attack, the manifesto of Umkhonto we Sizwe was distributed, announcing to all:

> Umkhonto we Sizwe will carry on the struggle by new methods. ... We of Umkhonto have always sought—as the liberation movement has sought—to achieve liberation without bloodshed and civil clash. We hope, even at this late hour, that our first actions will awaken everyone to a realization of the disastrous situation to which the Nationalist policy is leading. ... The time comes in the life of any nation when there remain only two choices: submit or fight. That time has now come to South Africa. We shall not submit and we have no choice but to hit back by all means within our power in defence of our people, our future, our freedom.

The manifesto went on to clearly articulate why Umkhonto had resorted to violence, citing the government's violent response to the ANC tactics of peaceful protest. Indeed, it seemed that the ANC would have to reverse its fifty-year-old policy of negotiation and nonviolence and resort to the only language that the apartheid government understood—violence. The Umkhonto leaflet continued:

> The government has interpreted the peacefulness of the movement as a weakness; the people's non-violent policies have been taken as a green light for a new government violence. ... We are striking out along a new road for the liberation of the people. ... Umkhonto we Sizwe will be at the front line of the people's defence. It will be the fighting arm of the people against the government and its policies of race oppression.[10]

THE RIVONIA TRIAL

Several years later, Mandela explained why he had finally turned to the use of violence:

> Without violence there would be no way open to the African people to succeed in their struggle against the principles of white supremacy. ... We were placed in a position in which we had either to accept a permanent state of inferiority, or to defy the government. We chose to defy the law. I did not plan it in a spirit of recklessness, nor because I have any love of violence. I planned it as a result of calm and sober assessment of the political situation that has arisen after many years of tyranny, exploitation and oppression of my people by whites.[11]

Although this turn toward violence was a limited and carefully considered decision, made perhaps in desperation, it was a decision that would enable the government to sentence Mandela to life imprisonment. Mandela had been arrested in 1962 for illegally leaving the country. While serving a five-year term of imprisonment, new information was found, linking him to Umkhonto; he was tried again in 1964 for treason. During his trial, Mandela never sought to deny his involvement as the leader of Umkhonto but merely sought to explain the factors that led to his decision to employ violence. He argued that faced with a regime as intractable as the Nationalists, there were no other options available to the ANC leadership at the time.

In any event, the government evidence discovered at Liliesleaf, the farmhouse in Rivonia outside Johannesburg that Umkhonto had been using as its headquarters for two years, was extremely incriminating. In addition to maps marking out possible targets for attack, it also contained a plan for an armed revolution aimed at seizing control of the government. Apparently, Mandela had thought this plan one member's harebrained scheme which he had never seconded; nonetheless, as the leader of Umkhonto he was held legally responsible for all the materials recovered at Liliesleaf. On the basis of this evidence of violent plans for terrorist attacks within South Africa Mandela was sentenced to life imprisonment on Robben Island, along with the others captured during the police raid at Rivonia, including Walter Sisulu, Ahmed Kathrada, and Rusty Bernstein.

While it may seem difficult to reconcile the idea of Mandela as the founder of Umkhonto with the tolerance and forgiveness he espoused after 1991, Mandela himself only turned to violence as a last resort, since twenty years of nonviolence had failed to advance the black man's cause in South Africa. Despite Mandela's overwhelming desire for peaceful coexistence, he is also a man of strong principles. Having decided that the violence seemed to be the only way to compel the government to engage in talks with the ANC, he refused to disavow violence until his requests were met.

A Battle of Wills

In the ensuing decades, the white leadership portrayed Mandela as a violent terrorist who was jailed because he was intent on forcefully taking over the South African government. At the same time, photographs and articles about Mandela, along with his own writings, were banned, making the apartheid government's version of "Mandela the terrorist" the only one available to the South African public. From the early 1980s, foreign governments and organizations took up a call for Mandela's release. This strong international pressure, along with mass disinvestment in South African businesses, eventually forced the South African government to offer Mandela his freedom if he agreed to stringent conditions, such as accepting the black homeland territories as independent states or renouncing violence. Mandela always refused, making it absolutely clear that he would renounce armed struggle only when the government agreed to enter into negotiations about a multiracial government in South Africa. Nationalist presidents such as P.W. Botha made much of Mandela's so-called refusal to renounce violence and justified his imprisonment as the government's refusal to negotiate with terrorists. But Mandela made it clear that his position had not changed because nothing in South Africa had changed. He repeatedly stressed that he would eagerly abandon the armed struggle if his requests for negotiations were met.

As international condemnation of apartheid grew, the South African government faced intensifying economic boycotts and other political repercussions. Finally, President F.W. de Klerk began to dismantle the segregationist system that had divided the country for so long. He lifted the ban on the ANC and ordered the release of Nelson Mandela in February 1990. Soon after his release, his requests met, Mandela announced the ANC's suspension of the armed struggle.

FREE AT LAST

Finally a free man, acknowledged by the South African government as the leader of the ANC, and about to enter into talks with then-President de Klerk, Mandela clearly and unequivocally began to speak of the need for blacks to forgive the perpetrators of apartheid. Retribution, he insisted, would be unproductive, resulting only in the needless loss of life on both sides. Leading by example, Mandela embarked specifically on a program of personal reconciliation with the administration that had jailed him for twenty-seven years, and with Afrikaner culture in general. In 1993 Mandela and de Klerk jointly were awarded the Nobel Peace Prize for their work in ending racial separation in South Africa.

In 1994 the ANC won an electoral majority in the country's first free elections, and Mandela was elected the new South African president. During his tenure as president, Mandela continued to speak of racial unity. For his part, he publicly embraced rugby, the national sport of white South Africa, donning the colors of the Springbok team in June 1995. Time and again he held out his hand in friendship to South Africans of all races and creeds. He also adopted a phrase coined by antiapartheid leader Archbishop Desmond Tutu, describing the new South Africa as the "rainbow nation." Mandela steered the rainbow nation through its first few years, focusing his attention not only on racial divisiveness but on health care, women's rights, and other issues that hampered the progress of the nation as a whole. He retired from his position in 1999, leaving South Africa to move forward into the twenty-first century as a nation radically different from the one in which he had grown up.

NOTES

1. Nelson Mandela, *Long Walk to Freedom: The Autobiography of Nelson Mandela.* Boston: Little, Brown, 1994, p. 569.
2. Debora Patta, *One Step Behind Mandela: The Story of Rory Steyn, Nelson Mandela's Chief Bodyguard, as Told to Debora Patta.* Rivonia, South Africa: Zebra, 2000, p. 9.
3. ANC Freedom Charter of 1955, www.anc.org.za.
4. Mandela, *Long Walk to Freedom*, p. 96.
5. Quoted in Charlene Smith, *Mandela.* Cape Town, South Africa: Struik, 1999, p. 28.
6. Quoted in Mary Benson, *Nelson Mandela: The Man and the Movement.* New York: Norton, 1994, p. 101.
7. Quoted in Barry Denenberg, *Nelson Mandela.* New York: Scholastic, 1991, p. 74.
8. Quoted in Smith, *Mandela*, p. 95.
9. Smith, *Mandela*, p. 19.
10. Quoted in David Mermelstein, ed., *The Anti-Apartheid Reader: The Struggle Against White Racist Rule in South Africa.* New York: Grove, 1987, pp. 218–20.
11. Quoted in Mary Benson, ed., *The Sun Will Rise: Statements from the Dock by Southern African Prisoners.* London: International Defence and Aid Fund for Southern Africa, 1979, p. 11.

CHAPTER 1

GROWING UP IN SOUTH AFRICA

NELSON MANDELA

A Country Childhood

Martin Meredith

The following piece by biographer Martin Meredith traces Mandela's early years growing up in the Transkei region of South Africa during the 1920s. Meredith situates Mandela's life within the context of a long history of Xhosa resistance to white colonial domination, which was responsible for progressively dispossessing the Xhosa of their land, livelihood, and political rights. Meredith explains how Mandela's own father, Henry Gadla, a headman of his village, refused to concede to British colonial infringement on traditional monarchical and bureaucratic institutions, and suffered heavy personal losses as a result.

Years after his father had died, while an adolescent at the regent's court at Mqhekezweni, Mandela would listen to other stories of resistance by the great Xhosa leaders, many of whom were subsequently exiled and incarcerated on infamous Robben Island where Mandela himself was to spend so many years.

Mandela was born in the simple surroundings of a peasant village on the banks of the Mbashe river in Thembuland. But for his royal connections, his childhood would have been no different from those of many others there. His great-grandfather Ngubengcuka, however, was a Thembu king, renowned for his skill in bringing stability to diverse Thembu clans [the Thembu are a subclan of the Xhosa people] in the early nineteenth century. And although Mandela was descended from only a minor branch of the dynasty—the Left-hand House—his link with the Thembu royal family was to have a marked influence on both his character and his fortunes.

His father, Gadla Henry Mphakanyiswa, was the village headman at Mvezo. A tall, respected figure, he presided over local ceremonies and officiated at traditional rites for such occasions as births, marriages, funerals, harvests and initia-

---

Martin Meredith, *Nelson Mandela: A Biography*. London: Hamish Hamilton, 1997. Copyright © 1997 by Martin Meredith. All rights reserved. Reproduced by permission of Penguin Books, Ltd.

tion ceremonies. Like most of his generation, he had had no formal education; he could not read or write. But he had a keen sense of history and was valued as a counsellor to the royal family. He was also wealthy enough at one time to afford four wives and sired in all thirteen children.

Mandela's mother, Nosekeni Nkedama, was the third of Gadla's wives. She bore four children, the eldest of whom, Mandela, was her only son but the youngest of Gadla's four sons. Like Gadla, she could neither read nor write. While Gadla adhered to the traditional Qaba faith, involving the worship of ancestral spirits, Nosekeni became a devout Christian, taking the name of Fanny.

TROUBLEMAKER

The Xhosa name given to Mandela at his birth on 18 July 1918 was Rolihlahla, which meant literally 'pulling the branch of a tree', but more colloquially 'troublemaker'. There were friends and relatives who later ascribed to his Xhosa name the troubles he would encounter. But the name by which he became popularly known was an English one, Nelson, given to him by an African teacher on the first day he attended school. For that, there was no ready explanation, only surmise that it was taken from the famous English admiral.

It was shortly after he was born that the Mandela household itself encountered serious trouble. Gadla's position as headman was dependent not only upon tribal lineage but upon the approval of white officials in the Cape colonial administration. After its annexation by Britain in 1885, Thembuland had come under the control of colonial magistrates who maintained a system of indirect rule through village headmen appointed to keep order among the local population as well as to represent their interests. The same system remained in place when Thembuland became part of the Union of South Africa, established in 1910, eight years before Mandela was born.

Well known for his stubbornness, Gadla fell into a minor dispute over cattle with the local magistrate and refused to answer a summons to appear before him. Gadla took the view that the matter was of tribal concern and not part of the magistrate's jurisdiction. He was dismissed for insubordination, losing not only his government stipend, but most of his cattle and his land, and the revenue that went with them. Facing penury, he sent Nosekeni and her young son to

Qunu, a village to the north of Mvezo, about twenty miles from the town of Umtata, where her family could help support her. It was there that Mandela spent his boyhood.

Life at Qunu

The landscape around Qunu—undulating hills, clear streams and lush pastures grazed by cattle, sheep and goats—made an indelible impression on Mandela. Qunu was the place where he felt his real roots lay. It was a settlement of beehive-shaped huts in a narrow valley where life continued much as it had done for generations past. The population there, numbering no more than a few hundred, consisted predominantly of 'red' people, who dyed their blankets and clothes with red ochre, a colour said to be beloved by ancestral spirits and the colour of their faith. There were few Christians in Qunu and those that there were stood out because of the Western-style clothes they wore.

The Mandela homestead, like most others in Qunu, was simple. Their beehive huts—a cluster of three—were built without windows or chimneys. The floors were made of crusted earth taken from anthills and kept smooth with layers of fresh cow dung. There was no furniture, in the Western sense. Everyone slept on mats, without pillows, resting their heads on their arms. Smoke from the fire filtered through the grass roof. There was no opening other than a low doorway. Their diet was also simple, mainly maize, sorghum, beans and pumpkins grown in fields outside the village and *amasi*, fermented milk stored in calabashes. Only a few wealthy families could afford luxuries like tea, coffee and sugar, bought from the local store.

Having four wives, each living in her own kraal several miles apart, Gadla visited them in turn, spending perhaps one week a month with each one. With his children, he was a strict disciplinarian. Complete obedience was expected, in accordance with Thembu tradition; questions were rarely tolerated. The life that Mandela led as a child was governed by strict codes of custom and taboo, guiding him through each state of adolescence. The number of taboos restricting the course of daily life for men, boys, girls and especially married women, ran into hundreds. Most were associated with sex, with key passages of life and with food. All were held in superstitious awe. Any transgression could incur the wrath of ancestral spirits, which was to be avoided at all costs.

Along with tribal discipline came the support of an extended family. The Mandela household in Qunu was often full of relatives, taking as much interest in the Mandela children as in their own. In Thembu tradition, as with many other African tribes, uncles and aunts were as responsible for the welfare of children as the children's own parents and were referred to as 'little fathers' and 'little mothers'. The family circle in which Mandela grew up was thus an affectionate one. Even though he remembered his father mainly for his stern countenance, Mandela tried to emulate him by rubbing white ash into his hair in imitation of the tuft of white hair above Gadla's forehead. Like Gadla, he had the distinctive facial features of the Madiba clan, high cheekbones and slanting eyes.

From the age of five, Mandela was set to work as a herdboy, looking after sheep and calves and learning the central role that cattle played in Thembu society. Cattle were not only a source of meat and milk but the main medium of exchange and the measure of a tribesman's wealth. As the price of a bride was paid in cattle, without cattle there could be no marriage. Moreover, the principal means of propitiating ancestral spirits were through the sacrifice of cattle. Significant events like funerals were marked by their slaughter.

Much of Mandela's time was also spent in the open veld in the company of members of his own age group, stick-throwing and fighting, gathering wild honey and fruits, trapping birds and small animals that could be roasted, and swimming in the cold streams—the normal pursuits of young Thembu boys.

THE MFENGU CHRISTIANS

What first set him on a different course was the influence of two villagers known as Mfengu. The Mfengu had arrived in Thembuland and neighbouring Xhosaland as refugees fleeing southwards from a series of wars and upheavals called the *mfecane* which accompanied the rise of the Zulu kingdom in the 1820s. Drawn from a number of different clans among the northern Nguni, the refugees, some moving in scattered bands, others in larger groups, were given the name of Mfengu to describe their position, as suppliants and were often treated with contempt and animosity. Lacking land and cattle, many formed a servant class for the Thembu and their Xhosa neighbours. But they were also more readily adaptable to serving the interests of white colonists. Mfengu levies fought as combatants on the colonial side in four frontier wars in the Cape Colony, helping to inflict defeats on the Xhosa. They were rewarded with land and cattle. A large area of what had been Xhosa territory was designated as Fingoland. They were also among the first to take advantage of Christian missionary education, acquiring new skills and finding employment as teachers, clerks, policemen and court officials.

Mandela's father did not share the common prejudice against Mfengu. Among his friends were two Mfengu brothers, George and Ben Mbekela, both Christian, one a retired teacher, the other a police sergeant. It was their suggestion that Mandela should be baptized and sent to the local mission-run school. Gadla, recognizing that an education was the only advancement available for his youngest son, accepted the idea.

At the age of seven, Mandela went to the one-room school in Qunu, crossing the boundary between 'red' people and 'school' people. To mark the occasion, Gadla presented him with a pair of his old trousers, cut off at the knee and fastened around his waist with a piece of string. Hitherto, the only clothing that Mandela had worn had been a blanket, wrapped around one shoulder and pinned at the waist. 'I must have been a comical sight,' he wrote in his autobiography, 'but I have never owned a suit I was prouder to wear than my father's cut-off trousers.'

Two years later, in the Mandela household in Qunu, Gadla died, leaving Nosekeni without the means to continue her son's education. The event changed Mandela's life dramatically. Because of his family ties to the Thembu royal house and to the Madiba clan dating back to an eighteenth-century Thembu chief, the young Mandela was taken up as a ward by Chief Jongintaba Dalindyebo, the acting regent of the Thembu people. Accompanied by his mother, he left the simple idyll of Qunu, walking across the hills westwards to Mqhekezweni, the provisional capital of Thembuland, where Jongintaba maintained his Great Place, and entered a new world.

MANDELA ARRIVES AT THE GREAT PLACE

The royal residence, consisting of two large rectangular houses with corrugated-iron roofs surrounded by seven thatched rondavels [Afrikaans word meaning round, thatched huts] all washed in white lime, was more impressive than anything the young Mandela had ever seen. As he approached, Jongintaba himself arrived in a Ford V8, to be greeted by a group of tribal elders who had been waiting in the shade of eucalyptus trees with the traditional salute, *'Bayete, Jongintaba!'*—'Hail, Jongintaba!'

In accordance with tribal custom, Mandela was accepted by Jongintaba into the Great Place as if he were his own child. He shared a rondavel with his only son, Justice, wore the same kind of clothes and was subject to the same parental discipline. The regent's wife, NoEngland, treated him with equal affection and, once his own mother had returned to Qunu, soon filled her place. Life at Mqhekezweni was too full of excitement for Mandela to miss for long the world he had loved at Qunu. Even the chores seemed more enjoyable. He took particular pride in ironing the creases in the trousers of Jongintaba's suits.

What impressed him above all was the influence of the chieftaincy. Under colonial rule, hereditary chiefs had retained a wide range of powers and functions. They continued to conduct traditional court cases, to collect tributary fees and dues, and to exercise considerable authority over the distribution of land. They constituted a central part of the colonial administrative system, held in high esteem by white officials, while enjoying at the same time the traditional support of the local population.

Watching at close quarters the way in which Jongintaba exercised his power as regent, Mandela became absorbed by the workings of the chieftaincy. At tribal meetings at the Great Place, when high-ranking councillors gathered to discuss both local and national issues, he observed how Jongintaba would take care to hear all opinions, listening in silence to whatever criticism was made, even of himself, before making a summary of what had been said and endeavouring to find a consensus of views. It was a style of leadership which made a profound impression upon him. He learned too of the proceedings of the traditional courts at Mqhekezweni, where chiefs and headmen from surrounding districts met to settle disputes and judge cases.

It was from these tribal elders, sitting around the fireside at night, that Mandela first heard stories of Robben Island. It was mentioned often by them when recounting the long history of conflict between white colonists and Xhosa-speaking tribes in the turbulent eastern frontier region of the Cape Colony during the nineteenth century. The name given to it in the Xhosa language was Esiqithini, a word which quite simply meant 'on the island'. Everybody knew which island was referred to and what it meant. For the Xhosa, it was a place of banishment and death.

XHOSA RESISTANCE AND ROBBEN ISLAND

The first Xhosa leader whom the whites sent to Robben Island was a warrior-prophet called Makana; he was also known by the name of Nxele, meaning "the left-handed." In 1819, in retaliation for a raid by colonial troops into Xhosa territory, Makana had led an army of 10,000 men against the British military outpost at Grahamstown, intending 'to chase the white men from the earth and drive them into the sea'. The attack, in broad daylight, failed. Four months later, after British forces had laid waste to a vast stretch of Xhosa territory, Makana gave himself up at a military camp, hoping to stop the slaughter. 'People say that I have occasioned this war,' he said. 'Let me see whether delivering myself up to the conquerors will restore peace to my country.'

Makana was sentenced to life imprisonment, taken in shackles to Port Elizabeth, put on board the brig *Salisbury* and delivered to Robben Island, 400 miles away, off the coast at Cape Town. It had been used since the seventeenth century as a prison colony for both criminal convicts and political dissidents. Within a year of his imprisonment, Makana, along with other inmates, helped organize an escape, seized a fishing boat and headed for the mainland three miles away. As the boat came into the breakers off Blauberg beach, it capsized. According to the survivors, Makana clung for some time to a rock, shouting encouragement to others to reach the shore, until he was swept off and engulfed by the raging surf.

Makana was never forgotten by his Xhosa followers. Many refused to believe that he was dead and waited for years for his return, giving rise to a new Xhosa expression, '*Kukuzakuka Nxele*', the coming of Nxele, meaning forlorn hope.

The fate of Maqoma, the greatest military commander the Xhosa ever produced, was also well remembered. Expelled from his native valley in 1829, Maqoma engaged in a series of wars against the British in an attempt to regain lost Xhosa lands. During the 1850s, his guerrilla force based in the Amatola mountains held at bay a British army for months on end, inflicting one defeat after another.

Twice Maqoma was shipped off to Robben Island. During his first term of imprisonment, lasting eleven years, he was allowed the company of his youngest wife and a son. But on the second occasion, at the age of seventy-three, he was sent back there alone. No one else on the island spoke any Xhosa. He received no visitors. According to an Anglican chaplain who witnessed his last moments in 1873, he cried bitterly, before dying of old age and dejection, 'at being here alone— no wife, or child, or attendant'.

After nine frontier wars, Xhosa resistance against British colonial rule finally ended. Once an expanding and aggressive nation, the Xhosa had lost great swathes of land to white settlers. In the process, Xhosa leaders squabbled and fought with each other as much as they did with the white colonists. Some chiefs defected to the colonial side. Others were willing enough to collaborate. In the most desperate act of resistance, the Xhosa slaughtered vast herds of their own cattle, believing the prophecy of a teenage girl, Nongqawuse, that it would help 'in driving the English from the land'. It resulted only in mass starvation, in which tens of thousands of Xhosa died, and enabled the authorities to take yet more Xhosa territory for white settlement.

Unlike their Xhosa neighbours to the south-west, the Thembu, a Xhosa-speaking people, managed to avoid most of the frontier conflict and lost little land to white settlement. Yet Thembuland, like all the other independent chiefdoms in the area, eventually succumbed to Cape control and became incorporated into a new region known as the Transkeian Territories. It was the largest area of South Africa not to fall into white hands. But just as much as the Xhosa, the Thembu had lost political control. The authority of their chiefs had become secondary to that of colonial officials, like the magistrates, as Mandela's father had found to his cost.

What stirred the young Mandela's imagination, as he listened to these tales of Xhosa history around the fireside, were the bravery and defiance shown by Xhosa leaders who stood against the whites' advance. The age of the chiefs was seen as a heroic time. The memory of men like Makana and Maqoma was carried down from one generation to the next to ensure that a tradition of resistance survived. They became the heroes of Mandela's youth.

Colonial British Missionary Culture

Another profound influence on Mandela at Mqhekezweni, pulling in a different direction, was the Church. The mission station there, centred around a white stucco church, was revered in Mqhekezweni as much as the Great Place itself. It was part of a century of endeavour by Wesleyan Methodist missionaries to carry Christianity to the African peoples of the Eastern Cape which had started when the Reverend William Shaw, a pioneer missionary accompanying a party of British settlers to the Cape frontier region in 1820, decided that a far greater potential for mission work lay in Xhosa territory to the east, 'a country abounding with heathen inhabitants'. Within a few years his chain of mission stations had reached 200 miles into African territory. One of the mission stations, Clarkebury, on the banks of the Mgwali river in the heart of Thembuland, was built on land donated by Mandela's great-grandfather, King Ngubengcuka. Anglican, Presbyterian and Moravian missionaries were also active in the Transkei region.

Before arriving in Mqhekezweni, Mandela had been to church only on one occasion, to be baptized in the Wesleyan chapel in Qunu as a prelude to attending school there. At Mqhekezweni, church was taken much more seriously. Jongintaba himself was a devout Wesleyan who regularly attended church each Sunday, together with his wife, NoEngland, and Mandela was expected to do the same. Once when Mandela missed Sunday service, preferring to take part in a fight against boys from another village, he was given a hiding by the regent.

The church was always full on Sundays, men dressed in suits, women in long skirts and high-necked blouses—a style favoured by missionaries at the time. The local minister, Reverend Matyolo, was a popular figure whose fire-and-brimstone sermons, seasoned with a dose of African animism, found a ready audience. But what impressed Mandela, even more than the rituals and ceremony, was the impact of missionary education. The African élite of the time—clerks, teachers, interpreters and policemen—were all products of missionary schools.

At the primary school at Mqhekezweni, a one-room building next to the royal residence, Mandela showed no particular flair, but he was a diligent learner and received special attention from his teachers, taking homework back every day to the Great Place, where an aunt would check it. The subjects he studied were standard: English, Xhosa, history and geography. They were taught, in the tradition that missionaries had long established, with a notable British bias, for the missionaries believed in the virtues of the British Empire, British culture and British institutions just as much as they did in the virtues of Christianity.

Thus Mandela grew up a serious boy, respectful of the chieftaincy, the Church and British tradition. At the Great Place, his solemn demeanour earned him the nickname Tatamkhulu, meaning Grandpa.

Mandela's Education

Virginia Curtin Knight

This excerpt from *African Biography* traces Mandela's childhood in the Transkei and his education there. Mandela was the first member of his family to attend school. His Methodist mother was encouraged to get Nelson an education, so she started him in a school in Qunu. From Qunu, Mandela continued his formal education at the British missionary boarding schools of Clarkebury and then Healdtown, concluding his studies at the University of Fort Hare, a historically black university where many of the current leaders of South Africa were educated.

Though [as president of South Africa] he became the toast of Western countries, outshining European and North American leaders of his era, Mandela kept in touch with a royal African heritage that molded him into a self-confident leader at an early stage in life. Mandela was born in Mvezo, a small, isolated Thembu village on the Mbashe River near Umtata, the Transkei capital. The Transkei is a land of sparkling streams and rounded green mountains in today's eastern South Africa. An area as large as Switzerland, the Transkei was home to the Xhosa people before whites arrived in the seventeenth century. The Thembu form one of seven groups that make up the Xhosa nation.

Mandela's father, Gadla Henry Mphakanyiswa, gave him the first name Rolihlahla, and he got his last name from his grandfather Mandela. As a show of respect, he is often called Madiba, his clan name. The name Rolihlahla means literally in Xhosa "pulling the branch of a tree." But Mandela said its informal meaning is more accurate: "troublemaker." On his first day in school [at Qunu], his British-trained African teacher gave each student an English name. Mandela was named Nelson. "Why she bestowed this particular name upon me I have no idea," Mandela wrote later. "Perhaps it had something to do with the great British sea captain Lord Nelson [1758–1805], but that would be only a guess.". . .

At Qunu, his mother became a Methodist and was given the Christian name Fanny. Mandela also was baptized a Methodist. The Methodist community persuaded Mandela's mother and father to send him to Qunu's one-room, Western-style school. He was the first member of his family to attend school.

THE GREAT PLACE

When Mandela was nine years old, his father died. After that, Mandela was raised at Mqhekezweni, the Thembuland capital in the Transkei, in the Great Place of Chief Jongintaba Dalindyebo, acting regent (ruler) of the Thembu people. As a local chief and counselor to Thembu kings, Mandela's father had been instrumental in getting Jongintaba chosen acting regent to rule until an infant prince came of age. Jongintaba repaid the counselor's favor by taking his son into the Great Place. Mandela was taken by his mother to the Great Place at Mqhekezweni where he was to be integrated into Chief Jongintaba's court and treated as a member of the royal family. Mandela remembers his mother's parting words as she left him in the majestic new world of the royal house (the chief even had a V-8 Ford): "Brace yourself, my boy!" It was motherly advice that Mandela could use for the rest of his life.

In the Great Place as a boy Mandela watched Jongintabe hold court on public affairs. Thembu men, no matter what their standing, were free to speak and make their arguments until a consensus (general agreement) could be reached— with Jongintabe summing up at the end of debate. "It was democracy in the purest form," Mandela recalled. He added in his book *Long Walk to Freedom:* "As a leader, I have always followed the principles I first saw demonstrated by the regent at the Great Place. I have always endeavoured to listen to what each and every person had to say before venturing my own opinion. Oftentimes, my own opinion will simply represent a consensus of what I heard in a discussion. I always remember the regent's axiom [rule or principle]: a leader, he said, is like a shepherd. He stays behind the flock, letting the most nimble go ahead, whereupon the others follow, not realizing that all along they are being directed from behind."

At Mqhekezweni, Mandela continued his education at

Christian schools, where he learned about British ideas, culture, and institutions. From Chief Jongintaba's Great Place he learned tribal culture and stories of past Xhosa heroes and glories. At the Christian church, Mandela learned another thing: how to eat with a knife and fork.

CHRISTIANITY IN 1920s SOUTH AFRICA

Christianity played an important role in Mandela's early life. Not only was his mother a Christian, but Mandela was baptized into the Methodist Church and educated at a series of missionary schools. For Mandela, as for other young black South Africans at this time, Christianity opened important doorways to education. Historian William Beinart explains here how, in 1920s South Africa, Christianity united ideas of liberation with local African ways of thinking—its adaptability to local contexts providing an appeal for many black South Africans at this time.

Christianity was one of the binding forces of 1920s' radicalism and Africanist thinking. It was still not the majority black religion, but its language reached far beyond the old mission communities. Some of the early independent churches had fragmented further by the 1920s. They were joined by a new religious force—fundamentalist Apostolic and Zionist churches. Most of these had their roots in the USA but adapted rapidly to the South African context incorporating African symbolism and practices. Many split again and a bewildering array of denominations emerged: [There were] nearly 1,000 African churches by 1945.

The attractions of Christianity were many and complex. As a religion of sacrifice, blood, saints, spirits, purification, and redemption it had much in common with pre-colonial African beliefs. The biblical world, evoking a pre-industrial and patriarchal society, clearly resonated with African ideas. For early converts missions had often been a refuge; now conversion was a route to literacy and education. Christianity provided universal belief and networks as well as a more individualist moral alternative to the bonds of rural communality. In the 1920s political messages of social as well as religious redemption were often drawn from the Bible. Increasingly, Christianity was moulded by African people into forms they found useful. Women, in particular, were the backbone of many churches.

William Beinart, *Twentieth-Century South Africa*. Oxford: Oxford University Press, 1994.

A Promise to Be Fulfilled

At 16, Mandela went through an elaborate Xhosa circumcision ceremony, a ritual that declared him a man. At the end of the ceremony, Mandela listened to a lamentation (an expression of grief) by Chief Meligqili: "There sit our sons, young, healthy and handsome, the flower of the Xhosa tribe.... We have just circumcised them in a ritual that promises them manhood, but I am here to tell you that it is an empty, illusory promise, a promise that can never be fulfilled. For the Xhosa, and all black South Africans, are conquered people.... They will go to cities where they will live in shacks and drink cheap alcohol, all because we have no land to give them where they could prosper and multiply. They will cough their lungs out deep in the bowels of the white man's mines.... Among these young men are chiefs who will never rule because we have no power to govern ourselves; soldiers who will never fight because we have no weapons to fight with; scholars who will never teach because we have no place for them to study."

Shortly after Mandela's circumcision, Chief Jongintaba told the young man he was being sent to school in a wider world. "It is not for you to spend your life mining the white man's gold, never knowing how to write your name," the chief told Mandela.

In his royal V-8 Ford, the chief drove Mandela to Clarkesbury Boarding School at Engcobo, one of the oldest Methodist missions in the Transkei. The chief left the young scholar with pocket money and a new pair of boots. In *Long Walk to Freedom* Mandela remembers his first days at the school: "On this first day of classes I sported my new boots. I had never worn boots before of any kind, and that first day I walked like a newly shod horse. I made a terrible racket walking up the steps and almost slipped several times. As I clomped into the classroom, my boots crashing on the shiny wood floor, I noticed two female students in the first row were watching my lame performance with great amusement. The prettier of the two leaned over to her friend and said loud enough for all to hear: 'The country boy is not used to wearing shoes,' at which her friend laughed. I was blind with fury and embarrassment."

His World Widens

In 1937, Mandela transferred to Healdtown, a Wesleyan college at Fort Beaufort, near East London, South Africa, still in the Transkei but 175 miles from home. His world was getting larger. Two years later at the age of 21, Mandela entered University College of Fort Hare at the Transkei town of Alice, also near East London. Fort Hare, the only residential (live-in) center of higher education for blacks in South Africa at the time, had been founded in 1916 by Scottish missionaries. By the time Mandela arrived for study in 1939, the university had evolved into a training ground for the African elite—some of them later to be heads of state—from southern, central, and eastern Africa.

At the end of his second year at Fort Hare, Mandela's studies were cut short by a tribal tradition. Chief Jongintaba decided it was time for Mandela to marry, picked out a wife for him, and set a wedding date. "He loved me very much and looked after me as diligently as my father had," Mandela said in a quote from Mary Benson's book *Nelson Mandela: The Man and the Movement*. "But he was no democrat and did not think it worth while to consult me about a wife. He selected a girl, fat and dignified."

To escape the arranged marriage, Mandela really opened up his world. He fled 550 miles north to Johannesburg, the city of gold where tens of thousands of people hurried to and fro all hours of the day and night. Mandela got a job on the police force at a gold mine. But Chief Jongintaba's agents soon found him, and he fled to Alexandra, a black township north of Johannesburg. There he met Walter Sisulu (1912–), a one-time teacher from the Transkei and a real estate dealer in Alexandra, who was bent on overturning the white-minority government.

Johannesburg

Fatima Meer

The following article, written by Fatima Meer, describes Mandela's arrival in the sprawling metropolis of Johannesburg, the inland city built around an enormous reef of gold-bearing ore. Upon learning of their imminent arranged marriages, and after Mandela was suspended from the University of Fort Hare for his attempts to organize the student body for better living conditions, he and his cousin Justice ran away to the city. Although they soon procured positions at one of the many mines in the area, Justice's father, the regent Jongintaba, traced their whereabouts and ordered them to return to the Transkei. Justice was compelled to leave Johannesburg, but Mandela succeeded in convincing his guardian that his best career prospects lay in remaining in the city to train as an attorney. In fact, Mandela soon was introduced to the charismatic Walter Sisulu, who helped him procure a legal position, as well as introducing him to Eveline, who would become Mandela's first wife.

Fatima Meer, a lifelong friend, colleague, and biographer of Mandela, supplements her account with letters that Mandela wrote from prison recalling his early years in Johannesburg.

In 1941 Johannesburg was wide and tall and cancerous. It had reaped the benefit of a European war and its industry in gold had been compounded by other industry, almost literally converting the rest of the country into its hinterland. Hundreds of thousands of male migrants poured in from the African reserves of the four Provinces, in search of the work the city offered.

As many came with proper authorization as did not, and as many found jobs in factories as found temporary accom-

Fatima Meer, *Higher than Hope: 'Rolihlahla We Love You': Nelson Mandela's Biography on His 70th Birthday.* Johannesburg: Skotaville Publishers, 1988. Copyright © 1988 by Fatima Meer. All rights reserved. Reproduced by permission.

modation in prisons. While there were jobs in eGoli, there was no housing, not even sufficient land for 'squatting', but there were 'non-European' townships established just after World War I before the white men totally contained the black with laws, mostly about where they could not live.

Sophiatown, Newclare, Martindale and Alexandra were stacked with rows and rows of single-roomed barracks, with forty or more people sharing a toilet and a tap. The only municipal housing provided close to the city was in the Western Native Township, a fenced-in compound of 2000 red-brick, three-roomed houses, planned for no more than 13,000 people.

MANDELA ARRIVES IN THE METROPOLIS

That was the Johannesburg into which Nelson stepped in 1941. Neither he nor Justice had the problem of authorization or accommodation, or job, at least not immediately. They had come to the epicentre of South Africa's industrial heart, to experience that heart and to come to grips with it, so that they could begin to understand their own place and their own destiny in their motherland.

They had one solitary address, in Crown Mines, where an old *induna* [royal official who ensured that the chief's orders were executed] of Jongintaba's was an overseer. They made their way to that destination. The induna was honored to extend his hospitality to the two members of the royal *kraal* [court].

But, within days of their arrival, Jongintaba's men tracked them down. Justice returned, for he had filial obligations he could not escape, but Nelson convinced his guardian that it was best for him to pursue his studies in Johannesburg and become a lawyer. Jongintaba realized that that would in fact be the culmination of his duty to [Mandela's father] Henry Gadla. So Nelson began his abode in Johannesburg, with the reassurance from his guardian that he would continue to care for him even in that great city, for as long as his assistance was required.

Nelson moved in with a family in Alexandra Township. He recalled his days there fondly, in a letter to his youngest daughter, Zindzi:

> Often as I walk up and down my cell or as I lie on my bed, the mind wanders far and wide, recalling this episode and that mistake. Among these is the thought whether in my best days outside prison I showed sufficient appreciation for the love

and kindness of many of those who befriended and even helped me when I was poor and struggling.

The other day I was thinking of the home in 46 Seventh Avenue, Alexandra Township, where I lived on my arrival in Johannesburg. At that time I was earning the monthly wage of £2 (R4,00) and out of this amount I had to pay the monthly rent of 13/4d plus bus fare of 8d a day to town and back. It was hard going and I often found it quite difficult to pay the rent and bus fare. But my landlord and his wife were kind. Not only did they give me an extension when I could not raise the rent, but on Sundays they gave me a lovely lunch free of charge.

I also stayed with Rev Mabata of the Anglican Church on 46 Eighth Avenue in the same township, and he and Gogo, as we fondly called his wife, were also very kind, even though she was rather strict, insisting that I should take out only Xhosa girls. Despite the fact that my political outlook was still formative, Healdtown and Fort Hare had brought me into contact with students from other sections of our people, and at least I had already developed beyond thinking along ethnic lines. I was determined not to follow her advice on this particular matter. But she and her husband played the role of parents to me rather admirably.

Mr Sehruna Baduza, originally from Sterkspruit, lived as tenant with his wife in 46, Seventh Avenue. He and Mr JP Mngoma, although much older than myself, especially the latter, were among some of my best friends in those days. Mr Mngoma was a property owner and father to Aunt Virginia, one of Mum's friends. Later I was introduced to Mr P Toyana, father-in-law to the brother of the late Chief Jongintaba Mzinzi. Mr Toyana, was a clerk at the Rand Leases Mine. I used to travel there on Saturdays to collect his rations—samp, mealie meal, meat, peanuts and other items.

Much later my financial position slightly improved, but I hardly thought of those who had stood on my side during difficult times; nor did I ever visit them except once or twice only. Both the Mabatas and the Baduzas came to live in Soweto and I visited the Mabatas on a few occasions. I met both Messrs Toyana and Baduza on many occasions but not once did I think of returning their kindness. Both in the late forties and early fifties Mr Baduza became a very prominent figure in the civic affairs of Soweto and our association was limited to that level. (1/3/81)

In another letter, he described an awkward moment as he familiarized himself with the city's consumerism:

Shortly after my arrival in Johannesburg in 1941, I bought some meat in a provision shop next to the Cathedral. When I reached my room in Alexandra, I asked Nobasini, then a young lady of about six, to tell her elder sister to cook it for me.

She had a short sharp mischievous laugh which she quickly suppressed. 'Ivuthiwe Buti' she said. It was smoked beef and as a 'mampara' [rogue] from the countryside, I thought it was raw meat. (2/10/77)

But there were also shocking experiences in those early Johannesburg days. He recalls one:

In 1941, I went to visit my teacher who had taught me in Standard Ten [Grade 12]. He was a good qualified teacher and a graduate, married to an equally well qualified nurse. They lived in Orlando East. I found the house shut and a terrible smell emanating from within, of herbs and medicines. It was clear that a professional herbalist was doing his job. His wife came out as I was about to knock on the door. She was pale with shock and said that her husband had become ill and was suffering from pain in the joints. She said that it had started when he had begun his studies in law, and accused me of bewitching him.

I was very troubled and went straight to Anton Lembede and told him of my experience. He only laughed.

In another letter he wrote:

Talking about Klerksdorp reminds me of some aspects of family history I never had the opportunity to relate to you, about some of the old families. On a Friday evening in the early 1940s, I entrained from Park Station to Klerksdorp. The train consisted of 3rd Class coaches only and was crowded and riotous. I reached the town at midnight. I took a taxi to my destination, I knocked on the door and the next moment I was part of the family. I was welcomed by a sporting, intellectual, tall, soft-spoken and steady person in many respects similar to Ngutyana. Early in the morning we went out sightseeing in a setting that differed from the open spaces in the South of Johannesburg only in that it was more wild with fairly thick bush and rookies. I immediately fell in love with the place because it reminded me of Mvezo on the bank of Umbhashe where I was born. We were together for several years until politics drastically cut down moments of pleasure. I am sure that when I return you will eagerly accompany me to that old spot in Klerksdorp and then to the south of the Golden City where history really begins. (15/5/77)

Meeting Walter Sisulu

While Nelson recalls his early days in Johannesburg with such affection, the impressions of a young nurse trainee who lived a few doors away on Eighth Avenue, Alexandra, were very different. She saw Nelson as a nice young man, fresh from the rural area, lost in the squalid dynamics of the sprawling township. She felt sorry for him and decided to help. She spoke about him to her friend, Albertina Totiwe, a fellow nursing student at the Johannesburg General Hospital, who in turn mentioned the home boy to her fiancé, the resourceful Walter Sisulu. If anybody could help the young man, she knew Walter could.

Walter had practically grown up in Johannesburg. His mother was a strong caring woman, highly respected both in her home area and in Orlando. No one referred to him by name, but they all knew of the white foreman who had come as a road builder to Engcobo, in the Transkei, many years ago, fell in love with the young Sisulu girl and then abandoned her and their two young children. MaSisulu never looked at another man. She devoted her life to her children. She took them to Johannesburg, found lodgings in Alexandra Township and worked as a washerwoman to put them through high school.

In 1941, she was one of the few fortunate ones with a house in Orlando, and she shared that house unstintingly with relatives, no matter how far removed from the home area.

Walter went to Alexandra to meet Nelson, and the two young men became friends almost instantly. Walter invited Nelson to stay with them at MaSisulu's house; Nelson accepted the invitation. Walter also gave him a part-time job in his office and helped him to enroll as a law student at the University of the Witwatersrand, and paid his fees.

Walter did not only draw him into his house, he also drew him into his world of politics and human concern, and in the course of time he drew him into marriage, to his cousin, the petite, pretty Eveline from Engcobo.

CHAPTER 2

MANDELA THE ACTIVIST

PEOPLE WHO MADE HISTORY

NELSON MANDELA

1948: The Nationalists' Victory and the ANC Response

Sheridan Johns and R. Hunt Davis Jr.

In 1948 the National Party (Nats) came to power in South Africa and officially implemented policies of apartheid through a series of wide-ranging laws. Here historians Sheridan Johns and R. Hunt Davis Jr. examine both these restrictive laws and the African National Congress's resistance to apartheid that steadfastly increased after the landmark election of 1948. The authors outline the important groundroots growth of the ANC after 1948, the split between the ANC and the Pan-Africanist Congress (PAC), the 1952 Defiance Campaign, and the landmark 1955 Congress of the People that resulted in the famous ANC Freedom Charter.

The year 1948 is the most critical year in South Africa's political history since the formation in 1910 of the Union of South Africa. The key political event of 1948 was the electoral victory of the National Party (NP), which elevated Dr. D.F. Malan to the prime ministership and led to a cabinet composed exclusively of Afrikaans-speaking ministers. Scholarly attention has generally focused on the construction of the apartheid edifice—the thoroughly rationalized and systematically implemented system of white supremacy that was far more extensive and oppressive than the segregation that had preceded it—as the major political development of the dozen or so years that followed the 1948 election and that ended with the shooting death of sixty-nine Africans at the hands of the police at Sharpeville in 1960. The emphasis on the political history of the period thus has been on the growing lock of the NP on the white electorate, the various pieces of apartheid legislation that the NP-

Sheridan Johns and R. Hunt Davis Jr., *The Struggle Against Apartheid, 1948–1960.* New York: Oxford University Press, 1991. Copyright © 1991 by Oxford University Press, Inc. Reproduced by permission.

dominated Parliament enacted, the African efforts to halt the growth of white supremacy and substitute in its place a vision of a more equitable society, and the government's efforts to quell the rising tide of black dissent.

The year 1948 also is noteworthy for those who study the black role in South African political history from an African-based perspective rather than primarily as a response to white political initiative, but it does not represent as sharp and as distinctive a dividing point. In the first instance, major changes of direction and emphasis had begun to take place in black politics earlier in the decade. African political leaders were more than ever before questioning and rejecting the paternalistic ideology of white trusteeship, with its notion of a possible assimilation of Africans into "white" civilization in the distant future. Thus they were already challenging the legitimacy of white supremacy before the electoral triumph of the NP and its apartheid ideology. Nonetheless, the NP did pose a new challenge to Africans. Through its rigid apartheid legislation it eliminated all possible points of political accommodation between African aspirations and continued white control....

NP STRATEGY

The NP seized the political initiative in 1948 and retained it into the early 1950s, pushing through its agenda of apartheid legislation without seeming to pay any heed, let alone making any compromises, to the political forces ranged against it. Political opposition did exist, however, and virtually each new piece of government legislation increased the level and intensity of struggle against the apartheid order. The government responded at first with increased police efforts to control the black opposition, expanding the police power of the state through measures such as the Suppression of Communism Act (1950) and the Public Safety Act (1953) and then using this legislation to curb African political organizations and activities through arrests, bannings, trials, and imprisonment.

African political strength was such, however, that reliance on police powers alone appeared insufficient to check it. The government thus sought other ways to respond to African political initiative. The Promotion of Bantu Self-Government Act (1959) was well suited to this purpose, for it served to deflect African politics away from the political center and to concentrate them instead on the peripheral 13 percent of the country that remained in African hands. These areas, successively termed *reserves, bantustans, homelands,* and *national states,* lacked exploitable resources and were vastly overcrowded. Their inhabitants were almost totally dependent economically on the remitted earnings of migrant workers employed on white-owned farms and in white-owned industries. The government thus held out to Africans the promise of full political control of what were supposedly their "own" areas but what in reality were huge rural slums incapable of existing independently from greater South Africa. In return for such a hollow gain, Africans were to relinquish all political claims to the country as a whole. . . .

THE SHARPEVILLE MASSACRE

In early 1960 South Africa found itself in the midst of an extensive political upheaval that has become known as the Sharpeville crisis. The political initiative passed into African hands, if only for a moment. Actions on the part of Africans caused the government to suspend the pass laws and brought the economy to a halt. Unprecedented international attention focused on South Africa. Also clear to Africans were the fear and uncertainty that gripped the white population. The acting prime minister, Paul Sauer, even went so far as to declare that "the old book of South African history was closed at Sharpeville." But the government soon regained its confidence and moved swiftly to reassert its authority. Africans, nonetheless, had been able to catch a glimpse of their potential power.

To understand how African political strength developed from being on the defensive in 1948 to the point of momentarily seizing the political initiative in 1960, one must go back to developments in the ANC and especially the founding of the ANC Youth League (ANCYL).

THE REVIVAL OF THE AFRICAN NATIONAL CONGRESS

Founded in 1912 by politically conscious Africans from all four provinces of the newly formed Union of South Africa to represent African opinion and interests, by the early 1930s the African National Congress had fallen on hard times. Indeed, for several years the ANC failed to hold its annual conferences and seemed in danger of dissolving altogether. By the late 1930s the organization had revived somewhat, but it still catered almost exclusively to the small African middle class and continued to pursue a moderate and deferential political course. But dramatic changes took place in the ANC during the 1940s, so that a much stronger, more militant organization came into existence and became better prepared to take up the challenge that the apartheid elections of 1948 were to pose. Simply put, the ANC of 1938 would have been totally unfit for the task of taking on the victorious National party, but the ANC of 1948 could do so.

Three developments undergirded the transformation of the ANC in the 1940s. The first of these consisted of the far-reaching economic and social changes that were associated with World War II and that created the conditions for a mass-based African political movement. The second was a new and more energetic president, the American-educated physician Alfred Bitini Xuma, who headed the ANC from 1940 until 1949. The third development was the emergence of a new generation of political thinkers and activists who were prepared to abandon the more polite and more conservative political discourse of their elders in favor of militant action. These new members formed the ANCYL to give organizational expression to their political activism.

World War II marked a watershed in the social and economic history of South Africa, second only to that wrought by the discovery of diamonds in 1867 and of gold in 1886. The principal impact of the war was to accelerate the growth of manufacturing in South Africa which before that time had been limited. This expanding industry in turn led to a growing demand for labor which, with so many whites in military service, was met to a large degree by blacks. This, in turn, meant a growing urbanization of the African population. At the time of the 1936 census, for instance, approximately 1.15 million of the country's nearly 6.6 million Africans lived in towns (compared with slightly more than 1.3 million of the 2 million whites). Over the next fifteen years, the African urban population more than doubled, to over 2.3 million. The black population of Johannesburg climbed in ten years by two-thirds, rising from about 229,000 in 1936 to nearly 385,000 in 1946....

Accompanying the increased flow of Africans from the countryside to the towns was another demographic change. In the past, the great majority of African urban immigrants had been adult males. But the massive wartime movement of entire families meant that for the first time women and children began to constitute significant portions of the African urban population. Underlying this new pattern of urban migration were both push and pull factors. The African rural areas had long been in decline because of decreasing soil productivity, the heavy outflow of able-bodied labor, lack of capital, and a growing overpopulation, among other factors. Their deterioration accelerated during the war years, forcing even greater numbers of their inhabitants to look elsewhere for the means to make ends meet. The expanding urban economy beckoned to the impoverished rural dwellers, pulling them into the cities where they more often than not settled permanently. Conditions were extremely harsh in the cities. Wages were often insufficient to meet family subsistence needs, and as many as one in four urban Africans lived in squatter camps consisting of dwellings made of hessian sacking, wood, corrugated iron, and cardboard.

The rapid growth of a permanent urban African population did much to change the political landscape of South Africa. Indeed ... one of the elements in the NP electoral victory was white concern with the so-called swamping of the cities (which by law and in policy were supposedly the preserve of whites). The urbanizing African working class was militant by its very nature, and its struggles both were more visible and posed a greater challenge to white power than did the hidden struggles of their rural brethren and forebears. Large-scale squatter movements involving many thousands of homeless people took shape during the mid-1940s. Africans in large numbers engaged in a series of bus boycotts to protest increased fares. Labor unions began to organize African workers on a significant scale, and a wave of strikes erupted during the war despite wartime regulations prohibiting them. In 1946 some seventy thousand gold miners went on strike. For the first time, then, the conditions existed for a mass-based African political organization.

The revival and restructuring of the ANC during the 1940s were very much an outgrowth of the wider social and economic changes taking place in South Africa. Although the organization had begun to climb back from the political nadir of the 1930s, its principal renewal dates from the December 1940 election of Dr. A.B. Xuma as president-general. Xuma's major contribution was that of a skilled organizer, as he both brought the provincial branches of the Congress and their often fractious factions under tighter discipline and asserted the authority of the national leadership. . . .

Yet another and equally critical feature of the Xuma era was the recruitment of a new generation of Africans into the ranks of the ANC. The new generation was better educated, reflecting the fact that more Africans than ever before, though still very few in terms of the total population, had access to higher education. By 1941 the new University College at Fort Hare, which had earlier been a secondary school, was awarding thirty bachelor's degrees annually. Both Mandela and [Oliver] Tambo were among the students of that period. Africans could also earn a B.A. degree through correspondence from the University of South Africa as well as attend the so-called white English-speaking universities. Further, in contrast with the founders of the ANC, the generation of the 1940s had no illusions about the efficacy of polite representations as a means of acquiring equal rights in a common society. The country's political history and the legislative record of entrenching white supremacy under every successive government since 1912 had clearly disabused them of any such hopes and aspirations. Finally, whereas most of the earlier ANC leaders tended to hold themselves aloof from the masses on the basis of class and cultural distinctions, the new generation realized that it would have to enlist the support of the masses if it were to overcome white supremacy. During the 1940s and 1950s, as the hitherto-separate working-class and middle-class cultural streams became increasingly juxtaposed and began to blend together to form a single vibrant and dynamic African urban culture, the ANC sought membership and support from all groups in the African population.

THE AFRICAN NATIONAL CONGRESS YOUTH LEAGUE

Impatient with African political progress to date, members of the new generation took up Dr. Xuma's call to youth in his 1943 presidential address to become more involved in ANC affairs, and in April 1944 they formed the ANCYL. It was from the ranks of this body that the African political leadership of the 1950s and 1960s, and even the 1970s and 1980s, emerged. The members were mainly young professionals who had been caught up in the intellectual ferment that characterized the wartime years. . . .

Discussion and debate within the ANCYL over the next

several years about the methods of struggle and the growing pressures for action led to the publication in 1948 of the "Basic Policy of Congress Youth League". This crucial document set forth several themes that were to resonate in African political thought in the years ahead: Africans are a people who "suffer national oppression" rather than being oppressed as a class; they were responsible for achieving their own freedom through building a mass liberation movement; and the goal of the liberation struggle, which would of necessity be "long, bitter and unrelenting," was a democratic society in political and economic terms in which the "four chief nationalities" (African, European, Indian, and Colored) would live free from racial oppression and persecution. Finally, it should be noted that the "Basic Policy" did not adopt the tone of racial exclusiveness that pervaded much of the Youth League's discussions and thinking. . . . Africans were to be accorded primary status in the struggle for liberation, but the goal was a free society for all South Africans. The ANCYL membership contended that the time was ripe for mass action, and they succeeded in committing their parent organization to embark on such a course.

The NP electoral victory accentuated the questions about tactics. The ANCYL executive committee, which included both Mandela and Tambo, drafted a "Programme of Action", which the ANC adopted at its annual conference in December 1949. It claimed for Africans the right of self-determination and called for the use of boycotts, strikes, civil disobedience, and other such weapons to "bring about the accomplishment and realization of our aspirations." For years, the ANC's approach had been, in the words of its 1919 constitution, "to record all grievances and wants of native people and to seek by constitutional means the redress thereof." The sharp contrast in the tone of the "Programme of Action" clearly indicated the new political mood and circumstances of the African population as they faced the new Afrikaner NP government, determined as it was to realize its vision of apartheid.

THE ANC RESPONDS TO APARTHEID

The new Malan government moved promptly to implement its electoral slogan of apartheid through the enactment of a major legislative agenda. This was the period of classical, or *baasskap* (bossdom), apartheid, when the government behaved as if South Africa was truly a "white man's country" and all other segments of the population should have absolutely no voice in the affairs of government. . . .

The NP government designed its apartheid legislation program to achieve four goals: racial purity, physical separation of the races, more effective political domination, and stronger control over the black population. Many of the acts served more than one purpose. Also, this new battery of legislation did not introduce white supremacy to South Africa but, rather, built on deeply rooted patterns of legislative segregation that had long been in existence.

The first legislative item on the apartheid agenda pertained to racial purity. This was the Prohibition of Mixed Marriages Act (1949), which made interracial marriages illegal. In 1950, Parliament enacted the Population Registration Act in order to classify all South Africans in one of four so-called racial groups (European, African, Colored, or Asian) and the Immorality Act, which prohibited all sex between whites and members of any other racial group.

A Turning Point in South African History

When the National Party (the "Nats") unexpectedly rose to power in 1948, it began to institute the system of "apartheid." Apartheid was maintained until 1994, when the Nats finally relinquished power, allowing South Africans of all races—not just whites—to vote in democratic elections. The following explanation of apartheid comes from a biography of Nelson Mandela in a South African history series entitled They Fought for Freedom.

In 1948, DF Malan's National Party was elected by which voters to form the national government of South Africa, and introduced 'apartheid' to the country. This Afrikaans word literally means 'separateness'. The National Party said that it meant 'separate development'—black and white people developing separately, each in their own areas and in the way that was best for them. In reality, however, it was a policy of white supremacy and white domination.

In the decades to come, apartheid caused much suffering and misery. People were classified according to the colour of their skin. Laws enacted in the name of apartheid prevented people of different colours from living in the same neighbourhoods, going to the same schools, or doing the same work. Black people were not allowed to marry white people. They could not use the same parks, lifts [elevators] or doors into public buildings. Black

Physical separation, of course, rested in part on the notion of racial exclusiveness. It also had major economic dimensions, for this category of legislation worked to entrench even further the already well-established white privilege. Having determined who belonged to what "racial" group, the government then enacted the Group Areas Act (1950), which gave it the power to designate an area as the exclusive preserve of a given group. This act, which [was] still in force [until 1994] continued to provide the government with the legal means to relocate large numbers of people for purposes of government policy. Two pieces of legislation affected Africans' rights to live in the cities. The Native Laws Amendment Act (1952) further restricted the right of Africans to live in urban areas, and the Natives Resettlement (Western Areas) Act (1954) provided the basis for prohibiting Africans from living in the central cities and for placing them in remote and isolated townships (the sprawling conglomeration of townships outside Johannesburg that consti-

---

people could not vote. Those black children who managed to go to school got an education inferior to that of white children. Black people virtually became slaves in the land of their forefathers. Things became so bad that apartheid was eventually declared a 'crime against humanity' by the United Nations.

In 1948, however, this was all still to come. While the votes were being counted after the election, Mandela was at an ANC meeting. The question of how to deal with a Nationalist government was not discussed, because nobody believed that the Nats (as members of the National Party were often called) would win the election. The meeting lasted a long time, and when Mandela and Oliver Tambo left the building it was almost dawn. They saw trucks delivering the early edition of the newspapers. The headlines of the *Rand Daily Mail* shouted— 'NATS WIN!'

'This is terrible!' exclaimed a shocked Mandela. 'The Nats' insane policies will make our fight even more difficult.'

'That may be true,' said Tambo, 'but in a way this is a good thing. I like this.'

'How can you say that?' asked Mandela, surprised.

Tambo replied, 'Well, the very wickedness of their policies will help us. It will become clear to everyone exactly who our enemy is. People will unite in the struggle against them.'

Karin Pampallis, ed., *Nelson Mandela.* Cape Town, South Africa: Maskew Miller Longman, 2000.

tutes Soweto had its origin in this act). Yet another piece of legislation in this category, the Prevention of Illegal Squatting Act (1951), dealt a further blow to Africans who were trying to maintain an independent agricultural existence outside the reserves, by giving the government the power to uproot so-called unauthorized African settlements on white-designated land.

MASS EVICTIONS

The cumulative effect of the legislation mandating physical separation has been disastrous for Africans. The most glaring example of the hardships that Africans have had to endure is the policy of forced removals. Although it is difficult to determine the exact total, the Surplus People Project estimated that between 1960 and 1983, more than three and a half million Africans were evicted from white farms, forced to relinquish land that they owned that was in predominantly white-owned rural areas (the so-called black spots), relocated in urban areas, or otherwise forced to abandon their homes to serve the purposes of apartheid policy. In addition to causing enormous social dislocation, forced removals have intensified African poverty through the loss of capital assets (land, housing, etc.), the rise in unemployment through loss of access to jobs, and the denial of schools, clinics, and other social services. More stringently than ever before, the South African government limited the right of Africans to maintain a permanent residence, to own property, or to earn an independent livelihood outside the 13 percent of the country legislatively mandated (by the 1913 Natives Land Act and the 1936 Native Trust and Land Act) as the African reserves.

Along with the legislation altering the demographic geography of South Africa, the government also enacted measures that enforced segregation in public facilities. At first the government relied on administrative edicts to extend the segregation that already existed. A court decision stating that separate amenities had to be equal, however, led to the passage of the Reservation of Separate Amenities Act (1953), which legislated that segregated facilities could be inherently unequal. The State Aided Institutions Act (1957) gave the government the authority to enforce segregation in libraries, theaters, and other public cultural facilities. Often termed *petty apartheid*, these measures have in more recent years been selectively ignored as the government has attempted to put a more human face on its policies.

In the political sphere the government sought to tighten even further the electoral monopoly of white South Africans. The Suppression of Communism Act (1950), for example, not only outlawed the Communist party but also defined communism in such broad terms that almost any form of political protest could be labeled communist and thus prohibited. Ironically, one effect of this act was to heighten the prestige of the Communist party and its members in antiapartheid circles and to create an environment in the ANC favorable to a united multiracial opposition to the state and cooperation with the left. The Bantu Authorities Act (1951) abolished the advisory Natives' Representatives Council, already nearly defunct, and in its place set up local authorities in the reserves, which were dominated by government-appointed chiefs. In the vision of the apartheid planners, these were to be the only sanctioned outlets for African political participation.

THE COMPLETE DISENFRANCHISEMENT OF BLACKS

A third key measure in the government's efforts to ensure a white electoral monopoly was the South Africa Amendment Act (1956) which removed Colored voters from the common voting roll and placed them on a separate voting roll to elect members of Parliament and provincial councils (who had to be white to sit in these bodies) to represent Colored interests. . . . African and Colored voting rights, limited to adult males who met certain educational and income or property qualifications, extended back to the Cape Colony's constitution of 1853 and were retained (for the Cape Province only) under the provisions of the 1910 Act of Union. The communal representation in Parliament that began for Africans in 1936 and Coloreds some twenty years later came to an end when the government abolished all parliamentary representatives for both groups (Africans in 1959 and Coloreds in 1969).

The fourth category of baasskap apartheid legislation consisted of measures of control—over movement, over participation in economic activity, over educational opportunities, and over the expression of political opposition. In order to enforce limitations on Africans' rights to live, work, or even move about areas of the country outside the reserves, the government expanded the existing pass system. This it accomplished with the Abolition of Passes and Consolidation of Documents Act (1952) which required all Africans above age sixteen, including women who had previously been exempt from the pass laws, to carry on their person at all times a reference book containing extensive personal data. Of course, acts designed for other functions, as well as the Abolition of Passes and Consolidation of Documents Act, also had major control functions.

ECONOMIC APARTHEID

Other legislation was designed to enhance the whites' economic control over Africans. This included the Native Labor (Settlement of Disputes) Act (1953), which made permanent the wartime prohibition of strikes by Africans that had been renewed regularly in the intervening years. Under the Industrial Conciliation Act (1924), African males were excluded from the legal definition of "employee" and thus from the right to engage in collective bargaining. A 1954 amendment extended the exclusion to African women, thus denying to all African workers the government-sanctioned collective bargaining machinery. The negative economic impact of apartheid on African labor was severe. For example, in the gold-mining industry (which set the standard for wage labor earnings), the earnings gap between white and black labor steadily widened in the 1950s and 1960s. In 1946 the average annual income of a white miner was 1,106 rands and of a black miner 87 rands (an earnings gap ratio of 12.7:1). By 1969 white miners averaged 4,006 rands per year, whereas black miners received only 199 rands (a ratio of 20.1:1). Over the same period, the index of real earnings (with 1938 as the base year) for white miners rose steadily from 99 to 172, while that of black miners first dropped from 92 to 89 before rising to 99. Clearly, white mine workers, who constituted about one-eighth of the total mine labor force, advanced their own economic interests at the expense of their black fellow workers, shackled as they were by harsh labor legislation. . . .

The Bantu Education Act (1953), with its creation of an entirely separate school system and curriculum for Africans, brought the education of Africans fully under the control of the state and sought to control them through their schooling. To a significant degree, the motivation behind Bantu Education was economic, for at its heart it was designed to safeguard whites from black competition. The Extension of University Education Act (1959) applied the logic of the 1953 act to higher education.

Finally, there were those measures designed to extend the police powers of the state to suppress the growing black opposition to apartheid, especially as it had manifested itself in the Defiance Campaign of 1952. Two critical such measures, both enacted in 1953, were the Criminal Law Amendment Act, which imposed heavy sentences for disrupting public order (e.g., for organizing and engaging in anti-apartheid demonstrations), and the Public Safety Act, which provided the government with the authority to declare a state of emergency in specific locales or throughout the country. By passing such legislation, the government was clearly responding to the rising tide of African protest against apartheid.

The NP government faced organized and militant African political opposition to the enactment of its legislative program. With the adoption of the Programme of Action the ANC had already signaled its intent to challenge white supremacy. Nonetheless, the steady barrage of apartheid legislation created a sense of immediacy and crisis in African political circles and forced the pace of political protest faster than might otherwise have been the case. In June 1952 the ANC, with support from the Indian Congress, individual Coloreds, and a handful of whites, launched the Defiance Campaign, in which thousands of trained volunteers courted arrest by staging sit-ins in facilities reserved for members of other races, in order to draw attention to segregation and to induce changes in government policies.

Nelson Mandela was one of the key leaders in the 1950s in setting forth an African political agenda that challenged government hegemony. Much of his work, however, had to be behind the scenes, because in September 1953 the government imposed a ban on him that forced him to resign from the ANC (though he continued his membership in secret) and prohibited him from attending meetings for five years (the authorities subsequently extended his bans until March 1961).

MANDELA AND COLD WAR POLITICS

Having emerged as one of the most prominent members of the Youth League, Mandela was elected its president in late 1950. In his presidential address to the December 1951 Conference of the ANCYL Mandela at length defined the nature of the struggle as well as the need of Africans to develop a coherent strategy. The struggle in South Africa, he stated, was part of a general global contest in which "the oppressed all over the world ... are irrevocably opposed to imperialism in any form." Furthermore, expounding a theme that was to recur regularly in the ANC literature in the years ahead, Mandela contended that "the ruling circles in America" were undergirding the efforts of the European colonial powers and "their servitors in South Africa" to maintain their rule in Africa. This was, after all, the era of the cold war in which the United States was giving its full backing to the Western European powers not only in Europe but also in their colonial empires. In addition, South African troops were part of the UN forces in Korea, and the British had a major naval base in South Africa. In short, this was an era in which colonialism remained politically acceptable in the West and in which the South African political system raised few questions. Mandela undertook a fuller exposition of this theme in a 1958 article entitled "A New Menace in Africa". Finally, in an era when memories of Nazi Germany were still fresh, Mandela charged the National party and the "financial lords" with moving the country in "the direction of an openly Fascist state." The forces of oppression were indeed powerful, he asserted, and "the struggle will be a bitter one," but in the end the people would prevail because their spirit could not be crushed.

If the people were to challenge effectively their national oppression, then it would have to be under the banner of African nationalism. For Mandela, this meant "the African nationalism propounded by the Congress and the Youth League." The issues to which he was alluding had to do with divisions inside African political ranks over the central question of how Africans were to be best mobilized. Was it to be on the basis of class origin, as the Communist party argued, or on the basis of common oppression and injustices, as the Indian Congress and white liberals argued, or exclusively on the basis of African nationalism, as Mda and some other Youth Leaguers (and Mandela previously) argued. Eventually the schism became too deep to bridge, and those calling for an "Africans only" policy broke with the ANC in 1958 and formed the PAC in 1959....

The ANCYL and its parent body, the ANC, Mandela stated,

had to grapple with several pressing issues. First, the government was using the Suppression of Communism Act to ban African leaders (Mandela was arrested under the provisions of the act in August 1952), thus posing the potential problem of how their organization was to carry on with its leaders restricted. Another issue also concerned organization—the need to develop a solid cadre of members to carry their message of "a free, independent, united, democratic, and prosperous South Africa" to the masses. A third issue had to do with "the participation of other national groups in our struggles." In Mandela's view, the successful resolution of these issues and the general need for a disciplined approach to the struggle was essential in order for the ANC to embark on its proposed Defiance Campaign in 1952. Mandela served as the volunteer in chief for the campaign.

THE DEFIANCE CAMPAIGN OF 1952

During the last half of 1952, more than eight thousand volunteers went to jail for disobeying minor apartheid regulations such as using whites-only facilities in post offices, railway stations, and so forth in what constituted the Defiance Campaign. The purpose of the campaign was to convince the government to abandon apartheid and to eliminate discrimination. Instead, as Mandela noted in his September 21, 1953, presidential address to the Transvaal branch of the ANC, the government launched "a reactionary offensive" of arrests, new repressive legislation (e.g., the Public Safety Act), and bannings. Not only had the "reactionary offensive" created turmoil in South Africa, but it also had "scared away foreign capital from South Africa" (according to government statistics, the net inflow of foreign capital dropped from 187 million rands in 1951 to 144 million in 1952 to 113 million in 1953). The speech was read in Mandela's name, as he was prohibited under the terms of his ban from attending the conference.

Although the Defiance Campaign had not achieved its stated goals, Mandela's address nonetheless conveyed a sense of accomplishment. In his view the ANC had now launched the fight against apartheid in a massive way, and the campaign had forced the government into the unaccustomed position of reacting to the African political initiative. A strategy was clearly emerging, one of action by "a real militant mass organization" (the ANC) in alliance with non-

African organizations (at this point limited primarily to the Indian Congress).

The major issues were also becoming clearer, according to Mandela. One was the increasing poverty of the people, heightened by the deleterious economic impact of the mounting apartheid legislation. Another was the intent of the government through Bantu Education to teach Africans that they were inferior to whites. . . .

Many within the ANC ranks had come to believe that the liberation of Africans from their national oppression as a people constituted the central feature of the anti-apartheid struggle at the same time that it also demanded a common front of all democratic forces arrayed against the fascist apartheid regime. Asians and Coloreds were natural allies, as they too suffered oppression as dark-skinned people. The real question had to do with the position of whites. "We are convinced," wrote Mandela in a 1953 article in the left-wing monthly *Liberation*, "that there are thousands of honest democrats among the white population who . . . stand . . . for the complete renunciation of 'white supremacy'". Mandela's argument had its roots in a deep-seated belief in nonracialism as well as in a pragmatism that saw the potential power of white allies working within the system for change. In addressing these whites, Mandela stated that there could be "no middle course" to the struggle. It was a false notion to believe, as the Liberal party did, that the struggle against apartheid had to be limited to constitutional and legal means, for the very constitutional and legal structure of South Africa was intended to maintain white supremacy. Democratic-minded whites would thus have to decide whether to throw in their lot completely with the extraparliamentary anti-apartheid movement or to abstain and remain on the sidelines.

CONGRESS OF THE PEOPLE

ANC efforts to develop a broad multiracial anti-apartheid alliance culminated in the Congress of the People which met at Kliptown outside Johannesburg on June 25–26, 1955. Some three thousand delegates, representing the ANC, the South African Indian Congress (SAIC), the South African Colored People's Organization (SACPO), the (white) Congress of Democrats (COD), and the multiracial South African Congress of Trade Unions (SACTU), convened in an open-air meeting as a self-declared national convention to endorse the Freedom Charter. Even though Mandela was certainly overoptimistic, in the light of subsequent events, in asserting that the movement that led to the charter "shall vanquish all opposition and win the South Africa of our dreams during our lifetime", he was correct in asserting its significance.

The Freedom Charter, with its unambiguous and forthright statement that "South Africa belongs to all who live in it, black and white," has remained for more than thirty years the single most important statement of the ANC's aims and purposes. The charter sets forth the vision of a South Africa with the full range of civil rights and liberties associated with Western liberal democracies, but it also was beyond standard Western constitutionalism to address the fundamental social and economic inequalities of South African life. In its pledge to restore the national wealth of the country to the people (including the redistribution of white-owned land and the nationalization of "the mineral wealth beneath the soil, the banks, and monopoly industry"); to provide fair and equitable working conditions for all workers, including equal pay to men and women for equal work; to commit the government to energetic education and cultural policies; and to call for wide-ranging social welfare measures, the charter recognizes that the deep-rooted and fundamental social and economic disparities in South Africa are the product of many decades of white supremacy and capitalist development. Thus the provision of full-scale political rights and liberties would not in and of itself resolve the country's enormous social and economic problems.

Mandela's Writings

Mandela regularly expressed his concern about African economic and social disabilities in his public statements, for he realized that these could easily be overlooked if the struggle concentrated exclusively on political rights. In the mid-1950s he directly addressed these matters in a series of articles for *Liberation*. In "People Are Destroyed", Mandela wrote about how "the actual workings of the hideous and pernicious doctrines of racial inequality" led to "the breaking up of African homes and families and the forcible separation of children from mothers, the harsh treatment meted out to African prisoners, and the forcible detention of Africans in farm colonies for spurious statutory offenses."

"Land Hunger" presents his analysis of how discriminatory land policies resulted in the impoverishment of the rural masses, compelling them to seek low-wage labor in the white-owned mines and on the large white-owned farms. In this article, Mandela also noted how the Bantu Authorities Act set up instruments of government that were "designed to keep down the people" rather than to provide a means for genuine local self-government. . . .

Mandela also used his series of articles in *Liberation* to return to a theme he had raised in his 1951 and 1953 presidential addresses—the threat of American imperialism. . . . Mandela believed that the United States was intent on expanding its economic and military hegemony while at the same time denying that it was engaging in imperialism. Yet "the American brand of imperialism is imperialism all the same," and it thus remained as deleterious to the interests of Africans and Asians as were the earlier European versions. The future of Africa, Mandela concluded, must be "in the hands of the common people."

The ANC's New Activist Agenda and Mandela's "M-Plan"

Stephen M. Davis

The African National Congress (ANC) was founded in South Africa in 1912 under the name South African Natives National Congress (SANNC) as a response to the founding of the Union of South Africa in 1910 (when South Africa gained independence from Britain). From the outset, the ANC was more of an elitist organization than a populist one, seeking to protect the rapidly decreasing rights of black South Africans after the establishment of the Union. Led by Pixley Seme, many of the early leaders were British-educated intellectuals who conceived the ANC as an organization focused on legal and constitutional change.

In the following excerpt from his book entitled *Apartheid's Rebels: Inside South Africa's Hidden War*, the Southern Africanist historian Stephen M. Davis analyzes the shift in ANC policies that occurred during the 1940s and early 1950s. He argues that at this time a new generation of leaders—Nelson Mandela, Walter Sisulu, and others—instituted fundamental changes in the ANC, transforming it from a small, largely ineffectual organization into a massive, popular movement of resistance. During this period, the ANC dramatically expanded its membership, changed its tactics to working closely with trade unions, and began to support dramatic and widespread strikes.

Of fundamental importance in the restructuring of the organization that would come to represent South Africa's black majority in the latter half of the twentieth century, was Nelson Mandela's "M-Plan," which

---

Stephen M. Davis, *Apartheid's Rebels: Inside South Africa's Hidden War*. New Haven, CT: Yale University Press, 1987. Copyright © 1987 by Stephen M. Davis. All rights reserved. Reproduced by permission.

aimed at implementing underground networks resistant to government infiltration. Mandela's vision was to retain the grassroots support base of the ANC as the voice of the people, while also protecting the national executive of the ANC by creating a structure of middle-level operatives that would communicate between the disparate levels of the organization. The goal was to divorce the ANC from the ineffectual "goodwill" relationship it had had with the South African government while at the same time cracking down on government informants within the organization's ranks.

While dissension among black workers led to mass demonstrations, strikes, violence directed against symbols of white power, and hundreds of deaths, the ANC maintained its aloof, constitutionalist approach, and so largely excluded itself from the fray. Until as late as the Second World War, in fact, the middle-class party remained largely apart from the mainstream of high-profile black protest, preferring instead to navigate channels of negotiation marked out by the government. Years of such efforts yielded the ANC few results, but trust in the possibility of compromise persisted.

Such faith reached new heights as South Africa entered World War II. The government, led by General Jan Smuts, was drifting leftward, and ANC leaders were convinced that the prime minister would move to abolish pass laws [the laws mandating that all black males carry an identity document, called a "pass," to track and control their movement] as a first step toward equal rights. To provide Smuts with political capital, ANC president Dr. Alfred Bitini Xuma persuaded a reluctant executive board to endorse the alliance against Nazi Germany. It was to be the ANC's last act of faith in white governmental goodwill.

GENERAL SMUTS'S BETRAYAL

General Smuts, under political fire from the growing pro-Nazi National Party, soon chose to abandon the option of lowering racial barriers. In a bid to retain power in the 1943 general election, Smuts spurned black aspirations, reassuring the whites-only electorate of his government's commitment to white supremacy.

The shock of Smuts's perceived betrayal forced the ANC

leadership to recognize the apparent futility of passive negotiation. Peaceful but forceful confrontation seemed the only path available. But with a total national membership of a paltry one thousand, Xuma could not recast the party's strategy without remaking the party itself. Therefore, he had the ANC fitted with a new activist platform, entitled "African Claims," which set out for the first time a comprehensive agenda of demands for political rights such as universal suffrage and equal pay for equal work. Xuma stripped the party of all remnants of official participation by traditional chiefs and reorganized it to encourage democratic selection of leaders and policy. Over thirty years after its founding as an organ of black opinion, the ANC was beginning the work of building a popular national membership amongst South Africa's diverse black population.

Methodically, Xuma sought to position his party as the chief voice of opposition to minority rule, quintupling the number of ANC cardholders to over fifty-five hundred by 1947. Fending off pressure to call mass demonstrations before the party was ready, he worked on building up the organizational skills to overcome communication problems, financial distress, and mounting governmental hostility.

The 1948 general election, however, confronted blacks, coloreds [those of mixed ancestry], and Indians with an even higher wall of white power. The Afrikaner-dominated National Party, swept into power by the white electorate for the first time, moved quickly to solidify and formalize the segregationist system it began to label "apartheid." By the time the new mass of legislation passed out of parliament in Cape Town, non-white South Africans faced tight government control over their schools, a ban on unionization, racial segregation by residential and commercial zones under the draconian Group Areas Act, further restrictions on opposition politics under the broadly worded Suppression of Communism Act, prohibitions on all interracial, sexual, and marital relations, and threats by authorities newly empowered summarily to banish urban-dwellers to the rural reserves.

Reverberations from the National Party's apartheid earthquake reached the inner councils of the ANC late in the year in the form of bitter political infighting. A new generation of impatient activists, gathered under the banner of the Congress Youth League, eventually wrested power from the old guard and launched the ANC's first mass protests. The 1952

Defiance Campaign, though marred by violence and near organizational anarchy, proved wildly popular, rocketing party membership past a hundred thousand.

With the new leadership's success came two problems that were to plague the ANC until the 1970s. One was the inflow of police informants among the flood of new members. Because the Congress could carry out few meaningful background checks on its tens of thousands of new constituents, police had no trouble planting agents throughout the ANC's political dominions. Having entered the Congress in the 1952 rush, many subsequently rose in its ranks while in the pay of security authorities and helped to implicate party executives in the "treason trials" of the late 1950s and early 1960s.

The second problem was a mark of how structurally unprepared the ANC was for the challenge of operating as a mass movement in a hostile environment. Under the weight of its huge new membership, the party proved incapable of maintaining an efficient nationwide network. By 1953, arrests and bannings of the uppermost stratum of ANC leadership threatened the Congress's potential to mobilize its newfound followers to carry out any of its plans.

Mandela's "M-Plan"

The near paralysis persuaded Nelson Mandela, a Congress Youth League founding member and a coordinator of the Defiance Campaign's trained volunteers, to launch a foresighted attempt to protect the ANC from repression. His "M-Plan" represented the first practical effort from within the Congress to prepare for the days of underground activity ahead.

The M-Plan's intention was to wean the ANC away from dependence on characteristics of organization most vulnerable to governmental pressure. Mandela envisioned the construction of a discreet but firm cellular network at the grassroots level in constant communication through a hierarchy of middle-level leaders with the national executive. But as it achieved only sporadic success in implementing the M-Plan, the ANC remained largely an undisciplined movement.

Rather than pausing to consolidate its Defiance Campaign gains, the bulk of ANC leadership quickly pressed on with nonviolent mass action in the conviction that the government could be persuaded to change its course away from apartheid. Born of this new activism was the Congress Alliance. Until the early 1950s, chief Youth League executives had so firmly rejected collaboration with communists that some, including Mandela and attorney Oliver Tambo, had proposed expelling the few who belonged to the ANC. However, the gathering momentum of governmental efforts to entrench apartheid spurred the two to seek allies in whatever guise they could be found. The ANC for the first time formed working relationships with communists and non-blacks in the South African Indian Congress, the white radical Congress of Democrats, the small South African Colored People's Organization, and the South African Congress of Trade Unions. In this constellation of congresses, an unprecedented multiracial political coalition, the ANC was the leading light.

THE FREEDOM CHARTER

In June of 1955 the group organized the Congress of the People in Johannesburg's Kliptown township, in which some three thousand delegates from the alliance's constituent parties adopted the Freedom Charter, later endorsed by the national executive as the ANC's principal political platform.

"We, the people of South Africa," the charter began, "declare for all our country and the world to know . . . that South Africa belongs to all who live in it, black and white, and that no government can justly claim authority unless it is based on the will of the people. . . ." Just as the preamble firmly placed the Congress on the side of multiracialism as opposed to black nationalism, so the remainder of the charter committed the ANC to principles of liberal democracy. It also gave the ANC a tinge of socialism with a nationalization plank which declared that "the mineral wealth beneath the soil, the banks, and monopoly industry shall be transferred to the ownership of the people as a whole. . . ." Yet the charter's provisions did not promise radically to alter South Africa's economic structure.

The work of painting the Congress in ideological colors appealing to the black public was brought to an abrupt end as a result of massive special branch security operations that culminated in the Treason Trial, for which arrests began in December of 1956. Accused initially were some 156 blacks and whites. For over four years, until all were judged innocent of high treason on March 29, 1961, the government was able successfully to withdraw many of the Congress's most important leaders from the political arena.

An Emerging Leader

Anthony R. DeLuca

In the following excerpt, professor of history at Emerson College, Anthony R. DeLuca tracks Mandela's increasing political activity and opposition to the South African government. The year 1948, when the National Party came to power and began to legislate apartheid's segregational policies into official state law, marked a pivotal shift in both South African history and in Mandela's life.

In his book entitled Gandhi, Mao, Mandela, and Gorbachev: Studies in Personality, Power, and Politics, *DeLuca analyzes Mandela in the context of other key twentieth-century leaders with compelling and charismatic personalities. Here, DeLuca focuses on Mandela's changing responses to the entrenchment of white power from the late 1940s, through the 1950s, and up until Mandela's arrest in 1962.*

The election of 1948 was a major turning point in the history of South Africa and the struggle for black freedom and independence. The surprising triumph of a Nationalist Dutch Afrikaans government under the leadership of Dr. Daniel Malan and the introduction of *apartheid*, which stood for a policy of "complete racial separation," sent shock waves throughout South Africa. Malan's raising the specter of the "*swart gevaar*, the black peril," so antagonized blacks that even such a patient, tolerant figure from the old guard as Z.K. Matthews [black professor at the University of Fort Hare] concluded that there was no hope in negotiating with Malan's racist government. In brief, *apartheid*, meaning segregation, was built upon the premise of *baasskap* or "bossship" and by way of extension the much larger notion of white supremacy. The formula was simple: "*Eie volk, eie taal, eie land*—Our own people, our own language, our own land," and it obviously echoed in tone and spirit the perni-

Anthony R. DeLuca, *Gandhi, Mao, Mandela, and Gorbachev: Studies in Personality, Power, and Politics.* Westport, CT: Praeger, 2000. Copyright © 2000 by Anthony R. DeLuca. All rights reserved. Reproduced by permission.

cious words and message of Adolf Hitler's venomous racism. The Dutch Reformed Church also played a prominent role in underwriting the government's racist message, as did a powerful, influential "secret society, the Broederbond," meaning Band of Brothers. What followed was a new wave of racist legislation, including the Prohibition of Mixed Marriages Act; the Immorality Act, outlawing sexual relations between blacks and whites; the Population and Registration Act, which defined groups by race; and the Group Areas Act, which divided living areas within cities on the basis of race.

POST-1948 RESISTANCE TO APARTHEID BEGINS

In response to the government's political offensive, the Youth League urged the ANC leadership to take action and engage the masses through a nonviolent, political campaign. In this particular context, it is important to note that [Mahatma] Gandhi's failure to concern himself with African rights did not prevent Mandela from studying Gandhi's campaigns of civil disobedience in South Africa and realizing the symbolic importance of passive resistance and the political meaning of going to jail for violating the law. Dissatisfied with the African National Congress' (ANC) failure to respond to the call for militant action, the Youth League organized a coup forcing the "autocratic" president-general Dr. A.B. Xuma out of office and replacing him with a more sympathetic Dr. J.S. Moroka. Reflecting the change in emphasis and direction, the New Program of Action called for more militant, less "decorous" forms of protest, including "boycotts, strikes, civil disobedience, and noncooperation." But on May 1, 1950, the call to action came from a different quarter. This time it originated with the Communist party and the Indian Congress, who called for a one-day general strike in the form of a massive, popularly supported "stay-at-home." Though genuinely impressed with the intense commitment of the communists and the Indians to the general strike, the ANC believed that they should concentrate on their own campaign and remained aloof from the political action. The government's response, however, was to crack down on the protesters, which led to the death of eighteen Africans and to the introduction of the Supression of Communism Act, outlawing the Communist party, extending the hated banning orders, curtailing freedom of movement and expression, and prohibiting virtually every form of political protest.

The ANC now joined forces with the Indians and the communists in calling for a National Day of Protest on June 26, 1950, and publicly dedicating themselves to the liberation of South Africa, "black, white, and yellow." In addition to providing the Indians with much broader support, the new forms of collaboration enabled the ANC to gain valuable "organizational experience" and "fund-raising" skills from their Indian allies. The success of the protest led to June 26 being designated Freedom Day within the movement. Mandela, who now found himself totally consumed by the struggle, also discovered that his attitudes toward communism were changing. By expanding upon his earlier exposure to Fabian socialism and reading the works of Marx and Engels, Lenin, Stalin, Mao, and other Marxist thinkers, he discovered in Marxism the virtues of a communal life he had already encountered in African culture, the appeal of an analytical perspective, based upon dialectical materialism with its emphasis on built-in profit mechanisms within a capitalist economy, and the desirability of reallocating wealth and resources from the haves to the havenots. He also acknowledged the Soviet Union's support for the liberation of colonial peoples, and while he did not convert to communism, he realized that he could work with communists.

THE DEFIANCE CAMPAIGN OF 1952

To counteract the government's campaign of formal, legal segregation, the ANC with Mandela serving as Youth League president agreed to join with South African communists and Indians in a Defiance Campaign scheduled for June 26, 1952, in the spirit of the first Day of National Protest. Admitting to having some reservations about the newly expanded political alliance, Mandela nonetheless participated fully in the protest. But he was careful to acknowledge that his willingness to embrace nonviolent protest based on Gandhi's model of "passive resistance" was not absolute but conditional, since the government's overwhelming military and police superiority dictated the choice to be one of nonviolence as a "practical necessity." He also realized that he had to convey to his followers that the very nature of nonviolent conflict ultimately required "more courage and determination" than more violent forms of aggressive political action. In his role as a political strategist, he also maintained that a boycott had to be viewed as a "tactical weapon to be employed if and when objective conditions permit" and not as an inflexible principle to be applied irrespective of the immediate circumstances. Since Mandela also believed that the British in India were far "more realistic and farsighted" than the Afrikaners in South Africa, he viewed the boycott more as a question of tactics than principle, because the approach could readily be changed to accommodate changes in the political situation.

Responsible for the nationwide effort to recruit volunteers for the Defiance Campaign, Mandela constituted a "magnificent figure," handsome and "immaculately dressed" in his elegantly tailored three-piece suits. Both blacks and whites found him attractive, including, according to one white observer, "white women, [who] were turning to admire him." It quickly became apparent to friend and foe alike that Mandela "was a born mass leader" who possessed a commanding, magnetic appeal. And while the campaign failed to reverse any of the government's repressive racist legislation, it provided the government with cause for concern about the future of African-Indian cooperation. It also led to the arrest and trial of the campaign's leaders, including Mandela, under the terms of the Suppression of Communism Act. But the campaign had an equally powerful impact within the ANC, which was transformed from an elitist group into "a mass-based organization," where the previous "stigma" of imprisonment now became an emblem of courage. In reviewing his own role in recruiting, organizing, and speaking on behalf of the Defiance Campaign, Mandela recalled how he felt empowered by the events and his ability to "walk upright like a man, and look everyone in the eye with the dignity that comes from not having succumbed to oppression and fear."

THE BANNING OF MANDELA

That dignity was tested again when Mandela and fifty-one other leaders of the ANC were banned. The detested practice of banning meant that the government could severely restrict the travel of individuals and prevent them from speaking or participating in the activities of named organizations. In Mandela's view banning was a form of "walking imprisonment," which created a yearning to escape from a form of "psychological claustrophobia." In reflecting upon his own experience as a victim of government banning, Mandela described the treatment he received as an "unconvicted criminal" and how he had been legally transformed into a criminal not for what he "had done, but because of what [he] stood for." The government's smothering tactics also led to a dramatic change in ANC strategy and to Mandela's drafting of the M-Plan, which was named for its author. According to the plan, the ANC would establish an intricate network of underground cells to prepare for the time when the government would outlaw its activities and force its membership to alter the nature of the struggle. . . . While Mandela was setting the M-Plan in motion, he also pursued his other life as a successful lawyer in Johannesburg and opened his own law firm, inviting Oliver Tambo—his friend, ally, and trusted confidante—to join him. They made for an interesting partnership. Unlike Tambo, who was more "reflective" and philosophically inclined, Mandela was a "passionate," "combative" man, who asserted himself whenever the occasion presented itself. He would, for example, intentionally enter court through the whites-only entrance, much to the dismay of court officials. And although practicing law in South Africa was not an easy task for a black man, he somehow managed to draw from the "racial tension in the courtroom" and distinguish himself by his wry wit, defiant manner, and "flamboyant" courtroom style.

Having declared Sophiatown a "black spot" on the South African landscape, the government's decision to move its people and make room for new white neighborhoods fanned the flames of resentment and dissent and presented the ANC with its next real challenge. In the atmosphere of "increasing repressiveness," Mandela emerged as a "rabble-rousing" speaker who ignited the crowds, redefined the movement, and moved in the direction of endorsing violence. In an address known as the "No Easy Walk to Freedom" speech, which borrowed its title from an article by [Indian leader] Jawaharlal Nehru, Mandela hailed the Defiance Campaign before members of the Transvaal conference of the ANC as a "battlefield" that unleashed powerful political and social forces among their people. He also took this strategic opportunity to outline his own views on the deteriorating physical and economic situation confronting blacks in South Africa. Blacks, for example, were compelled to comb the countryside for work out of fear of being arrested as a result of their inability to pay the "poll tax." Moreover, those who were arrested often provided cheap labor to sustain the fortunes of white South African businesses and farms. Mandela also endorsed the idea of replacing the "old forms of mass protest" with "new forms of political struggle" and quoted Nehru's belief that "there is no easy walk to freedom anywhere and many of us will have to pass through the valley of the shadow of death again and again before we reach the mountain tops of our desires."

In 1953 the passage of the Bantu Education Act extended the policy of racial subjugation. The new legislation clearly reflected the racist presses of Dr. Hendrik Verwoerd, the Minister of Bantu education, who rigidly believed that "There is no place for the Bantu in the European community above the level of certain forms of labor" and that "natives" needed to "be taught from childhood . . . that equality with Europeans is not for them." Viewing the act as a form of "education for ignorance" in which indoctrination prevailed over free inquiry," Mandela described the South African system as lifelong submission to menial labor and subordination to white man's role. Under Verwoerd the state also imposed a more rigorous system of censorship by tightening its grip on the press, literature, and entertainment and gaining control over the media which became a powerful instrument for promoting anticommunism and rigid social conformity. The information restraints were also accompanied by new, tougher forms of interrogation and torture, which pointed South Africa ever further in the direction of a police state.

CONGRESS OF THE PEOPLE

In 1955 the ANC was instrumental in coordinating the Congress of the People. A multiracial gathering that included Indians, Coloureds [people of mixed racial ancestry], and whites within a predominantly black audience, the congress was a unique event in South African history. Mandela, who had approved the invitation to the congress, viewed it as a beautifully poetic document that spoke of "the wide lands and the narrow strips on which we toil, . . . of taxes and of cattle and of famine . . . OF FREEDOM!, . . . OF COAL, GOLD, AND DIAMONDS!, . . . [and of the dark shafts and the cold compounds," that undermined the cohesiveness of the family spirit. The congress itself created a "South Africa in microcosm" and openly reflected the socialist orientation of its leadership. Its Freedom Charter called upon all men and women irrespective of color and religion to create a free and democratic state, based upon popular rule with "EQUAL RIGHTS" for "ALL NATIONAL GROUPS," with the ability of all people to "SHARE IN THE COUNTRY'S WEALTH!" and participate in the distribution of the land among "THOSE WHO WORK IT!" By calling for the nationalization of wealth and its distribution among the people, the Charter set forth a revolutionary "programme of action."

Mandela's life as a public advocate for change increasingly thrust him into the political spotlight, and his life as a self-proclaimed "freedom fighter" caused him to reflect upon the need "to remain in touch with his own roots" and guard against the temptations of the "hurly-burly of city life." He also confronted the convoluted nature of his world when he wanted to give money to a white woman begging on the street, only to realize that in South Africa "to be poor and black was normal, to be poor and white was a tragedy." When the government announced its plan to create "bantustans" or homelands on marginal land with poor soil and inhospitable living conditions as separate territories of development for the black people of South Africa, the intention was clear. The Nationalist government had decided to turn South Africa into a patchwork of "ethnic enclaves" or "Reserves" in "poverty-stricken areas" in violation of the principles of "*democracy*," "*sovereignty*," and "self-determination." Supported by the tribal chiefs, who viewed their authority as hereditary and not elective, the government exploited the divisions within the African community and pursued a policy of *apartheid* on a grand scale by relegating 70 percent of the population to live on only 13 percent of the land.

Confronted with this challenge, Mandela turned to the pen and published a series of articles in the left-leaning journal *Liberation* from June 1953 to May 1959, outlining his political views. He cataloged the widespread human suffering brought about by inadequate food, disease, poor medical care, and people's hunger for land. He also condemned the abusive labor policy, which contributed to the cycle of misery and frustration among South Africa's blacks. He openly criticized the government's desire to create a pool of migrant laborers, separated from their families and forced to live in hostels as a means of undermining the emergence of a powerful African labor movement. And he condemned the "forcible detention of Africans . . . for spurious statutory offenses" as a means of creating a "vast market of cheap labor" to feed South Africa's economic expansion. He and his colleagues also exposed white reluctance to advocate the "democratic principle [of] 'one adult, one vote'" and labeled the Liberal Party's "high-sounding principles" of economic growth and expansion reactionary, because they perpetuated the *de facto* existence of the underclass. Moreover, he openly accused the white Liberal government, despite its denials of being inspired by any of Hitler's ideas, of being a "fascist regime" and of raising the "specter of Belsen and Buchenwald [two Nazi concentration camps]" in South Africa.

THE TREASON TRIAL

On December 5, 1956, Mandela and other members of the ANC leadership were arrested for high treason and sent to jail. Mandela would later admit that his own "foolhardy behavior" and inattention to detail had contributed to his arrest. When the accused appeared for their trial, their vans were greeted with a triumphant salute from ANC supporters. In court they were forced to sit inside a cage hemmed in "like wild beasts," until the court acceded to the protests of the defense to have the cage removed. In presenting the charges, the prosecution cited the Freedom Charter as evidence of communist intent and of a desire to overthrow the state. Faced with the charge of violent revolution and aware that the scales of justice were tilted against them in a predominantly Afrikaner court, the defendants chose to turn their trial into a countertrial and indict the government, its unjust racial policies, and the tyrannical domination of 13 million blacks by 3 million whites.

During a recess in the preparatory phases of the trial, Mandela happened to spot a beautiful young woman, Winnie Nomzano, on the streets of Johannesburg, only to see her again in his office a few weeks later. What followed was a whirlwind romance in which Mandela by his own admission both courted Winnie Nomzano and politicized her. In love and in awe of a man who was able to inspire such "confidence, faith, and courage," she simultaneously entered his life and the political world of the ANC. He in turn found new hope in their relationship and marriage, at a time when women had become openly active in the freedom struggle and had begun to contribute new strength to the movement. He believed, however, that despite an upsurge in political activism Winnie found it difficult to fashion "her own identity in my shadow." Their union produced three children, who possessed their father's warmth and magnanimity, despite his reputation as a stern authority figure and disciplinarian, and the crusading, restless spirit of their mother.

Although the outcome of the Treason Trial, as it came to be known, hinged on the government's ability to prove its case that the ANC had in fact "plotted violence," the future of the trial was also influenced by developments and events outside the courtroom. One such development was a defection by "exclusivists," who, under the influence of Marcus Garvey's doctrines of "Africa for the Africans" and "Hurl the Whiteman into the sea," broke from the ANC and in 1959 formed the Pan Africanist Congress (PAC) led by Robert Sobukwe. But while Mandela also emphasized the importance of maintaining African leadership and control of the movement, he preferred to alter the tone of Garvey's message to read as follows: "While I was not prepared to hurl the white man into the sea, I would have been perfectly happy if he had climbed aboard his steamships and left the continent of his own volition."

THE PAC IS FOUNDED

From the very beginning, the relations between the two organizations were, in Mandela's words, "more competitive than cooperative." Opposed to collaboration with whites, Indians, and communists, the PAC insisted on a black movement for black people only and accused the ANC of "selling out" to foreign interests. It is interesting to note that although PAC's conduct hardly made them the darlings of the South African government, Mandela believed that their avowed anticommunism made them "the darlings of the Western press and the American State Department." In March 1960 PAC announced its own pass campaign, calling upon blacks to leave their passes at home and surrender peacefully to government authorities. What followed was a cycle of protest, repression, and the imposition of martial law, following the eruption of the Sharpeville massacre. Of the sixty-nine Africans dead, most had been shot in the back while trying to flee the confrontation. According to Mary Benson, Mandela's biographer, "the people went berserk . . . as riots swept the country." News of the bloody event penetrated the courtroom and reverberated around the world, prompting the international community to follow events in

South Africa more closely and the UN Security Council to pass a resolution holding the South African government responsible for the shootings.

Meanwhile, Mandela was arrested at home as part of the official crackdown and placed in a cell where the stench, cockroaches, and vomit-soiled blankets served as a rude introduction to a new political reality. In keeping with the *apartheid* spirit, food was rationed, with blacks getting smaller proportions than Coloureds or Indians. Blacks were also denied bread on the assumption the blacks did not like bread, because it represented a "more sophisticated . . . 'Western' taste." Sharpeville also provoked a government crackdown, including the decision to outlaw both the ANC and PAC under the Suppression of Communism Act.

The Sharpeville massacre also marked a turning point for the opposition, as younger, more radical black political leaders advocated going underground and adopting more violent guerrilla tactics. It also had an impact on the significance of the Treason Trial, which now became, in Mandela's words, "a test of the power of a moral idea versus an immoral one." He, in fact, used the trial as a platform to denounce imperialism, lecture on commercial exploitation, and expose the fallacy of foreign investment as a means of raising people's standard of living by citing "low wages, . . . poverty, . . . misery, . . . illiteracy," and the rise in "squalid tenements" as proof to the contrary. When the government, basing sections of their case on Mandela's writings and speeches, tried to portray him as a communist, he took the opportunity to thank the communists in his testimony for the support the ANC had received, while scrupulously making the point that he was not a communist. He also warned of a new, different type of foreign intervention in which Europeans would pay greater attention to the ANC's economic pressure in South Africa. When the court finally rendered its verdict and declared the accused not guilty, it did so on the grounds that the government had failed to prove that the ANC had "acquired or adopted a policy to overthrow the state by violence," irrespective of all its inflammatory rhetoric. The victory, however, was bittersweet because Mandela and his colleagues realized that in future proceedings the government would make sure that the courts would return a guilty verdict.

Following the Treason Trial, Mandela made an electrifying appearance at the All-In African Conference, which served as a "unity forum" for a loosely knit alliance of opposition groups. Made up primarily of blacks, but including some white representatives, the conference called upon the government to convene a "national convention." If the government refused to comply, the participants set in motion plans for a three-day stay-at-home to begin on May 29, 1961. As the secretary of the national action committee, Mandela was responsible for drafting the letter to the government and coordinating the stay-at-home. When the protest drew less support than had been expected, Mandela decided to call it off in its second day, despite what he described as a show of "solid and massive support throughout the country," which included enthusiastic university students, "Coloured People," and the "entire Indian community," who participated in the action. He did, however, single out the "treacherous" press for its biased reporting and the malevolent police for its "fraudulent" announcement of the stay-at-home's collapse. He also began to question whether it was "politically correct to continue preaching peace and non-violence when dealing with a Government whose barbaric practices have brought so much suffering and misery to Africans." On behalf of the people, who produce the mass of wealth of the country, he argued that militant "noncollaboration is the weapon we must use to bring down the government." Moreover, he also came to the conclusion that since he had been forcibly "denied the right to live a normal life," he had no choice but to go underground, "live the life of an outlaw," organize a guerrilla campaign, and embrace the use of violence as a political weapon.

THE BLACK PIMPERNEL

For Mandela "living underground require[d] a seismic psychological lift," which turned him into a "creature of the night." As South Africa's "Black Pimpernel," an obvious adaptation of the fictional Scarlet Pimpernel of the French Revolution, he surreptitiously made his way through the country in an assortment of motley disguises. With all his energy now focused on making the case for revolution in the immediate political environment, he believed, as had Fidel Castro, that the movement should not rigorously follow "textbook conditions" or slavishly adhere to the Marxist concept of inherent contradictions in the social structure to justify the use and timing of violent political action. What was most important was to lead the people and not allow them to move ahead of the revolutionary leadership. It is interesting to note that in his reading of Edgar Snow's *Red Star over China* Mandela believed that "it was Mao's determination and nontraditional thinking that led him to victory." To achieve its goal, the ANC decided to form a new organization, *Umkhonto we Sizwe* (the Spear of the Nation), also known as MK, which was to remain separate from the ANC and organize the underground struggle against South Africa's racist regime through the use of violent means, including explosives. In June 1961 Mandela released a letter in which he spoke with conviction, passion, and the charismatic voice of an inspirational leader, quoting Abraham Lincoln to support the creation in South Africa of "a democratic government of the people, by the people, and for the people." In his letter he also announced his refusal to submit to arrest and declared his commitment to fight the government because "The struggle is my life. I will continue fighting for freedom until the end of my days."

Mandela found temporary "sanctuary" in the Liliesleaf-Farm located in Rivonia, a northern suburb of Johannesburg, which provided a temporary safe haven for MK's guerrillas within the confines of what he described as an "idyllic bubble." The decision to pursue sabotage as the primary form of violence reflected the movement's desire to inflict as little harm as possible on individuals and to focus its attack on military targets, communications, and transportation as a means of frightening away foreign capital and investments and calling attention to the plight of South Africa's black community. MK chose December 16, the day Afrikaners traditionally celebrated their victory over the Zulus in 1838, to stage its attack. In this instance the explosions hardly constituted a celebration for whites, although they did serve as a signal to both blacks and whites that a "powerful spear" was now aimed at the "heart of white power." Once again, the movement insisted that it had been forced to resort to violence because the government "had interpreted the peacefulness of the movement as weakness."

In February 1962 Mandela led the ANC delegation to the Pan African Freedom Movement conference in Addis Ababa. The trip, which was designed to search for outside support, funds, and opportunities for military training, provided Mandela with an opportunity to see more of the world, experience the absence of color bars in public places, observe a black man doing a "white man's job" flying an airplane, and luxuriate in the thrill of feeling like "a free man . . . for the first time in my life." In words that recalled the legacy of Martin Luther King, Jr., he described the feeling of "being judged . . . not by the color of my skin but by the measure of my mind and character." In Ethiopia he was deeply moved by the presence of Haile Selassie and the sight of black generals commanding black soldiers honoring black leaders in the presence of a black head of state. In Addis Ababa he delivered a passionate speech, identified by the phrase, "A Land Ruled by the Gun," in which he attributed the shift "away from the path of peace and non-violence" to the minority government's willful determination to maintain "its authority over the majority by force and violence." To reinforce the sense of dedication among his own people to the goals of national liberation, he stressed his unwavering commitment to popular self-reliance and his faith in the people of South Africa to combine their efforts and engage in "united action" to achieve their freedom.

In Egypt Mandela learned more about ancient African art and architecture and contemplated the impact [Egyptian president] Gamal Abdel Nasser's socialist reforms would have on the people of South Africa. But it was in Algeria that he encountered the model of a struggle by an indigenous people against colonial rule imposed from abroad that most closely corresponded to the situation at home. The underground freedom fighter then made his way across Europe to visit England, where his candid anglophile assessment praised the style and manners of the British, the quality of British officials he met, and the majesty of Westminster Abbey, the tower of Big Ben, and the houses of Parliament. On his way home he stopped in Ethiopia for military training and affirmed his belief that military training must be combined with appropriate forms of political training "to create a just and fair society."

Life with Him Was Always a Life Without Him

Winnie Mandela

The following selection is from Winnie Mandela's 1984 memoir of her life with Nelson, entitled *Part of My Soul Went with Him*. Her story was written with the assistance of Mary Benson and Anne Benjamin while Winnie was in confinement in the small town of Brandfort, South Africa. Looking back nearly thirty years to 1956, Winnie recalls the first time she met Nelson and the whirlwind romance that followed.

In fact Nelson and Winnie met during the Treason Trial, an enormous affair in which 156 people had been arrested for their alleged involvement in a plot to overthrow the government. The trial dragged on for several years, during which time Mandela appeared in court during the day and maintained his busy legal practice at nights and on weekends. Although the court ultimately failed to convict the accused for lack of hard evidence, the defendants' victories proved to be short-lived, for almost as soon as the trial ended, the state was hunting for new evidence with which to indict Mandela and others.

I saw Nelson Mandela for the first time in the Johannesburg Regional Court. He was representing a colleague of mine who had been assaulted by police. I just saw this towering, imposing man, actually quite awesome. (*Giggles.*) As he walked into court, the crowd whispered his name. He doesn't even know about this incident.

The second time was in the company of [ANC activist] Oliver Tambo and Adelaide Tsukudu (later his wife). Oliver comes from Bizana, the same village I come from, so I knew him slightly, and Adelaide and I were living at a hostel, the

Winnie Mandela, *Part of My Soul Went with Him*, edited by Anne Benjamin. New York: W.W. Norton & Co., 1985. Copyright © 1984 by Rowohlt Taschenbuch Verlag GmbH, Reinbek bei Hamburg. All rights reserved. Reproduced by permission of the publisher.

Helping Hand Club, and were close friends. I had just got off the bus from Baragwanath Hospital and they drove by and offered me a lift. Adelaide said she was starving so we stopped at a delicatessen. Oliver found he had no money but they noticed Nelson in the shop and Oliver said, 'Tell him to pay.' Which he did, and when he came out with Adelaide, Oliver introduced me as 'Winnie from Bizana'.

First Dates

Soon after, I got a telephone call from Nelson. He invited me to lunch and said he would send a friend to fetch me. I was of course petrified—he was much older than me and he was a patron of my school of social work. We had never seen him, he was just a name on the letterheads; he was too important for us students to even know him. So when I got this call, I couldn't work for the rest of the day. And when I prepared to go and meet him, I took out every schoolgirl's dress I possessed. Nothing seemed suitable—in those days we had almost knee-length frilled dresses that made one look even younger and more ridiculous. And when I ultimately found something more dignified—it wasn't even mine. I felt so uncomfortable.

It was a Sunday. He always worked right through—Saturdays, Sundays, Mondays, the days were the same. I was driven to his office where he was buried in files, there were stacks and stacks of files all over, and it was just about lunch-time.

We went to an Indian restaurant. I tasted Indian food for the first time—a little country bumpkin from Pondoland. I had associated most of the time with my professional colleagues and I hadn't really known much about Johannesburg social life. It was such a struggle to eat. I couldn't swallow. I was almost in tears because of this hot, hot curry. And he noticed and embarrassingly gave me a glass of water and said, 'If you find it too hot, it helps to take a sip of water.' And he was enjoying that hot unbearable food!

As we were eating, he couldn't swallow one spoonful without people coming to consult him—it was an impossible set-up. It went right through that very first appointment. And I felt so left out, I just didn't fit in.

Leaving the restaurant, going to his car, we took something like half an hour. Nelson couldn't walk from here to there without having consultations. He is that type of person, almost impossible to live with as far as the public is concerned.

He belongs to them. I didn't know that that was to be the pace of my life. I was just stunned and fascinated.

When we got back to the office it was the same story—there were people everywhere. So we drove out of town and walked in the veld, and he told me he had in fact phoned to ask if I could help raise funds for the Treason Trial. He never even asked me what my political affiliations were or whether I had any views at all. And I never dreamt of asking: how do I fit in, in this whole complex structure?

When we were walking back to the car, the path was rocky and my sandal strap broke. I was walking with difficulty, barefoot, so he held my hand as my father would hold a little girl's hand, and just before we got in the car, he said, 'It was a lovely day,' and just turned and kissed me.

The following day I got a phone call to say I would be picked up when I knocked off from work. He was there in the car dressed in his gym attire. He was a fanatic from the fitness point of view, so he was in his training clothes. That's where I was taken, to the gym, to watch him sweat out!

That was the pattern of my life right through the week. I was picked up—one moment I was watching him, then he would dash off to a string of meetings. He would just have time to drop me off at the hostel.

Even at that stage, life with him was a life without him. He did not even pretend that I would have some special claim to his time.

So if you are looking for some kind of romance, you won't find it. What he always did was to see to it that one comrade was there to pick me up. Even if I didn't see him for a week, I would be industriously collected and taken back to the hostel every day, and then of course the car must dash back to fetch him and take him to his meetings. I never had any frivolous romance with him—there never was time for that.

He took me to meet a lot of his friends. Almost every night there were consultations in the suburbs; there were meetings in the townships. Nobody asked questions, people were just comrades. I was also extremely involved in my own way, in my social work, in a lot of cultural activities and a large number of women's organizations.

Marrying Mandela

One day, Nelson just pulled up on the side of the road and said, 'You know, there is a woman, a dressmaker, you must go and see her, she is going to make your wedding-gown. How many bridesmaids would you like to have?' That's how I was told I was getting married to him! It was not put arrogantly; it was just something that was taken for granted. I asked, 'What time?' I was madly in love with him at that stage, and so was he with me in his own way. It was such a mutual feeling and understanding that we didn't have to talk about it.

He arranged for me to be driven to Pondoland to tell my family. I got there and for a whole day I couldn't bring myself to speak of it to my father. And then I couldn't do it directly, I told him through my stepmother. He was very shocked. Nelson was held in such high esteem and was such an important person in the country that my father couldn't imagine how I had found my way to him when I had been sent to do social work. My father was extremely proud.

But the family was also very concerned about the fact that Nelson had three children[1] and that I might not be able to cope. I never knew when he actually got divorced: I couldn't bring myself to ask such a thing right through our so-called courtship. And they were concerned about Nelson's future—after all, he was on trial for treason. Well, they were able to read history better than I was. But one becomes so much part and parcel of Nelson if you knew him that you automatically expected anything that happened to him to happen to yourself, and it didn't really matter. He gave you such confidence, such faith and courage. If you became involved in our cause as he was, it was just not possible to think in terms of yourself at all.

For him it was a total commitment which goes back to the days of his youth. Growing up in that tribal set-up in the countryside seemed to give him his background; he is a traditionalist. I don't mean in the stifled, narrow sort of way. Rather in the sense that what he is in the struggle, he is because of the love of his country, the love of his roots. He used to philosophize about the elders—white-haired, heavily bearded old men smoking their pipes beside the huge fireplaces outside the *kraal* [homestead]—about their wisdom which he admired so much. It was those elders who instilled that pride in him, and love of his people. It's an incredibly strong bond—he himself as a person comes second to this love for his people, and the love of nature.

---

1. Mandela's two sons and daughter lived with their mother in Johannesburg.

In June 1958 he was granted four days' permission to leave Johannesburg for us to get married—besides being an accused in the Treason Trial he was also banned—and I insisted on getting married at home in Pondoland, because nothing could have pleased my father better and I wanted Nelson to see my background. It was an initiation for the kind of life we were heading for anyway because we had to dash back without even completing the usual marriage ceremony in the traditional manner. After the marriage in my home, we were supposed to then get married in his home as well. As far as the elders in the family are concerned, we haven't finished getting married to this day.

It was both a traditional marriage and to some extent a Western ceremony. Of course Nelson paid *lobola* [a symbolic "bride price"] for me; I never found out how much it was. It is not talked of in terms of money but in terms of cattle. (For years, Brigadier Coetzee, who is now head of the Security Branch, kept Nelson's letter from my father, in which he acknowledged the *lobola*. And during my interrogation in 1969, I remember this horrible Swanepoel saying: 'Poor Nelson, he must have been terribly stranded to pay so much for a woman like you!')

The day Nelson comes out of prison, we must go and complete the second part of our ceremony. I still have the wedding cake, the part of that cake we were supposed to have taken to his place. I brought it here to Brandfort. It crumbled a bit when they dumped our things. It is now in my house in Orlando, waiting for him.

CHAPTER 3

TRIAL AND PRISON

PEOPLE
WHO MADE
HISTORY

NELSON MANDELA

Remembering Rivonia

Nelson Mandela

The following extract is from Mandela's autobiography that he began to write in secret in 1974. Although Mandela's original was confiscated by the authorities, his friends and comrades managed to smuggle out a copy, which Mandela recovered and completed after his release in 1991.

After Mandela returned from his tour of African states, where he gathered political and financial support for Umkhonto we Sizwe (MK), he returned to South Africa secretly and proceeded directly to Liliesleaf Farm in Rivonia, the MK hideout. Two days later he set out for Durban in disguise, in order to meet with the head of the African National Congress (ANC), Chief Albert Luthuli, and report to him on his pan-African tour.

Soon after Mandela's party had left Durban for the four-hundred-mile return drive to Johannesburg, their car was stopped by police near Pietermaritzburg, an hour or so from Durban, and Mandela was arrested and taken into police custody. At the time, Mandela felt certain that the police had been tipped off by informants within the ANC; in later years it became evident that the CIA had been integrally involved in the operation, for at the time Mandela's pro-Communist stance had been seen as a threat to U.S. interests in South Africa (since South Africa supplied the United States with plutonium).

After spending some weeks in jail, Mandela was put on trial. He received a five-year sentence: three years for inciting people to strike and two years for leaving the country illegally without a passport, and soon after was moved to Robben Island for imprisonment. Although, at the time, five years was the longest prison term that the South African court system had yet handed down for a political sentence, the police

Nelson Mandela, *Long Walk to Freedom.* New York: Little, Brown & Co., 1994. Copyright © 1994 by Nelson Rolihlahla Mandela. All rights reserved. Reproduced by permission of the publisher.

had not yet discovered the hideout at Liliesleaf Farm, which contained a cache of incriminating documents. Thus at that point, they were unable to provide evidence that Mandela was the leader of MK and that the organization was planning guerrilla activities.

Unfortunately, however, Mandela was not far into serving his sentence when he was suddenly transported back to Johannesburg. Liliesleaf Farm in Rivonia had been discovered, and Mandela and other MK members were to face another trial. In this, the famous Rivonia trial, the state was seeking the death penalty for the accused saboteurs.

One day a captain came to our cell and commanded the four of us to pack our belongings. Within minutes my comrades were taken away, leaving me in the cell by myself. Very early the next morning I was taken back to Pretoria. The Department of Prisons released a statement to the press that I had been removed from the island for my own safety because Pan Africanist Congress (PAC) prisoners were planning to assault me.

I was kept in solitary confinement at Pretoria Local. But prisoners are resourceful and I was soon receiving secret notes and other communications from some of the ANC people there. I had a communication from Henry Fazzie, one of the MK cadres who had undergone military training in Ethiopia and been arrested while attempting to return to South Africa. They were among the first ANC members to be tried under the Sabotage Act.

Through the prison grapevine, I attempted to help them with their defence and suggested they contact Harold Wolpe. I later heard that Wolpe was in police detention. This was my first intimation that something had gone seriously wrong. One day, as I was being led away from the courtyard after exercise, I saw Andrew Mlangeni. I had last seen him in September 1961 when he was leaving the country for military training. Wolpe, Mlangeni—who else was under arrest?

Early in 1961, [Mandela's wife] Winnie had been banned for two years. I heard from another prisoner that Winnie had recently been charged with violating her bans, which could lead to imprisonment or house arrest. I had no doubt that she violated her orders, and I would never counsel her not to do so, but it concerned me greatly that she might spend time in prison.

One morning in July 1963, as I was walking along the corridor to my cell, I saw Thomas Mashifane, who had been the foreman at Liliesleaf Farm. His presence there could mean only one thing: the authorities had discovered Rivonia.

A day or two later I was summoned to the prison office where I found Walter [Sisulu]; Govan Mbeki; Ahmed Kathrada; Andrew Mlangeni; Bob Hepple; Raymond Mhlaba, a member of the MK High Command who had recently returned from training in China; Elias Motsoaledi, also a member of MK; Dennis Goldberg, an engineer and a member of the Congress of Democrats; Rusty Bernstein, an architect and also a member of the COD; and Jimmy Kantor, an attorney who was Harold Wolpe's brother-in-law. We were all charged with sabotage, and scheduled to appear in court the next day.

THE POLICE RAID LILIESLEAF FARM

I gradually learned what had happened. On the afternoon of 11 July, a van drove up to the farm and dozens of armed policemen and several police dogs sprang out. They surrounded the property and entered the main building. The police confiscated hundreds of documents and papers, though they found no weapons. One of the most important documents was Operation Mayibuye, a plan for guerrilla warfare in South Africa. In one fell swoop, the police had captured the entire High Command of Umkhonto we Sizwe. Everyone was detained under the new Ninety-Day Detention Law. The raid was a coup for the state.

We were brought before a magistrate and charged with sabotage. A few days later we were allowed to meet Bram [Fischer, head attorney for the accused], Vernon Berrange, Joel Joffe, George Bizos and Arthur Chaskalson, all of whom were acting for us. I was still being kept separately as I was a convicted prisoner, and these sessions were my first opportunity to talk with my colleagues.

Bram was very sombre. He told us that the state had formally advised him they would ask for the supreme penalty permitted by law, the death sentence. Given the climate of the times, Bram said, this was a very real possibility. From that moment on we lived in the shadow of the gallows. The mere possibility of a death sentence changes everything. From the start, we considered it the most likely outcome of the trial. Far lesser crimes than ours had recently been punished by life sentences.

On 9 October 1963, we were driven to the Palace of Justice in Pretoria for the opening of 'The State versus the National High Command and others', better known as the Rivonia Trial.

THE RIVONIA TRIAL BEGINS

The Palace of Justice was teeming with armed policemen. All around the building police officers with machine guns stood at attention. As we got out, we could hear the great crowd singing and chanting.

When we entered the courtroom, we each turned to the crowd and made a clenched-fist ANC salute. In the visitors' gallery our supporters shouted *'Amandla! Ngawethu!'* [Power! To the People!] and *'Mayibuye Afrika!'* [Freedom Africa!]. This was inspiring, but dangerous: the police took the names and addresses of all the spectators in the galleries, and photographed them as they left the court. The courtroom was filled with domestic and international journalists, and dozens of representatives of foreign governments.

Our judge in the Rivonia Trial, Mr. Quartus de Wet, judge-president of the Transvaal, was one of the last judges appointed by the United Party before the Nationalists came to power, and was not considered a government lackey. The prosecutor was Dr. Percy Yutar, deputy attorney general of the Transvaal, whose ambition was to become attorney general of South Africa.

We were charged with sabotage and conspiracy rather than high treason because the law does not require a long preparatory examination (which is highly useful to the defence) for sabotage and conspiracy. Yet the supreme penalty—death by hanging—is the same. With high treason, the state must prove its case beyond a reasonable doubt; under the Sabotage Law, the onus was on the defence to prove the accused innocent.

Bram Fischer stood up and asked the court for a remand on the grounds that the defence had not had time to prepare its case. He noted that a number of the accused had been held in solitary confinement for unconscionable lengths of time. The state had been preparing for three months, but we had only received the indictment that day. Justice de Wet gave us a three-week adjournment until 29 October.

On 29 October, we again entered the Palace of Justice;

again the crowds were large and excited; again the court was filled with dignitaries from many foreign embassies.

We went on the attack immediately—Bram Fischer criticized the state's indictment as shoddy, poorly drawn and containing absurdities such as the allegation that I had participated in certain acts of sabotage on dates when I was in Pretoria Local. Yutar was flummoxed. De Wet was impatient with Yutar's fumbling and told him so. He then quashed the indictment.

For that moment we were technically free, and there was pandemonium in the court. But we were rearrested even before Judge de Wet left his seat. Lieutenant Swanepoel clapped each of us on the shoulder and said, 'I am arresting you on a charge of sabotage', and we were herded back to our cells. Even so, this was a blow to the government, for it now had to go back to the drawing-board in the case it was calling the trial to end all trials.

The state redrew its indictment and we were back in court in early December. The new charges were read: we were alleged to have recruited persons for sabotage and guerrilla warfare for the purpose of starting a violent revolution; we had allegedly conspired to aid foreign military units to invade the republic in order to support a communist revolution; and we had solicited and received funds from foreign countries for this purpose.

Yutar argued that from the time the ANC had been driven underground, the organization had embarked on a policy of violence designed to lead from sabotage through guerrilla warfare to an armed invasion of the country. He asserted that we planned to deploy thousands of trained guerrilla units throughout the country, and these units were to spearhead an uprising that would be followed by an armed invasion by military units of a foreign power.

We wondered what evidence the state had to prove my guilt. I had been out of the country and in prison while much of the planning at Rivonia had taken place. When I saw Walter [Sisulu] in Pretoria Local, I urged him to make sure that all my books and notes were removed from the farm. But during the first week of the trial, when Rusty Bernstein applied for bail, Percy Yutar dramatically produced the sketch of the Fort and the accompanying note about escape that I had made while detained there. [Mandela discussed but rejected a possible escape from jail. The telltale note was supposed to have been destroyed but never was.] Yutar exclaimed that this was evidence that all of the accused meant to escape. It was a sign that nothing of mine had been removed from Rivonia. Later, I was told that my colleagues at Rivonia had decided to preserve my escape note because they thought it would be historic in the future. But in the present, it cost Rusty Bernstein his bail.

OPERATION MAYIBUYE

The keystone of the state's case was the six-page Plan of Action confiscated in the Rivonia raid. Operation Mayibuye sketches out in general form the plan for the possible commencement of guerrilla operations, and how it might spark a mass armed uprising against the government. It envisions an initial landing of small guerrilla forces in four different areas of South Africa and the attacking of preselected targets. The document set a goal of some 7,000 MK recruits in the country who would meet the initial outside force of 120 trained guerrillas.

The prosecution's case rested in large part on their contention that Operation Mayibuye had been approved by the ANC Executive and had become the operating plan of MK. We insisted that Operation Mayibuye had not yet been formally adopted and was still under discussion at the time of the arrests. As far as I was concerned, it was a draft document that was not only not approved, but was entirely unrealistic in its goals and plans.

The plan had been drafted in my absence, so I had very little knowledge of it. Even among the Rivonia Trialists there was disagreement as to whether the plan had been adopted as ANC policy. Govan [Mbeki], who had drafted the document with Joe Slovo, insisted that it had been agreed upon. But all the other accused contended that the document, while drawn up by the High Command, had not been approved by the ANC Executive or even seen by Chief Luthuli.

The state case continued during the Christmas season of 1963, ending on 29 February 1964. We had a little over a month to examine the evidence and prepare our defence. There was no evidence against James Kantor; he was not even a member of our organization and should not have been on trial at all. For Rusty Bernstein, Raymond Mhlaba and Ahmed Kathrada, the evidence of involvement in conspiracy was slight and we decided they should not incriminate themselves. In Rusty's case, the evidence was negligible; he had merely been found at Rivonia with the others. The remaining six of us would make admissions of guilt on certain charges.

Bram was deeply pessimistic. Even if we proved that guerrilla war had not been approved and our policy of sabotage was designed not to sacrifice human life, the state could still impose the death sentence. The defence team was divided on whether or not we should testify. George Bizos, though, suggested that unless we gave evidence and convinced the judge that we had not decided on guerrilla war-

---

DRUM MAGAZINE REPORTS ON THE RIVONIA TRIAL

Throughout the 1950s and 1960s, Drum *magazine recorded the conflict in South Africa through compelling photographs and writing that brought the apartheid struggle out of the townships and into the larger environment of South Africa and the world. The following excerpt is from an article in the December 1963 issue titled "South Africa Goes on Trial." Here the author suggests that in the eyes of the international community, the South African government is as much on trial for its apartheid policies at Rivonia than any of the anti-apartheid defendants.*

All South Africa is on trial: its political leaders, its people, its government. For the men now charged at the country's three major sabotage trials are not alone in their predicament. The very people who introduced the legislation under which the men are being charged, are themselves on trial—on trial before the world.

At the United Nations, at meetings of international jurists and at special gatherings in many countries, the South African government has been condemned both for its Sabotage Act and for putting these men on trial. There are scores of sabotage trials throughout the country, but the world's attention is focused on the three major hearings and, in particular, on the Pretoria trial which arose out of the spectacular Rivonia raid. Not since the Treason Trial has there been so much world interest in South African judicial proceedings. The three trials are completely separate and the charges against the men in each one are different. Whatever the outcome, *Drum* says that it is a tragedy that outstanding and brilliant men like Nelson Mandela, Walter Sisulu, Billy Nair and Neville Alexander should be standing trial today instead of being able to play active—and vital—roles in running the country.

Jurgen Schadeburg, ed., *Nelson Mandela and the Rise of the ANC.* Parklands, South Africa: A.D. Donker and Jonathan Ball, 1990.

fare, he would certainly impose the supreme penalty.

I would be the first witness and therefore set the tone for the defence. We decided that instead of giving testimony, I would read a statement from the dock, while the others would testify and go through cross-examination.

I spent about a fortnight drafting my address. I asked Bram Fischer to look it over. Bram became concerned and got a respected advocate named Hal Hanson to read it. Hanson told Bram, 'If Mandela reads this in court they will take him straight out to the back of the courthouse and string him up.' Bram begged me not to read the final paragraph, but I was adamant.

On Monday 20 April, under the tightest of security, we were taken to the Palace of Justice, this time to begin our defence. Winnie was there with my mother, and I nodded to them as we entered the court, which was again full.

Bram announced that certain parts of the state's evidence would be conceded by the accused, and there was a buzz in the court. But he went on to say that the defence would deny a number of the state's assertions, including the contention that Umkhonto we Sizwe was the military wing of the ANC. He stated that the defence would show that Umkhonto had not in fact adopted Operation Mayibuye, and that MK had not embarked on preparations for guerrilla warfare.

Then Bram said, 'The defence case, My Lord, will commence with a statement from the dock by accused No. 1, who personally took part in the establishment of Umkhonto, and who will be able to inform the court of the beginnings of that organization.'

MANDELA'S STATEMENT FROM THE DOCK

I rose and faced the courtroom and read slowly.

After I had finished, the silence in the courtroom was complete. I had read for over four hours. It was a little after 4 in the afternoon, the time court normally adjourned. But Justice de Wet, as soon as there was order in the courtroom, asked for the next witness. He was determined to lessen the impact of my statement, but nothing he did could weaken its effect.

The speech received wide publicity in both the local and foreign press, and was printed, virtually word for word, in the *Rand Daily Mail*. This despite the fact that all my words were banned. The speech both indicated our line of defence and disarmed the prosecution, which had prepared its entire case based on the expectation that I would be denying responsibility for sabotage. It was now plain that we would not attempt to use legal niceties to avoid accepting responsibility for actions we had taken with pride and premeditation.

Accused No. 2, Walter Sisulu, was next. Walter withstood a barrage of hostile questions to explain our policy in clear and simple terms. He asserted that Operation Mayibuye and the policy of guerrilla warfare had not been adopted as ANC policy. In fact, Walter told the court that he had personally opposed its adoption on the grounds that it was premature.

Govan, Ahmed Kathrada and Rusty Bernstein testified to their membership of the Communist Party as well as the ANC. Although Rusty was captured at Rivonia during the raid, the only direct evidence that the state had against him was that he had assisted in the erection of a radio aerial at the farm. Kathy, in his sharp-witted testimony, denied committing acts of sabotage or inciting others to do so, but he said he supported such acts if they advanced the struggle.

Raymond Mhlaba was one of the leading ANC and MK figures in the eastern Cape, but because the state did not have much evidence against him, he denied he was a member of MK and that he knew anything about sabotage. The defence rested. All that remained were the final arguments and then judgment.

Defence counsel Arthur Chaskalson rose first to deal with some of the legal questions raised by the prosecution. He rejected Yutar's statement that the trial had anything to do with murder, and reminded the court that MK's express policy was that there should be no loss of life. When Arthur began to explain that other organizations committed acts of sabotage for which the accused were blamed, de Wet interrupted to say he already accepted that as a fact. This was another unexpected victory.

Bram Fischer spoke next and was prepared to tackle the state's two most serious contentions: that we had undertaken guerrilla warfare and that the ANC and MK were the same. Though de Wet had said he believed that guerrilla warfare had not yet begun, we were taking no chances. But as Bram launched into his first point, de Wet interjected somewhat testily, 'I thought I made my attitude clear. I accept that no decision or date was fixed upon for guerrilla warfare.'

When Bram began his second point, de Wet again interrupted him to say that he also conceded the fact that the two organizations were separate. Bram, who was usually prepared for anything, was hardly prepared for de Wet's response. He then sat down; the judge had accepted his arguments even before he had made them. We were jubilant—that is, if men facing the death sentence can be said to be jubilant. Court was adjourned for three weeks while de Wet considered the verdict.

A Verdict Is Reached

On Thursday 11 June we reassembled in the Palace of Justice for the verdict. We knew that for at least six of us there could be no verdict but guilty. The question was the sentence.

De Wet pronounced each of the main accused guilty on all counts. Kathy was found guilty on only one of four counts, and Rusty Berstein was found not guilty and discharged.

'I do not propose to deal with the question of sentence today,' de Wet said. 'The state and the defence will be given opportunities to make any submission they want tomorrow morning at ten o'clock.' Court was then adjourned.

We had hoped that Kathy and Mhlaba might escape conviction, but it was another sign, if one was necessary, that the state was taking a harsh line. If he could convict Mhlaba on all four counts with little evidence, could the death sentence be far behind for those of us against whom the evidence was overwhelming?

That night, after a discussion among ourselves, Walter, Govan and I informed counsel that whatever sentences we received, even the death sentence, we would not appeal. Our decision stunned our lawyers. Walter, Govan and I believed an appeal would undermine the moral stance we had taken. We had from the first maintained that what we had done, we had done proudly and for moral reasons. We were not going to suggest otherwise in an appeal. If a death sentence was passed, we did not want to hamper the mass campaign that would surely spring up. Our message was that no sacrifice was too great in the struggle for freedom.

I was prepared for the death penalty. To be truly prepared for something, one must actually expect it. We were all prepared, not because we were brave but because we were realistic. I thought of the line from Shakespeare: 'Be absolute for death; for either death or life shall be the sweeter.'

On Friday 12 June 1964 we entered court for the last time. Nearly a year had passed since the fateful arrests at Rivonia.

Security was extraordinarily high.

Before sentence was passed, there were two pleas in mitigation. One was delivered by Harold Hanson and the other by the author Alan Paton, who was also national president of the Liberal Party. Hanson spoke eloquently, saying that a nation's grievances cannot be suppressed, that people will always find a way to give voice to those grievances.

Though Paton did not himself support violence, he said the accused had had only two alternatives: 'to bow their heads and submit, or to resist by force'. The defendants should receive clemency, he said, otherwise the future of South Africa would be bleak.

But de Wet seemed absorbed in his own thoughts. He nodded for us to rise. His face was very pale, and he was breathing heavily. We looked at each other and seemed to know: it would be death, otherwise why was this normally calm man so nervous? And then he began to speak.

> The function of this court, as is the function of the court in any other country, is to enforce law and order and to enforce the laws of the state within which it functions. The crime of which the accused have been convicted, that is the main crime, the crime of conspiracy, is in essence one of high treason. The state has decided not to charge the crime in this form. Bearing this in mind and giving the matter very serious consideration I have decided not to impose the supreme penalty which in a case like this would usually be the proper penalty for the crime, but consistent with my duty that is the only leniency which I can show. The sentence in the case of all the accused will be one of life imprisonment.

The police were extremely nervous about the crowd outside. They kept us underground for more than half an hour, hoping people would disperse. We were taken through the back of the building and entered the black van. To avoid the crowd, the van took a different route, but even so, we could hear the crowd shouting *'Amandla!'* [freedom], and the slow beautiful rhythms of *'Nkosi Sikelel' iAfrika'* [Xhosa song that is now South Africa's national anthem].

AFTERMATH

That night, I ran over the reasons for de Wet's decision. The demonstrations throughout South Africa and the international pressure undoubtedly weighed on his mind. International trade unions had protested. Dock-workers' unions around the world threatened not to handle South African goods. The Russian prime minister, Leonid Brezhnev, wrote to Dr. [Hendrik] Verwoerd [prime minister of South Africa, 1958–1966] asking for leniency. Members of the United States Congress protested. Fifty members of the British Parliament had staged a march in London. Alec Douglas-Home, the British foreign secretary, was rumoured to be working behind the scenes to help our cause. Adlai Stevenson, the US representative at the UN, wrote a letter saying that his government would do everything it could to prevent a death sentence. I thought that once de Wet had accepted that we had not yet initiated guerrilla warfare and that the ANC and MK were separate entities, it would have been difficult to impose the death penalty; it would have seemed excessive.

Verwoerd told Parliament that the judgment had not been influenced by the telegrams of protest and representations that had come in from around the world. He boasted that he had tossed into the waste-basket all the telegrams from socialist nations.

Every evening, in Pretoria Local, before lights were out, the jail would echo to African prisoners singing freedom songs. We too would sing in this great swelling chorus. But, each evening, seconds before the lights were dimmed, as if in obedience to some silent command, the hum of voices would stop and the entire jail would become silent. Then, from a dozen places throughout the prison, men would yell *'Amandla!'* This would be met by hundreds of voices replying *'Ngawethu!'*

The Defense Strategy

Joel Joffe

The extract that follows was written by Joel Joffe, an attorney for Mandela and many of the other accused, in collaboration with Rusty Bernstein and others involved in the trial. Joffe recounts the difficulties of planning the legal defense. The defense team had a mere five weeks in which to pore through thousands of pages of documents, they were forced to break for several hours at midday so the jail wardens could eat lunch, and their strategy discussions were taped and censored. Nonetheless, despite these difficulties, the defense team was composed of some of the best legal talent in South Africa including Bram Fischer, the brilliant, understated lawyer and activist.

The central issue Joffe discusses in this account is the debate over whether the accused should testify or not during the trial. Counsel believed that it was unwise to do so, for it would be very easy for Mandela and the others to unwittingly incriminate themselves in some way. But for various reasons, the accused, and Mandela in particular, argued that they had an important obligation to take the stand and explain their position. In fact, against the advice of counsel, Mandela chose this course, and delivered a brilliant and compelling speech that lasted over five hours, and ended with the famous words: "During my lifetime I have dedicated myself to the struggle of the African people. . . . It is an ideal which I hope to live for and to achieve. But if needs be it is an ideal for which I am prepared to die."

We had five weeks in which to prepare our defence. It was at once simple in so far as so much was admitted by us, and yet extremely complicated. Because of the sheer volume of evidence, especially documentary, the defence virtually di-

Joel Joffe, *The Rivonia Story*. Cape Town, South Africa: Mayibuye Books of the University of the Western Cape, 1995. Copyright © 1995 by Joel Joffe. All rights reserved. Reproduced by permission.

vided into two separate sections. On the one hand consideration had to be given to the individual position of each accused, the extent of the evidence against him. On the other hand, there was the overall consideration—which to the accused seemed to be the most important—that of establishing the true facts of the movements in which they had been engaged and their true aims as distinct from the gross distortions presented by the prosecution. . . .

The lives of the accused were at stake. The State case alleged that they had already embarked on the organisation of armed insurrection and guerrilla warfare; that in pursuit of this plan they had already arranged for the intervention of military forces of foreign powers against the Republic of South Africa. By way of aggravation of sentence, the State had led much evidence of cases of murder, and of sabotage where murder could be said to have been attempted. With this case accepted by the court, the peril to the lives of the accused was real and grave.

The accused denied absolutely that they had decided to launch guerrilla warfare, though they admitted that all their planning was based on a realisation that if all else failed, the time would come when they would turn to guerrilla warfare. They were quite prepared for it and ready to admit it. But that time had not, in their view, been reached at the time of their arrest. They had not contemplated direct intervention by foreign military forces at all, and most of them in fact thought that even to visualise such a prospect was a political error. It was then vital for us to clarify the significance of the document 'Operation Mayibuye' on which the State relied to establish its allegations, and which the prosecution described as "the corner-stone of the State case".

TO GIVE EVIDENCE OR NOT

It seemed almost certain that the three I have named, [Rusty] Bernstein, [Raymond] Mhlaba and [Ahmed] Kathrada, would all have to go into the witness box and give evidence. So far as the others were concerned, there was a very serious question in our minds over whether they should give evidence.

At the commencement of our preparations, our legal team was inclined to the view that they should not. We argued that they could say little that would prove that guerrilla warfare had not been decided upon or initiated—nothing that could not be as well or better deduced by counsel, from documents. Under cross-examination they might make statements or admissions which could damage the chances of argument on their behalf being believed. Our hesitation to put them in the witness stand was based on the assumption that [prosecuting attorney] Dr. Yutar would not cross-examine the accused on matters of politics; he would stick closely to the law, and the facts. On matters of politics he had shown himself throughout this case to be a complete amateur. . . .

Whenever opportunity permitted during the State case, the accused had been discussing amongst themselves their versions of the facts. They had laid down for themselves a very clear basic principle: they would state the facts as fully as possible, but they would not under any circumstances reveal any information whatsoever about their organisations, or about people involved in the movement, where such information could in any way endanger their liberty. They would reveal what was necessary to explain and justify their political stand, provided only that it implicated no one other than themselves, and that it did not in any way undermine the safety and continued existence of their organisations which were still operating illegally.

We explained to them that once in the witness box, they were obliged to answer all questions put. They insisted, quite simply, that they would refuse to answer any questions which they thought might implicate their colleagues or their organisations. We told them that in doing so they might well antagonise the judge and make their case worse, not better. They were unimpressed. They felt from the outset that because of their standing in their movement and in the country, it was not only their right but also their obligation to go into the witness box and explain precisely what they had been aiming to do and why. Thus, the record would be put straight and the falsifications and distortions of the State against them would be answered in public. . . .

Mandela's Stance

The next problem was how to present the case they wanted. At first, working on the assumption that the accused would go into the witness box in numerical order—either all of them or only some—we assumed that Mandela would be first and would take the first hammering from the prosecution. We started preparing the evidence we would lead, but the more preparation we did, the more unhappy he and his colleagues became. They had begun to realise that the case which they wished to put to the world—their side of the case—would not emerge forcibly through Mandela in the witness box. It would come out in a jumble of bits and pieces, led in the spasmodic fashion which question and answer necessarily provides. There would be no cohesive statement which they and their supporters in the country and abroad would be able to build upon, or even to understand. Second, they began to feel that Mandela's voluntary entry into the witness box for cross-examination would appear to be a retraction from the position he had taken during his own trial on the charge of incitement in which he had been sentenced to the five-year term he was currently serving. At that trial he had refused to enter the witness box. He had made a strong statement from the dock attacking the institutions of white supremacy, including particularly white supremacist justice, in terms of which, he had said, he was being tried by an all-white court, white magistrate, white prosecutor and white police investigating officers. Under such circumstances he had said, equal justice, real justice could not be done. And accordingly, he had told the court, he refused to plead before such a court. Let the court decide his case as it chose!

Would it be possible on this occasion, to give evidence without apparently contradicting that stand on principle, which had had an exhilarating effect on his followers at the time.... It was these two factors that finally led all the accused to the decision, Mandela himself being the most insistent supporter of this point of view, that he should not go into the witness box for cross-examination. We decided that, instead he would make a carefully prepared, lucid and exhaustive statement of the political aims of the accused, their attitudes and their work, which would stand as the frame into which we would set the defence of all the others. Thereafter, the others would go into the witness box for cross-examination....

Mandela, the Leader

It was during this period that I, and I think all the counsel, began really to know the men for whose lives we were fighting. Their personalities began to emerge clearly before us, and their differing characters, qualities and capabilities showed themselves. Nelson Mandela emerged quite naturally as the leader. He has, in my view, all the attributes of a leader—the engaging personality, the ability, the stature, the calm, the diplomacy, the tact and the conviction. When I first met him, I found him attractive and interesting. By the time the case finished I regarded him as a really great man. I began to notice how his personality and stature impressed itself not just on the group of the accused, but on the prison and the prison staff themselves. Somehow Nelson was treated in a particular way—not quite with deference, for that is not the word—rather with respect. Everyone in the jail from the Colonel down to the most unenlightened, uneducated and unfeeling warder, treated him in a special way. I think they realised that, with Nelson, they were dealing with a bigger man than themselves, though this did not mitigate their hatred for all that he stood for. In some ways, coupled with their fear and their contempt there was a strange inverted awe for one whom they regarded as a "Kaffir," better educated, more able than they could ever hope to be. It was perhaps part of Nelson's greatness that he never dictated, nor made himself a law unto himself. He would always consult, discuss, argue, and finally be guided by the opinions of his colleagues around him. Yet he was never a follower; he was one who worked and moved with the group and at its head.

And so sitting daily huddled around a table, with little notes passing backwards and forwards, and obscure conversations with coded key words which we hoped only we understood, we prepared the case for the defence. While the others worked at their own evidence, Mandela worked steadily at his statement to be made from the dock. But at no time did we disclose to the prison authorities or to the prosecution that he would not go into the witness box.

I have said before that I don't think Dr. Yutar ever came to understand the accused or their attitude to the charges against them. Certainly in this preparation for the defence innings it seems to me he went wildly astray. On the day that court reassembled, it appeared to us that he had prepared himself as though the only man to be cross-examined was Nelson Mandela. In a normal case Mandela was the one accused who would certainly have taken the stand to exonerate himself on the basis that his culpability was minimal because he had been in jail throughout the period of the main offence. And Yutar, I think, imagined this case would run like any other. In his failure to understand the accused, he must have imagined that Mandela would behave as the run-of-the-mill criminal does in court: lying, distorting, concocting alibis and explanations, and relying on every possible legalism. I believe that it was on this basis that Yutar prepared himself to tackle Mandela, and what he fully expected would be Mandela's lies about himself, his activities, his organisation, his leaders, his own part in the conspiracy and the plans and tactics of Umkhonto we Sizwe. In this, perhaps more than anything else in the case, Yutar revealed how deeply he was out of his depth.

On Monday, 23 April, the courthouse was packed with spectators. Dozens of uniformed police were inside and outside the building, mingling with the plain-clothes detectives, friends and relations of the accused, and interested outsiders, mainly African. There was a large contingent of students from the Pretoria University, hostile to the accused. As the crowd milled about in Church Square outside the Palace of the Justice, a special branch photographer rested his telephoto lens on the shoulder of a sergeant and took snapshots of spectators to be tagged and filed amongst the anti-government dossiers at Security Police headquarters.

We went down to the cells below the court to have a last discussion with the accused before the session began. By this time the colour bar even in the Supreme Court was breaking down. At the start of the case Bernstein, [Dennis] Goldberg and [James] Kantor had been regularly locked up in a "Europeans Only" cell, while all the non-whites were locked up in a "Non-European" cell. The two groups were only brought together at our special request for consultation or immediately before time for them to be ushered into the court. By now, however, the arrangement had broken down, partly because the accused themselves markedly ignored the colour demarcation unless instructed on each occasion to abide by it, partly because it was part of the atmosphere of the case that colour lines did not operate either between the accused or between the accused and counsel. Nelson was calm and completely unperturbed by the task before him.

FISCHER OUTLINES THE DEFENCE

In court, as planned, Bram Fischer led off for the defence. He summarised what the defence would state, what it would try to prove; which parts of the State case it conceded and which it would deny.

"Amongst the matters which will be placed in issue by the defence are the following: First, that Accused Nos. 1 to 7 (that is, all except Kantor, [Andrew] Mlangeni and [Elias] Motsoaledi) were members of the National High Command of Umkhonto we Sizwe. The defence evidence will show that the accused Goldberg, Kathrada and Bernstein were not members of the High Command of Umkhonto or members of Umkhonto at all. The defence evidence will also explain what the relationship was between Mandela, [Walter] Sisulu and [Govan] Mbeki, and with Umkhonto and the High Command of Umkhonto. It will also show what the relationship was between Goldberg and Umkhonto, and between Mlangeni and Umkhonto, and Motsoaledi and the African National Congress.

"Second, my Lord, in issue will be the allegation by the State that Umkhonto was a section of the African National Congress, to use the phrase so frequently used by the State, 'the military wing' of the African National Congress. The defence will seek to show that the leaders both of Umkhonto and of the African National Congress, for sound and valid reasons which will be explained to your Lordship, endeavoured to keep these two organisations entirely distinct. They did not always succeed in this for reasons which will also be explained, but we will suggest that the object of keeping the two organisations separate was always kept in mind and every effort was made to achieve that object.

"Thirdly, my Lord, it will be put in issue that the African National Congress was a 'tool' of the Communist Party, and that the aims and objects of the African National Congress were the aims and objects of the Communist Party. Your Lordship will remember that great point was made of this in the State's opening. The defence will deny this emphatically, my Lord. It will show that the ANC is a broad national movement, embracing all classes of Africans within its ranks, and having the aim of achieving equal political rights for all South Africans. The evidence will show further that it welcomes not only the support which it received from the Communist Party but also the support which it receives from any other quarter. Now on this point, the evidence will show how Umkhonto we Sizwe was formed, and that it was formed in order to undertake sabotage only when it was considered that no other method remained for the achievement of political rights. Finally, on this point, my Lord, the defence will deny the allegations made in the state's case that Umkhonto or the African National Congress relied, in order to obtain support, on what was referred to as being "the alleged hardships" suffered by people.

"All this will be relevant particularly to the fourth point, and that is this—the fourth issue—that Umkhonto had adopted a military plan called "Operation Mayibuye" and intended to embark upon guerrilla warfare during 1963 or had decided to embark upon guerrilla warfare."

Mr. Justice de Wet: Will that be denied?

Mr. Fischer: That will be denied. Here the evidence will show that while preparations for guerrilla warfare were being made from as early as 1962, no plan was ever adopted, and the evidence will show why it was hoped throughout that such a step could be avoided. In regard to the last issue, the court will be asked to have regard to the motives, the character and political background of the men in charge of Umkhonto we Sizwe and its operations. In other words, to have regard amongst other things to the tradition of non-violence of the African National Congress; to have regard to the reasons which led these men to resort to sabotage in an attempt to achieve their political objectives; and why, in the light of these facts, they are to be believed when they say that "Operation Mayibuye" had not been adopted, and that they would not have adopted it while there was some chance, however remote, of having their objectives achieved by the combination of mass political struggle and sabotage.

Bram paused at this point, while the judge finished making notes. He then said: "the defence case, my Lord, will commence with a statement from the dock by Nelson Mandela who personally took part in the establishment of Umkhonto, and who will be able to inform the court of the beginnings of that organisation and of its history up to August 1962 when he was arrested."

This statement seemed to cause consternation. Dr. Yutar was behaving as though he could not believe his ears. As Nelson rose slowly, adjusting the spectacles which he wore only for reading, Yutar jumped to his feet. His voice rose to that falsetto which we came to know as the crisis call of the prosecution. "My Lord!" he squeaked, "My Lord. I think you should warn the accused that what he says from the dock has far less weight than if he submitted himself to cross-examination!".

The judge looked at him rather sourly, "I think Mr. Yutar,

that counsel for the defence have sufficient experience to be able to advise their clients without your assistance".

Yutar seemed unable to get his breath back. Bram, somewhat less biting than De Wet, replied in the gentlemanly manner which he could never abandon, even when he was very annoyed. He appreciated, he said, his learned friend's advice. But "neither we, nor our clients are unaware of the provisions of the Criminal Code". Mandela, let it be remembered, was himself a qualified attorney with several years of practical experience in the courts before his conviction and sentence in 1962.

Mandela Speaks

Standing in the dock he began very slowly, very quietly, reading the statement which he had prepared, in a flat even voice. At no stage did he raise his voice very much, or change from the slow, measured speech with which he had started. His voice carried clearly across the court. Gradually as he spoke the silence became more and more profound, until it seemed that no one in the court dared move or breathe.

He started from the days of his youth, explaining how he had come into the national movement, what had led him first of all to the African National Congress and later, from the African National Congress to the founding of Umkhonto we Sizwe in which he himself had played a leading part. He explained why Umkhonto we Sizwe had chosen sabotage of a particular type, that is to say, attacks against government buildings and installations where no loss of life could be involved. Throughout its existence, he said, Umkhonto had recognised that the time might well come when it would have to turn to more militant struggle and guerrilla warfare. That time had never been reached. His explanation was at once legal and political. He set out the political reasoning which had guided himself and the African National Congress in all that had been done and the reasoning which led him now to believe that what had been done was not only right, but the only possible course of action for them. He described how he had travelled abroad on a mission for the African National Congress and how, while abroad, he had himself received military training. He had solicited and been promised that men from the liberation movement in South Africa would be trained by friendly African States in the arts of guerrilla warfare and military arts generally. He had returned from this mission to South Africa, and taken up the struggle again, living an underground life until his arrest. In this clandestine life as a politician and organiser, he had lived and worked in hiding at Rivonia. He dealt with the character of the Rivonia house and of the fact that, to his knowledge, this house had been used also by members of the Communist Party for their own political affairs.

Once he had been anti-communist. But he had learned from his experience that his duty to his people made it necessary that he co-operate with the Communist Party, as the African National Congress had cooperated with it. The Communist Party alone he said, had shown a willingness to throw in its lot with the national liberation struggle of the African people. He explained his attitude to communism, and the Communist Party, denying that he himself was a member of the Communist Party though he found much to admire in their programme and behaviour. He had been influenced, he said, by Marxist thought, and so in fact had almost all the significant leaders of the national movement in every country in Africa. In a short, detailed and documented statement of the way in which Africans live in South Africa, he threw back in the teeth of the prosecution the allegation that the African National Congress had been motivated by imaginary or bogus allegations of grievance. He showed that in fact the grievances of the African people were very real indeed, and very genuine. He finished, with his voice slightly roused, in a peroration on the aims of the African National Congress.

"Africans want to be paid a living wage. Africans want to perform work which they are capable of doing, and not work which the government declares them to be capable of. Africans want to be allowed to live where they obtain work, and not be endorsed out of an area because they were not born there. Africans want to be allowed to own land in places where they work, and not be obliged to live in rented houses which they can never call their own. Africans want to be part of the general population, and not confined to living in their own ghettos. African men want to have their wives and children to live with them where they work, and not be forced into an unnatural existence in men's hostels. African women want to be with their menfolk and not left permanently widowed in the reserves. Africans want to be allowed out after 11 o'clock at night and not to be confined in their rooms like little children. Africans want to be allowed to travel in their own country and to seek work where they want to and not where the Labour Bureau tells them. Africans want a just share in the whole of South Africa; they want security and a stake in society.

"Above all, we want equal political rights, because without them our disabilities will be permanent. I know this sounds revolutionary to the whites in this country, because the majority of voters will be Africans. This makes the white man fear democracy.

"But this fear cannot be allowed to stand in the way of the only solution which will guarantee racial harmony and freedom for all. It is not true that the enfranchisement of all will result in racial domination. Political division, based on colour, is entirely artificial and, when it disappears, so will the domination of one colour group by another. The ANC has spent half a century fighting against racialism. When it triumphs it will not change that policy.

"This then is what the ANC is fighting for. Their struggle is a truly national one. It is a struggle of the African people, inspired by their own suffering and their own experience. It is a struggle for the right to live.

"During my lifetime I have dedicated myself to the struggle of the African people. I have fought against white domination, and I have fought against black domination. I have cherished the ideal of a democratic and free society in which all persons live together in harmony and with equal opportunities."

At this moment he paused, a long pause, in which one could hear a pin drop in the court, and then looking squarely at the judge he finished: "It is an ideal which I hope to live for and to achieve". Then dropping his voice, very low, he added: "But if needs be it is an ideal for which I am prepared to die".

He sat down in a moment of profound silence, the kind of silence that I remember only in climactic moments in the theatre before the applause thunders out. Here in court there was no applause. He had spoken for five hours and for perhaps thirty seconds there was silence. From the public benches one could hear people release their breath with a deep sigh as the moment of tension passed. Some women in the gallery burst into tears. We sat like that for perhaps a minute before the tension ebbed.

Mr. Justice de Wet turned to Bram and said, almost gently: "You may call your next witness".

Bram called on Walter Sisulu.

Life on Robben Island

Mac Maharaj

Satyandranath "Mac" Maharaj was sent to prison on Robben Island in 1965 after being convicted of sabotage. He was to spend twelve years there, a sentence that overlapped with those of Mandela and other Rivonia convicts. After his release, in 1978, Maharaj was interviewed by a member of the International Defense and Aid Fund for South Africa (IDAF), a humanitarian organization committed to disseminating information and aiding victims of apartheid. This interview took place while Maharaj was in London, and was published in the United Kingdom by IDAF. It thus provided crucial news of Mandela, who had been banned in South Africa since his imprisonment, and was thus largely absent from South African newspapers, while the international press had access to him only on the rarest of occasions. Maharaj's testimony was an important source of information for the many people who saw Mandela as representing the struggle against apartheid.

In this extract from the interview, Maharaj describes both practical information about the harsh living conditions on the island, and also discusses Mandela's views, his attitudes, and his morale.

After South Africa's April 1994 elections, which signaled the end of apartheid and ushered in Mandela as president, Maharaj was appointed minister of transport in the new South Africa.

Q. *What kind of cell does Mandela have?*

A. He has been living in a concrete cell, outside walls of grey stone 7 ft by 7 ft and about 9 ft high. It was lit with one 40 watt globe. It had originally no furnishings except for a bed roll and mat, no bench, no table, nothing. Then as a result of demands made by us some were provided with small

Mac Maharaj, "Interview with 'Mac' Maharaj," *Nelson Mandela: The Struggle Is My Life*. London: IDAF, 1990. Copyright © 1990 by IDAF Publications Ltd. All rights reserved. Reproduced by permission.

tables 2 ft by 2 ft 6 in and later on it was extended to all the prisoners in that section and they built post office type counters against the wall without benches, you had to stand and work. They then provided benches and one wooden shelf, just a plank to keep your books on but we ourselves got cardboard paper and plastic and made cupboards for ourselves. Somewhere around 1973–74 when Nelson was ill he was granted a bed for the first time, so in his cell there is a bed. Then I think, oh yes, as a result of his back trouble he received a chair instead of a bench.

Q. *Does he have hot water to wash in?*

A. From the beginning of our imprisonment up to 1973 we only had access to cold water. There were periods when they changed the water for bathing to sea water instead of brack water. They reverted to brack water for washing and provided fresh water brought from the mainland in drums for us to drink from. They introduced hot water into the isolation section in 1973—a little earlier in the main sections of the prison. There are communal showers. Now again, typically of the administration, you will find that these facilities which you begin to enjoy are then used as forms of punishment. It is difficult to talk of hot water for showering without remembering that in mid-winter we will find that when we are engaged in some struggle against the authorities, suddenly there is no hot water and that will go on for weeks and weeks. The same thing will happen with the taped music they were playing for us. Once you've got used to it the next thing it is used as a form of punishment—it is taken away. Of course they do not say it is a form of punishment but you will find that it's out of order for six months or a year.

Q. *What toilet facilities are available?*

A. In the single cell section we have communal toilets to which we have no access except when the cells are opened. In your cells when you are confined—and you spend an average of 15 hours on weekdays, and during weekends up to 17 hours or more in your cell—you are provided with a sanitary pail, and you are given a plastic bottle which takes about 1½ pints of water for drinking purposes or any other use while you are locked up.

Q. *What diet does Mandela have? How does it compare with that of other prisoners?*

A. Right at the beginning of his imprisonment and when Nelson got to Robben Island as part of the Rivonia group he was offered by the head of prison security a special diet. Nelson refused because he realised that it was a subterfuge based not on his actual medical condition but merely a roundabout way of giving him a diet different from his colleagues. So his diet has been the normal prisoners' diet which of course discriminates on the basis of whether you are African, Coloured, or Indian. Just to illustrate how it works: there is porridge for breakfast (maizemeal porridge) for all—but African comrades are allowed half a tablespoon of sugar—Indians and Coloureds [South Africans of mixed ancestry] one tablespoon. . . .

Mandela's Routine

Q. *What work has Mandela done on the island? What is he doing now?*

A. When Nelson was sentenced in 1962 he was kept in Pretoria Central jail in solitary confinement. He was then shifted to Robben Island in 1963—he stayed two weeks on Robben Island without work, confined to his cell. Suddenly he was taken back to Pretoria into solitary and then brought to trial in the Rivonia case. He was sentenced in June 1964, taken with his comrades to Robben Island, kept in a zinc section (a temporary section) in total isolation and solitary confinement and then brought to the present single cells which were specially built for the Rivonia men. There they were first kept in total isolation.

They were then put to breaking stones in the yard with a four-pound hammer, crushing them to little pieces. This is where I joined them and we did that job until February 1965 when we were taken to the lime quarry, which meant digging limestone with a pick and shovel, cutting it and loading it on to trucks. This work was our main form of activity right until 1973–74. It was interspersed with very short bouts of other work—at one time building a road to the airport of Robben Island and at other times repairing the surface of the hardground road. In 1973–74 we were taken for the first time to the sea where we collected seaweed with our bare hands. This was alternate work, we sometimes did seaweed work, sometimes the lime work. The lime work was one the authorities had promised the Red Cross they would stop and despite their promises they only stopped it somewhere around 1975.

The latest report I have is that since I left the island at the beginning of November 1976 the comrades in the single cells have not been out to work at all and have therefore spent virtually a year and a half in total inactivity. This is at a time when their studies have been curtailed, which means that most of those in the single cells are not studying. They are therefore confined once more, as we were when we were breaking stones, to the little quadrangle which is slightly larger than a tennis court and they therefore have no chance of even seeing a blade of grass except when they go out to receive visits.

Q. *Tell us about this quadrangle?*

A. It's supposed to be an exercise yard and in about 1975 they allowed us to construct a volleyball court in it. We constructed it ourselves and adjusted it into a sort of tennis court—but with 30 prisoners you must appreciate you can't all play tennis and not all of them are fit enough to play tennis. In fact, I have one comrade who says that at present they are not working and it is completely monotonous, he says weekends have lost their meaning; every day is just the same. And of course, we have repeatedly demanded creative work: pottery, carpentry, basket-making, where you work at your own speed and you do something creative and can see what you are producing. But the authorities have been adamant in refusing this kind of work.

Q. *What is a routine day for Mandela on the island? Could you give a brief summary of a day for the single cell prisoners?*

A. I'll give a typical day of the last two years of my prison life, that is between 1974 and 1976.

You are woken up at different times in winter or summer, earlier in summer, later in winter. Summer at five, winter about six. When you are woken up you go out through the corridor into a section where there are communal baths and toilets. You are allowed about half an hour for everyone to wash and to clean their sanitary pails. There are about four sinks where all 30 may wash and shave. It is mandatory that you shave, as well as clean your sanitary pail. If you want to have a bath you must have it within that half an hour.

Then you collect your food. The food is brought in drums into the section, left at the gate where it is collected and we then dish it out ourselves, organising ourselves into teams voluntarily to do this work. You have your breakfast and within an hour from opening the doors you are supposed to fall in, unless of course the warders are late. You then go out to work. There were times in the early years when we were allowed the luxury of walking to our workplace, which enabled us to see something of the island, but then they began to move us by truck to prevent us from coming across any other prisoners. You get to work and you go down to work, say clearing seaweed, and you go on doing this until lunchbreak, which is an hour's break. The food is brought in drums, we dish it out and we sit down on the ground—open air, no tables—for eating utensils we are provided with a spoon and a steel plate. You knock off work at any time between half past three and four, the timing being determined by the fact that you must be back in the prison and given about half an hour for all the prisoners to have a bath and the food to be dished out and cleared by the prisoners. Then you are locked up by half past four or quarter to five so that the warders can sign off by five and the next shift of warders can come on. And from five if you are not allowed study privilege you are allowed to be up and about in your cell until eight o'clock when you are supposed to be in bed. Those who are allowed to study at the level of matriculation (which is roughly the equivalent of ordinary level GCE [grade 12]) are allowed until ten o'clock at night to study; those who are allowed university status could go on until eleven. When you are supposed to go to sleep the lights remain on and you are meant to be in bed, not even reading. If a warder finds you reading after those hours he can have you charged and punished for it. In the early 1970s they introduced a canned music service. This music was played from lock-up or from about six to eight P.M. Neither at Christmas, New Year or any other occasion are you allowed to sing or whistle, either individually or communally. That is the typical day.

Q. *Are you allowed to talk to each other when you are in your cells, in the evening or at any other time?*

A. When we got there we were told that this was solitary confinement, which meant that we were not allowed to talk to each other at all, even when we were in our cells. In the cells there are windows overlooking the corridor and cells on either side of the corridor, and it is possible to whisper to your neighbour. But that was illegal and we were punished. Of course they justified this on the grounds that we were in solitary confinement. One of our lines of attack was that they had no right to put us in solitary confinement. The first sign of caving in from the authorities was to say that we were no longer in solitary confinement but in 'isolation'. And then we challenged that and said isolation conditions don't permit them to stop us from talking, and secondly that these conditions did not conform to isolation, and thirdly we were not supposed to be under isolation. Eventually as a result of defying these orders we reached a tacit understanding where a prisoner may talk to his fellow prisoners from his cell up to eight pm. Then of course when the music came it became impossible to talk. In any case those studying don't want to hear the others shouting and talking across to each other.

We are therefore now allowed to talk at work. The name 'isolation' for the section has been dropped by the authorities and they now refer to it as the 'single cells'.

Q. *When are the prisoners in the single cells allowed into the courtyard?*

A. Now that they are not working their life will be the way it was on some days (when I was in prison) when, for lack of warders or some other reason, you didn't go out to work even though it wasn't a public holiday. You'd be let out later, say by eight o'clock in the morning, you'd be left in the confines of that quadrangle until eleven or 11.30; given your lunch; locked up in your individual cells; let out between two and 2.30 and again allowed access to that quadrangle; and then again by 3.30 your food would come in and by four o'clock you'd have your food and by 4.30 at the latest you'd be locked up again.

Q. *Is any day—for example Sunday—different?*

A. On Saturdays and Sundays you are locked up for longer periods. You are opened up later and closed earlier. At lunch breaks on weekends and public holidays you do not have access to your fellow prisoners; you are locked in your individual cells. Otherwise the days are the same. But, I run away from the description of monotony because in a certain sense it is true the days are monotonous but in another sense every day is also a different day for a prisoner because of the fact that you are able to talk with each other and develop friendships, you develop comradeship and find that you have new things to talk about. You also re-live some old things over and over again. . . .

IMPRESSIONS OF MANDELA

Q. *What personal impressions do you have of Mandela?*

A. Well firstly, as a personality, Nelson is a very friendly

Mandela Rejects Conditional Release

Soon after the South African government imprisoned Nelson Mandela in 1967, it began to come under pressure from the international community to release him. As the years passed, the government also became increasingly anxious about the aging Mandela's deteriorating health, fearing that if he died in prison he would be seen as a martyr forever (and his captors condemned). According to Mandela biographer B.M. Sinha, the government, therefore, spent years trying to think up conditional ways to release Mandela without compromising their own pride or acknowledging the unjustness of the regime that had imprisoned him in the first place.

Pretoria had begun contemplating, as early as 1969, some face saving ways of releasing Mandela. It offered him in 1969 freedom if he publicly renounced violence as means of political struggle and settled in the Transke Bantustan (i.e. beyond the borders of 'white' South Africa). He was also promised a government post. Mandela, who was then going through torturous days of imprisonment on Robben Island, according to his co-prisoner, "Mac" Maharaj, emphatically rejected the offer saying he would rather remain in jail than become a traitor.

Pretoria repeated this offer again and again and Mandela contemptuously rejected it. Pretoria sought to gain from the repeated offer and in 1985 propagated that Mandela was willing to accept the condition and would come out of jail any moment. Mandela scotched the rumour about his accepting the conditional release by sending a letter to his daughter, Zinzi, on February 1, 1985, and having it read out to a mass meeting in Jabulani Stadium in Soweto. The letter said:

> I am surprised at the conditions that the Government wants to impose on me. I am not a violent man.
>
> It was only then when all other forms of resistance were no longer open to us, that we turned to armed struggle. Let Botha show that he is different to Malan, Strijtom and Verwoerd. Let him renounce violence. Let him say that he will dismantle apartheid. Let him unban the people's organisation, the African National Congress. Let him free all who have been imprisoned, banished or exiled for their opposition to apartheid. Let him guarantee free political activity so that people may decide who will govern them.
>
> I cherish my own freedom dearly but I care even more for your freedom.
>
> Your freedom and mine cannot be separated. I will return.

B.M. Sinha, *Nelson Mandela: From the Shadow of Death to the Light of Freedom.* New Delhi: Competition Review, 1990.

and warm person to meet, but one also feels that he maintains a distance. To get to know him really well takes time—in my own case it took a lot of time before we became intimate friends. When I did get to know him well I realised that initially I hadn't really known him after all; his initial friendliness makes one think one knows him.

Secondly, he has obviously cultivated a deliberate policy of concealing his anger. In his political line in the early years he gave vent to the anger he felt. In prison he has got his anger almost totally under control. That control has come about through a deliberate effort by Mandela, for political reasons as well as personal.

His warmth comes out in his real sense of concern for his comrades in prison. In an unobtrusive way he finds out if anybody has problems and he tries to spend time with them if they do. Although he is completely committed to the African National Congress (ANC) his approach to *all* prisoners is always warm.

When something is worrying him, he does not come out with it easily. Both his eldest son and his mother died while I was in prison with him—both deaths were severe blows to him. He was very close to his son. When he returned from hearing the news, he just stayed in his cell and kept out of the way. However, [Rivonia convict] Walter Sisulu noticed that he was quiet and went to his cell and asked him what was wrong. Nelson then confided in him, and Walter stayed with him a long time, talking to him. By the next morning Nelson was his usual self again.

In relation to his personal problems, Mandela never complains to other prisoners. However, when taking complaints to prison authorities concerning his personal problems and the problems of other prisoners, he shows tremendous persistence and stubbornness.

In his manner he is kind, gentle and warm, but he has steeled and hardened himself. When he acts he wants to act in a cool and analytical way, and then follows through his decision with tremendous perseverance.

Q. *How do you assess the morale of Mandela and the other prisoners in the special section, and on the island generally?*

A. In many ways, like all of us Nelson has been changing over the years. I think that the basic change in Nelson is that as he has been living through prison his anger and hatred of the system has been increasing but the manifestations of that anger have become less visible to a person. They are more subdued, more tempered. They've become more cold and analytical in focusing on the evils of the system. His morale has been such that he has been one of the men that has inspired all who came into contact with him. He isn't the only one, there are many who've played this role, in truth all of us in our own small way have helped each other, but Nelson has been outstanding. He has had the confidence of all prisoners whatever their political persuasion and has been accepted by all as a spokesman of the whole prisoner community. He has often sought and guided us in the campaigns we've waged so that even though we were fighting on losing ground, that is, ground controlled by the enemy, the campaigns we waged would at least bring us some benefit.

His confidence in the future has been growing. I do not recall a time when he showed any despondence or gave us any clue that he may be thinking in the back of his mind that he would never live through prison. He has always shown this belief in private and in public, and I believe I can say this, knowing him intimately, not even when [his wife] Winnie was in jail, detained, or when news came out of her torture or whatever demoralising actions were taken by the enemy, has Nelson flagged. His spirit has been growing, and I think the reasons for this high morale amongst us are very deeply related to our conditions. First of all, I believe that the enemy's treatment is counter-productive, it's a dead loser. You never fail to be reminded every moment in prison that you are there not just as a prisoner but as a black man, and that alone tells you that the only way to survive, even if you haven't thought it out, is to fight back.

It is a very important element in our morale that we are able to find ways to fight back: we feel we have something to do, we have a programme in prison, we want to put our demands. Our central issues are: a) release, unconditionally; b) interim treatment should be that of *political* prisoners; c) remove all racial discrimination. Now that on its own is a limited programme which we know we cannot win altogether, since it is dependent on the wider struggle, but it has given us something to fight for. The fact that we come to prison as political fighters and are kept together gives us this opportunity to act as a collective.

The next element has been the recognition that our freedom won't come from negotiation with the enemy. The enemy could only afford to release us from a position of strength, and any semblance of strength that it may have had, say between 1965 and 1969 when it could claim, as it kept on claiming, that South Africa was calm and peaceful—although this had been achieved at the cost of a terrible campaign of intimidation and terror—has now been lost. Today every day brings the regime more and more against the wall. So that any such act will be perceived as an act of weakness, and it is clear that our release won't come from them and we see that it is related directly to the struggle outside. There our morale and spirit is helped by the fact that, even with all the repression and intimidation, our operations have continued to survive underground. The struggle has carried on despite the blunders and the casualties. The jail doors have been drawing in more and more people, testifying to the presence of the organisation, to the fact that it continues to live, continues to fight. Then the mood of our people: the evidence from round about the 1970s of a mounting mass of campaigns from our people, a rising tide of anger culminating in the explosions of Soweto [black ghetto that witnessed violent uprising against apartheid] and post-Soweto, all these have shown us that the conditions are there for our victory.

Q. *How is Mandela regarded by the other prisoners on the island?*

A. Well, first of all Nelson Mandela is accepted and recognised by the Congress and its allied bodies as one of its leading members. His image in prison is that of the first commander-in-chief of Umkhonto we Sizwe. He therefore is seen as symbolising the new phase in our struggle—a phase where we have turned our backs on the view that non-violent struggle will bring us our victory. He therefore symbolises that spirit, that aspiration, and he symbolises the recognition that to talk of change by violence is not enough, that violence has got to be organised and that campaign of violence has got to be rooted in the masses. This is the image that Nelson has. In prison of course his stature has grown, just as it has grown internationally. As I said, in the campaigns in prison, his guidance and leadership and advice have made him accepted by all political movements in prison as a spokesman of the prisoners. This was true too of the 'younger generation' of prisoners, those who began to come in from the so-called 'black consciousness' groups from 1973 and the young people imprisoned after Soweto. What was interesting was that, after all these years of imprisonment, with the organisations driven underground and these young men and women growing up under Bantu education, educated by the enemy as he desires, exposed only to the propaganda of the enemy, with no knowledge of the history of our struggle and only surreptitious information given in darkness, none the less their first connection was Nelson Mandela, this was the first thing they'd ask you about. This indicated that his name was even by that generation accepted as a leader in the country. Of course this has interesting implications, because the enemy has tried to show that what happened in Soweto and post-Soweto was exclusively the work of some new crop, 'historically unrelated', with no roots. But their very questions and interest and acceptance of Nelson show that there is an organic connection. Furthermore, no black group which claims to be standing for the rights of the black man and for the ending of national oppression, however much they may differ even on tactics and theory and strategy, fails to mention Nelson Mandela when it talks of a future South Africa. Thus not only does the ANC recognise him as a leader, but he is accepted as a national leader in the country as a whole by all the people whatever their colour, and no future plans can afford to exclude him from their calculations.

Mandela Was an Inspirational Prisoner

Eddie Daniels

Eddie Daniels was an apartheid activist and a member of the Liberal Party who was convicted of sabotaging government property (he attacked electric pylons and government installations). He arrived on Robben Island in late 1964, and spent his entire fifteen-year sentence with Nelson Mandela, Walter Sisulu, Ahmed Kathrada, and the others convicted at Rivonia.

Although Daniels was released in 1978, Nelson Mandela was a banned person and any mention of him, or of his presence on Robben Island, was grounds for arrest and imprisonment in South Africa. In 1986, when this account was published in Johannesburg's *Weekly Mail*, a liberal newspaper, Mandela was still banned, and although the political situation was nominally less repressive than during the 1970s, Daniels was still risking arrest by speaking with the *Mail*'s journalists.

In his account, Daniels praises Mandela, commenting on both his commanding presence and inspirational leadership, as well as his unstinting kindness and humanity.

I spent my full fifteen years with Nelson from the very first day until the last when I was taken to Pollsmoor [Prison] and discharged. Nelson is a tremendous figure, an inspiration. He is everything that is noble and good. How do you describe a person who, when you are at rock bottom, is a shining example of how to behave in adversity, who by his walk would inspire you, by his touch would inspire you, by his little talks would inspire you.

I joined Nelson in a special section of the prison. It was a

Eddie Daniels, "Account by Eddie Daniels," *Weekly Mail*, March 21–27, 1986. Copyright © 1986 by *Weekly Mail*. Reproduced by permission.

bit rough. The food wasn't up to much. We slept on a cement floor, with three blankets that were very thin. If I held my blanket up I could see through [it]. The setting was quite grim. The aim of the authorities was to destroy our morale by giving us very poor food, very thin blankets, and poor clothing. When one is very, very cold, one does feel a bit demoralized.

All the political prisoners at that time were allowed one visit and one letter every six months. Strange as it may seem, even though we were allowed only one letter every six months, sometimes those letters were accidentally "lost" and our families might get a permit too late, so you might not get a visit or a letter for a full year. Times have changed, because the political prisoners fought very hard, and we succeeded in bringing about changes in the prison.

Pushed over the Edge

In this rather grim setting, a man like Nelson stood out like a shining star. There were other leaders of other political organizations. I was a member of the Liberal party [and] the only member of the African Resistance Movement (ARM) in prison, and there were other organisations, [including] the Pan Africanist Congress (PAC) and the Unity movement. With due respect to all of them, the leadership of the African National Congress (ANC), namely, Nelson Mandela and Walter Sisulu, was really in a class of its own.

There were occasions when we went on hunger strike, when we used to challenge the authorities for some reason or other, and the warders would always come to Nelson and challenge him, [asking] why this was taking place. Nelson would always have to face the thrust of the authorities, and he always carried himself with dignity, no matter what the situation was like.

It is said by the government that Nelson is a terrorist. He is no terrorist. He is a kind, honest, humble, and peace-loving man. Nelson is a family man. He has been pushed into this position, and being a man of calibre, he has accepted it. He is prepared to carry out what he considers to be his duty. Nelson will never give undertakings that will demean him. If Nelson gives an undertaking, he will honour it. He is that type of a person. Nobody in the government can compare to him.

Nelson, like me, was pushed over the edge by the cruel laws of the land.

We have two people in this country, Chief Albert Luthuli and Bishop [Desmond] Tutu, who have been awarded the Nobel Peace Prize. Chief Luthuli, in his book *Let My People Go*, said after 35 years of knocking on closed doors, pleading for the people: "The doors have still not opened."

Bishop Tutu last week went to see the government after the trouble in Alexandra Township, pleading with the cruel people who make these cruel laws, asking them for mercy.

Nelson felt he could not take that road. Nelson founded Umkhonto we Sizwe [MK, "Spear of the Nation"].

The government talks about negotiations with the ANC. Negotiations have been going on a long time. Jimmy Kruger came to see Nelson on the island. Le Grange came to see Nelson on the island. Brigadier Aucamp was actually a political appointment by the government as a go-between the ANC and Pretoria.[1]

When we used to face the Prison Board, they would often ask us political questions, and the ANC made the point that we are not prepared to discuss political matters with them. Under the leadership of Mandela, we said, "Send your political representatives to us, and we will talk to them. We will only discuss prison matters with you."

MANDELA IS AN INSPIRATIONAL FIGURE

Here is another example which shows you the kind of man that Mandela is. I had a diary in which I had noted the names of warders involved in assaults and their victims. The warders captured it in a raid. We had a very bad officer in command at that time. The police were putting people in straitjackets, beating people, and jumping on them. I was next in line, and I was quite frightened. I found it very difficult to sleep that night, and the next morning was still full of fear. I went into the yard to fetch my plate of porridge, and when I came back Nelson was sitting in my cell. I got such a thrill seeing him sitting there, and then he said to me: "Eddie, you just go ahead and face them the way you want to face them." Nelson was an inspiration.

And another small point will give more insight into Nelson: There is a shrine on Robben Island for a political prisoner who died there many years ago. Nelson got the permission of the commanding officer for us to go and pay our

---

1. Kruger, Le Grange, and Aucamp are all figures in the South African police force.

respects. When we went to the shrine, under guard, someone walked in wearing his shoes. Nelson said, "Please let us respect this shrine," and so we all removed our shoes and paid our respects and went back with a bit of inner peace.

Nelson was very good at negotiations and everybody, including the warders and the commanding officers, all held him in high esteem. They always greeted him, and he is a very courteous person and always replied.

Nelson is, of course, a nonracialist. After the death of John Harris (a member of the ARM hanged for the 1964 bomb at the Johannesburg station), I had a memorial service in my cell. There was an occasion at around that time when Nelson made a speech in which he mentioned John Harris. He said, "Here is a white man who died fighting apartheid." Nelson would always give credit where credit was due, and he especially made this point because there were a number of organisations present that were very antiwhite. He wanted to press the point . . . that a person is not judged on the color of his skin but on what kind of person he is.

Among the post-1976 political prisoners, there was a strong antiwhite element. One day in 1979 this led to fighting in the cells, and a number of the ANC people were stabbed and hurt. The authorities arrested some of the other men, and when the court case came up, the men had to give evidence against the others. Nelson said he wouldn't give evidence, and the whole case was dropped. This shows the kindness and the greatness of Nelson, and the move won the respect and even the applause of everyone else in the prison—in this way a lot of what may have been hostility between the young and the old guard or between one organization and another was actually done away with.

When I was ill one day, lying in my bed pretty helpless, Nelson came into my cell. I remember he had his bowly (chamber pot) under his arm, and he bent down and picked up my bowly and said: "Eddie, I will see you later." And he took my bowly to clean it.

Again you see he is a giant of a man, a giant that can walk with beggars and with kings and be at home in any company. And here was I, an insignificant individual and this great man, an international figure, came down to clean my bowly.

There is a joke Nelson tells about himself quite often. When he was a lawyer in Johannesburg he saw a lady, a white lady, trying to park her car. Nelson, being the kind and honest gentlemen that he is, came to help her. Eventually she parked the car and offered him a sixpence. Nelson said, "No, thank you," and she replied, "Well, if you want a shilling, I will give you nothing now." Nelson loved telling jokes about himself.

He is tremendous. The way he walks, the way he talks. When he touches you, he is an inspiration. When one is rock bottom one looks for something to lift you, to warm you, and I often think to myself that Nelson and Walter [Sisulu] have this power to lift others.

Mandela's commitment is to his country. He will die for what he believes in. This is the man Mandela who I know, a man who I am proud to have met, a man who inspired me, and a man who has won my lasting respect.

A Warden Remembers Robben Island

James Gregory with Bob Graham

James Gregory was posted to Robben Island in late 1966 to serve as a censor of letters, newspapers, and the minimal written material that the political prisoners were allowed. He also supervised the rare family visits that were allowed in the prison's later years. In the course of time, he came to be the personal jailer of Nelson Mandela, and moved with him from Robben Island to Pollsmoor Prison in 1982 and subsequently to Victor Verster Prison in late 1988, from which Mandela was released in January 1991.

In his book, which Gregory wrote after Mandela's release, he tracks his own personal development: from the young Afrikaner taught by his education, his friends, his society, and the media to hate the imprisoned African National Congress (ANC) leaders and think of them as brutal terrorists, to the mature man who would come to deeply respect Mandela, Walter Sisulu, and others, and feel shame for his former beliefs.

The following selection describes Gregory's first days at Robben Island, his impressions of the prison, and his first interactions with Nelson Mandela.

He seemed to stand taller and straighter than any of the others with an aura that made a statement. 'I am a leader. You will not intimidate me.' Even in his drab prison clothes Nelson Mandela was different. As I stood to one side of the yard in the shade, just watching these men, the Poqo [Xhosa word for "standing alone" given to an underground military organization that splintered from the Pan Africanist Congress in the 1960s], I could feel his inner strength. I knew this man would be a difficult one to overcome.

James Gregory with Bob Graham, *Goodbye Bafana: Nelson Mandela, My Prisoner, My Friend.* London: Headline, 1995. Copyright © 1995 by Editions Robert Laffont. All rights reserved. Reproduced by permission of the publisher.

This was the prison within the prison which was officially called the Solitary Block. It was designed specifically to separate the leadership of the Poqo from the militants and rank-and-file members of each of the organisations. It was a purpose-built one-storey rectangular structure surrounding a solid cement courtyard, a little larger than the size of a tennis court. The grey, soulless centre had cells on three sides; the fourth, a twenty-two-foot high wall, was topped by a catwalk which was patrolled by German shepherd dogs.

Standing in the shade of the wall, on the western side, I felt their eyes flicking towards me and away again, yet in the moment of contact they penetrated me, trying to figure me out. Lengthy direct eye contact was rare; these men were sitting mostly in ones or twos, although occasionally in larger groups, while others were walking, strolling around the courtyard.

The three lines of cells were known as sections A, B and C. Mandela and the rest of the Poqo were in section B, which lined the eastern side of the quadrangle. The other two sections were solitary confinement areas, largely left empty. I looked across to the line of windows, seventeen in all, tiny square double windows, with their four bars cemented into the walls on the inside. The windows had been left open to allow what little breeze there was to take away the stench of incarceration. In total the entire section contained ninety single cells. I had been told it was known to the rest of the prison population as *Makhulukutu*, after the leader group. In prison jargon, the Poqo were known as 'The *Makulu* Span', the big team.

I was aware of an unease among the inmates, a change. Small groups who had been sitting cross-legged on the courtyard began to stand up, there was a buzz about the place; something was definitely happening. I soon realised it was the sudden appearance of Vosloo, one of the senior warders in the prison. The Poqo were at once alert. It was the first indication of their in-built radar and network which warned them of visits before they occurred, before any senior officers actually showed up in their section.

Vosloo took me into B section which housed the Poqo.

'Come, Gregory, come see where these kaffirs and koelies[1] live.'

---

1. derogatory terms for black and Indian South Africans

Inside the corridor the heat and smell hit me. Disinfectant, mixed with the unmistakable stench of sweating bodies and urine. The unforgettable smell of incarceration which was to remain with me for much of the next three decades.

'Go, have a look for yourself,' encouraged Vosloo. 'Familiarise yourself, see where we keep these animals. See how well we look after them; better than they deserve, man. Better than what they have come from.'

Mandela's Cell

The floor of the corridor was bare, grey cement, but it was polished as a mirror, the way the Zulus had polished the inside of the huts in their kraals [homesteads]. The row of fluorescent tubular lights down the middle of the corridor which were always left on glistened off the floor and pale-green gloss-painted walls. Slowly, I paced out the line of thirty cells, looking at the names above each door. Here, first inside the barred gate at the entrance, on the left-hand side, was [Elias] Motsoaledi, an ANC terrorist. At the far end of his cell, through his barred windows, I could catch a glimpse of the harbour and beyond, the enticing beaches of Bloubergstrand. That was nice, to let him see the forbidden fruit, I thought. Slowly down the corridor, fourth on the right, Mandela. His details were listed on a card which at one time had been white, but was now yellowed with age; he had already been here two years. It bore his details: N. Mandela. 466/64. It told me he had been the 466th prisoner to be admitted on the island in 1964. Not for him the benefit of a room with a view. No, his barred cell looked out on to the courtyard.

The cell was sparse, neatly cared for. The *sisal*, or straw mat, used as a bed, was rolled up inside the right-hand wall, the three thin, grey blankets neatly folded beside it. In one corner was the rusted iron bucket known as a *balie*, which was used as a toilet. It had a porcelain lid which was invariably turned upside-down to contain enough water to allow them to shave or wash their hands and faces. Beside the folded blankets were two strips of old, grey fraying cloth. I was later to discover one was a face-cloth, the other a towel. This was a man's possessions.

Vosloo talked mechanically of the daily routine. 'They are awakened at 5.30 each morning, and they must prepare themselves to be ready for cell opening at 6.45.

'They must have their cells neatly ready, mats and blankets rolled and folded. And they must take their balies and wash them in the bathroom and shower area.

'Then they must go out into the courtyard and wait for their breakfast, which they don't deserve. Man, these kaffirs are never happy, they are always complaining about the food. They don't know how well off they are. They eat better in here than they ever did at home.'

I wasn't about to argue with Vosloo, but I already knew the food was not the sort I would feed to a dog. It was unpalatable and looked disgusting. The breakfast of mielie pap was wheeled into the courtyard and slopped into metal bowls that were often dirty from the day before. The coffee which accompanied it was a revolting swill of black liquid, unlike any coffee I had ever seen before. This was a mix of ground-up maize, baked until it was black, then boiled.

I wandered into Mandela's cell wondering how such a tall man could stretch out along the narrow space. Years later Mandela would tell me how, when the men from the Rivonia trial were brought to the section, the floors and walls were still running with water; they had been built hurriedly and the cement had not yet dried. When they had complained of the damp, the commanding officer, called Wessels and one of the old, hard school, had told him that their bodies would absorb the moisture. Inside the cell the window looked even smaller, perhaps one foot square, at eye-level. The view on a dull day would have been a scant scene of the courtyard and the grey stone wall opposite. This day it was just a blinding mass of white light from the unforgiving sun which shone through his barred window.

Each cell had a second window also barred, facing into the corridor, and two doors: an inner, five-barred metal grille gate and a second, outer door of solid oak. I paced the room in my size ten shoes. It was almost square, three steps by three steps.

Slowly, absorbing the feel of the section, I wandered down the line of cells, the homes of the Poqo, men I had been taught to despise: [Raymond] Mhlaba, [Andrew] Mlangeni, [Ahmed] Kathrada, [Walter] Sisulu, men I thought I already knew from the infamous deeds I'd read and heard about.

At the end of the corridor the stench of the area increased: the toilet and shower area, a lower, flat space, its puce-coloured walls chipped and flaking.

Vosloo walked slowly behind me, inspecting cells, flicking and poking with his stick. At the bottom of the corridor we turned right into the isolation area; it was darker, more sinister.

'This here, man, is where we keep Tsofendas.' The name was etched larger in the hearts of Afrikaners than any other: this was the madman who had taken a knife to [South African president known as the "architect of apartheid"] Hendrik Verwoerd and stabbed him to death.

Outside the cell a guard sat, a notebook on his lap. 'We watch this madman twenty-four hours a day. We write down every word he says; they're the orders from Pretoria.' I looked through the window and saw the killer sitting hunched up in the corner of the cell, his knees drawn tightly up to his chest. His eyes were shut and he was gibbering to himself.

Vosloo was beside me again: 'Come, man, that's the end of the tour.'

I was still uncertain of what my job was here in the B section. I asked Vosloo, 'What precisely do I do?'

'Nothing, just keep a watch over the Poqo. It's easy, they are kaffirs.'

Outside in the sunshine, the prisoners were walking, lapping the courtyard on their oval route to nowhere, their faces either staring at the ground or straight ahead. It was an eerie sight. I went over to another guard but he shied away. 'No, keep away, we are not allowed to stand together and talk. Vosloo doesn't like that.'

I began to walk, bored and confused about how I was best to spend my time. Several times I cast a glance at Mandela, but he was deeply engrossed in conversation. Three laps of the courtyard and I could feel the sweat coming, so I headed for the shade of the verandah, close to the bathroom and toilet corner. The prisoners simply ignored me.

This was a weekend and the prisoners were excused work; I had imagined they would at least do something, exercise or play a game of volleyball, something. But not this.

MEALTIME

My eyes were drawn back to Mandela as he stood talking. I could pick out his compatriots from the pictures I had seen. Walter Sisulu, Mac Maharaj, Ahmed Kathrada and Laloo Chiba. They walked their laps of the courtyard, always animated until they reached within ten yards of where I stood and then ... silence. At noon the food was wheeled in, a mixture of mielie rice and ground-up mielies called *samp*. It was supposed to contain vegetables although they were as rare as an ice-cube in the Karoo Desert. There was also a drink called *phuzamandla*, meaning drink of strength, made from powdered mealies and yeast, which is stirred with milk and served as a thick milkshake-type drink. However, the concoction wheeled into the courtyard was a thin, weak variety which looked like dirty water.

The prisoners knew the routine well and took their food and headed for their own cells. There was almost silence as I walked into the corridor of B section although occasionally as someone spoke it echoed all along the hall. I closed each of the inner metal-barred grille doors with hardly a glance from the occupant. At Mandela's cell his back was turned to me. I went on to the next.

As I closed the final cell I handed the keys to a warder at the end of the area and headed off for my own lunch, an enjoyable two-course meal of meat and vegetables followed by good strong coffee. I smiled at the difference between the food I had seen dished up in the B section and the food I was served. That's what serving a life sentence should be about: punishment of the stomach as well as the mind.

At 2 o'clock I unlocked the cells again and let them wander out into the courtyard, where I had picked my spot again beneath the verandah in the shade.

The afternoon was an almost dreamy time and I felt myself drifting off in the heat of the day; it was hard to concentrate, watching this endless stream of prisoners strolling around the courtyard. At 4.00 a shrill whistle sounded which made me spring to attention, suddenly awake again. The prisoners lined up to be counted, their eyes forward, refusing to focus on Vosloo as he counted them. As they were dismissed they headed again for the cell area where they were allowed half an hour to clean up. I watched Mandela carefully and observed how he was the centre of so much activity. As they walked around the courtyard he was frequently joined by other prisoners who walked with him then departed again. As they walked from the count-up and inspection, he was again the focus of attention from his colleagues. Several times they would approach him, ask a question or tell him something, and he would stand and nod or shake his head, often talking earnestly. It was clear this man was the leader of the group.

The sun had cast a shadow over the entire courtyard as they filed away to B section for their own clean-up period. The walls seemed to close in on the smell of forty bodies that had been in it throughout the day. It was the locker-room smell of sweat and toil, intensified by heat and humidity. The shadow of the walls closed the entire courtyard as I stood at one end listening to the songs now emanating from the bathroom area.

I walked slowly down the line of cells, outside the windows, listening to the sounds of the Poqo as they sang of their homes and sang of their struggle. It was the nostalgia and harmony which reminded me of the kraals when the Zulus would sing. I had learned as a child, and I realised again as I stood listening to the prisoners, the songs of the black man contained more than just melody and words, they were the African way of conversing, of commenting, of observing. I knew there was so much I could learn from listening to these songs.

Vosloo and the other guards had vanished for half an hour, but reappeared suddenly at 4.30 when supper was delivered in large metal containers. I wandered over to the meal area and watched as the same mielie pap porridge was delivered on the plate with a slap. I thought again, if the courts had not carried out the death sentence by hanging these terrorists, then to spend the rest of one's life being served this kak was a punishment in itself. There were pieces floating in the pap which I was told were vegetables, carrots or beetroot thrown in and occasionally meat. But they looked like burned kernels of corn to me.

I had read the regulations carefully and knew there was a distinction between the food served to black prisoners and the food served to the coloureds and Indians. Now I was seeing it first-hand as the few coloureds in the area were served with a small hunk of bread and a dollop of margarine, half-melted and close to becoming rancid. The bread was known as *katkop*, cat's head, after the shape of the bread when it was hacked into quarters. Whatever it was, the blacks never received any. They were treated differently from other races, even in prison.

As with lunch, the food was eaten in silence. By 5 o'clock Vosloo gave me my final task of that day: to lock up, count the numbers and to fill in each form to ensure everyone was accounted for. As I walked through the corridor of B section, I looked in at each prisoner in their cramped cell. Not one bothered to look at me, their eyes busy elsewhere, averted. I was a nonentity, part of the enemy that they had avowed to defeat. As I closed several doors, Mandela's and Sisulu's among others, I remember from that first day, their deep voices came from behind it with a simple 'Good night'. How strange that a courtesy should be extended in such circumstances.

Vosloo and the other officers were anxious to get away and, as the junior warder, I stayed locked into the corridor area until the night-shift showed up.

Night-Shift

Now, with the disappearance of Vosloo, the talk started in the cells, from one prisoner to another. It was an invaluable insight into the thinking of these men. Not for them pointless complaining about their situation; they were intent on conversing about higher matters—religion, social issues, concepts in physics and chemistry, literature and art. That evening just listening to them was a beginning to my understanding of how different these men in B section were. It was a group of men unlike any the people who trained us at Kroonstad had ever mentioned. I'd expected something very different.

The night guys came, with their flasks of tea and coffee and packages of sandwiches. I had not met them and when they saw me they were hesitant, distinctly cool. I was a newcomer and I had a specific role to play, that of censor, so I was, therefore, a man to be wary of. That evening the look from the night guard was one of disgust.

Without being introduced, he started on me. 'Man, why do you let these kaffirs make so much noise? They are breaking the rules, there should be silence.'

The night warder stormed up and down the corridor, yelling in Afrikaans: *'Stilte in die gang!'* Quiet in the passage. I felt very much the junior warder, being reprimanded.

'You must keep them quiet. They want to talk, but it is not allowed.' I said I was listening to what they said, that some things were interesting.

'Ag, that is just kaffir and koelie talk. It's just nonsense and it's not allowed.'

I was to learn later that there was no call of 'lights-out'. The forty-watt bulbs in each small cell would burn all night long, as they did through the days.

As I walked slowly home that evening, the sun setting in the hills behind Bloubergstrand, I went over the day and how strange and almost dreamlike it had all seemed. What had I expected? What had I been told to expect from the people at Kroonstad? These blacks were terrorists and they wanted to kill me. But here they were in my control now, and they were just ordinary people. When I had been introduced they responded politely. My mind was spinning; this was not what I had expected at all. They were different.

CHAPTER 4

LEADING THE RAINBOW NATION

PEOPLE WHO MADE HISTORY

NELSON MANDELA

Mandela Is Released from Prison

René du Preez

The following piece is written by veteran South African journalist René du Preez. Du Preez was one of many newspeople who was standing outside Victor Verster Prison on Sunday, February 11, 1990, when Nelson Mandela was unconditionally released after twenty-seven years in captivity. South Africans were hoping that the release of Mandela was imminent because, in previous months, the South African president at the time, F.W. de Klerk, had released Oliver Tambo, Walter Sisulu, and other ANC political prisoners, and had ceased to ban the African National Congress (ANC) and the Pan-Africanist Congress (PAC). But when on Saturday evening de Klerk suddenly announced that Mandela would be released the following day, joy and disbelief gripped the country. Nelson Mandela had been imprisoned and banned for so long that most people younger than their forties had never seen him or even a photograph of this iconic figure. Du Preez captures the mood of exaltation that overtook the thousands who thronged the streets between the town of Paarl, where the prison was located, and the city of Cape Town, where Nelson and Winnie Mandela were proceeding to address the nation.

It was a typical Cape summer's day, scorching hot. But unlike other summer Sunday afternoons, when the Cape's open beaches are packed to capacity, this day, 11 February, was very special.

A moment in time that the whole world had been waiting for since five o'clock the previous day.

It was the day South Africa's best-known, and most ad-

René du Preez, "Nelson Mandela Is Released from Prison," *Nelson Mandela and the Rise of the ANC*, edited by Jurgen Schadeberg. Johannesburg: Jonathan Ball Publishers and Ad. Donker Publishers, 1990. Copyright © 1990 by JRA Bailey. All rights reserved. Reproduced by permission of the publisher.

mired son, Nelson Rolihlahla Mandela, was to be released after having spent twenty-seven years in jail.

And nowhere was the fervour stronger than in Cape Town, for some fifty kilometres away in Paarl, where the town's large farming population mostly seem more interested in the upkeep of the sprawling, lush lawns surrounding their large Dutch-styled homes, their precious vines and rugby than the injustices that prevail in this country, Mr. Mandela was to be released from the Victor Verster prison.

The prison, nestled snugly below a beautiful mountain range and surrounded by the area's wealthy farmers, had been 'home' for Mr. Mandela for just over a year, after he had spent much of the other twenty-five years on Robben Island.

When Mr. Mandela and ten others first appeared in the Rivonia treason trial on 9 October 1963, their appearance shared the news headlines in this country with the marriage of Port Elizabeth singer Danny Williams to a white British woman called Bobbi Carole.

But let's go back to the day most of the world had been waiting for, 11 February.

THE ANNOUNCEMENT

When State President F.W. de Klerk finally made the long-awaited announcement late the previous day that Mr. Mandela would be released at three o'clock on Sunday, Cape Town, noted for its 'laid back' style of life, moved into a kind of frenzy that had never been experienced before.

With hooters blaring, impromptu parties being organised all over the townships and busloads of ordinary folk riding around the Sea Point area with ANC flags and clenched fists protruding through the windows, shouting 'Viva Mandela' and 'Viva ANC!', Cape Town had suddenly come alive.

In fact, not even the peace declaration after World War II compared with the excitement that was generated by the announcement of Mr Mandela's release.

Taverners in the townships of Langa, Guguletu and Nyanga reported that they were 'dry' long before the witching midnight hour.

One taverner told *Drum* [magazine]: 'You would think the world is coming to an end tomorrow at three. I'm completely sold out of everything I had in stock, and I'm not the only one. And can you blame the people, for tomorrow will be the most joyous day in the history of black South Africans because their long-lost father is returning.'

With fireworks punctuating the cool evening air and thousands of people making arrangements to travel to Paarl to witness one of the greatest events in this country's history, Cape Town simply refused to sleep that night.

Hundreds of international press photographers and journalists camped outside the prison in order to get the best possible vantage point so that they could get the 'first' pictures of the famous prisoner, pictures that would earn them thousands of American dollars.

With the sun beating down on the multitude who had congregated outside the gates to the entrance of the Victor Verster prison and the many thousands more who had lined the route from Paarl to Grand Parade in Cape Town, it was to be a long wait, but a moment nobody was prepared to miss, irrespective of the scorching heat.

Policemen, photographers, journalists and followers all shared the same tap in an effort to quench their thirst.

In fact, the long wait in the sun was all about sharing. People joked. They sang. They shouted slogans. They laughed. They cried. They fainted. But never an incident.

The police, who kept a low profile while the United Democratic Front (UDF) marshals controlled the wildly excited crowd, were left amazed at the discipline that prevailed.

With the magic hour of three o'clock finally having arrived, one could almost feel the electricity that was being generated from an audience, of which most were not even born when Mr. Mandela was sentenced to his long prison term.

Mandela Walks Out

At two minutes past three, Mrs Winnie Mandela and her entourage arrived at the gates below slowly making their way down the one hundred metre drive to Mr Mandela's 'home'.

The singing became louder. The slogans became stronger. The excitement reached fever pitch. Control became more difficult. But still no Mr. Mandela.

'Please be patient,' UDF marshals shouted.

'We've been patient for twenty-seven years,' shouted back a young, khaki-clad ANC member, much to the delight of those within hearing distance.

'They are an hour late,' shouted someone else and the response from a neighbour was immediate, 'I hope they have not changed their minds.'

Then it all happened.

It was just after four when Mr. Mandela and his wife Winnie, holding hands and waving to a now delirious crowd, alighted from a black limousine and walked the few metres to the gates.

Pandemonium broke loose as people and the press surged forward for a glimpse of a face that the whole world had been wanting to see for twenty-seven years and one that everybody hopes will bring peace and harmony to this troubled country of ours.

At first one sensed a touch of nervousness and uncertainty about Mr. Mandela's behaviour, almost as if he seemed uncertain whether to smile or cry.

But having been encouraged by Winnie to raise his right arm and show a clenched fist, it must have been the first time in all those many years that he really realised he was in actual fact a free man.

As it turned out, the crowd had only about five minutes in which to feast its eyes on the tall figure of their hero with his black and grey hair and impeccably dressed in a conservative grey suit.

But at moments like these, length of time is irrelevant, for they have been privileged to actually see the man who is sure to cast a larger than life shadow on South African politics for the rest of our lives and on the lives of all those who are destined to follow us.

Then followed a slow and tedious journey to Cape Town for the Mandelas.

THE PROCESSION

Thousands, both black and white, lined the route from Paarl to the Grand Parade, waving ANC flags and shouting good wishes, and one wonders whether in his wildest dreams Mr. Mandela ever expected to receive such a huge and warm welcome from the people of Cape Town.

There was a poignant moment during the three-hour drive when Mr. Mandela bounced a baby boy on his knee while his cavalcade was held up in a traffic jam.

The incident occurred near the University of Cape Town when a woman rushed into a friend's home to tell them that Mr. Mandela was in a car outside.

A man, holding a baby, came rushing out of the house and Mr. Mandela asked for the child, who was then passed through the window where Mr. Mandela bounced him on his knee.

At one time the organisers estimated the crowd to be a quarter-million strong, but because of the intense heat and cramped space on Grand Parade and its surrounds, about half the crowd opted to return home to their television sets when it became known that Mr. Mandela would not be arriving at the City Hall to deliver his first speech in twenty-seven years before seven o'clock.

His eventual arrival was greeted with deafening applause, a sound that rang so sweetly and sincerely that it brought tears to the eyes of thousands.

When Mr. Mandela began to read his speech in the fading light, the people of Cape Town clung onto every word he said with intermittent shouts of 'Long live Mandela!' and 'Viva ANC!'

After having completed his speech in near darkness, a white bank of cloud hovered above Table Mountain before settling on the mountain like a table cloth, ready to serve a man who has sacrificed the better part of his life for the cause of justice.

Yes, the people of the Mother City had done their duty by paying homage to a man who will go down in history as South Africa's greatest son.

Mandela's Philosophy of Post-Apartheid Forgiveness

Don Boroughs

For decades, people in South Africa expected that only a violent and bloody revolution would topple the white apartheid government from power. When Nelson Mandela was released from prison and talks began between the ruling National Party (NP) and the African National Congress (ANC) with the aim of moving toward democratic elections, South Africans could barely believe that such negotiations were happening in a peaceful manner. Indeed, one of the reasons often cited for this near-miracle of nonviolent transition was the lack of revenge exhibited by the ANC leaders who had been imprisoned by the NP government for decades. Without doubt, the leading proponent of this spirit of forgiveness and reconciliation was Nelson Mandela, who made an enormous effort to reconcile with his former captors and enemies in the NP. On numerous occasions, Mandela spoke of his desire to include South Africans of all races and religions in the rebuilding of the new South Africa.

In the following excerpt from *U.S. News & World Report*, reporter Don Boroughs examines Mandela's role as a catalyst for the widespread movement of forgiveness and reconciliation that was enthusiastically embraced by other leaders, as well as many churches and courts, in post-apartheid South Africa.

The new South Africa did not dawn brightly for Wazil Ismail. Five years ago, on the eve of the country's first democratic elections, a blast from a car bomb ripped through the front windows of his butcher shop and blew the rear door off its

Don Boroughs, "Proving That One Man Can Make a Difference," *U.S. News & World Report*, vol. 126, May 24, 1999, p. 36. Copyright © 1999 by U.S. News & World Report, Inc. All rights reserved. Reproduced by permission.

hinges. Ismail was fortunate to survive; 10 people were killed by the bomb, planted by white terrorists. But he feared the country was headed toward civil war. "We were expecting a lot more violence after the elections," says Ismail, standing behind rows of hanging sausages. "Anything could have happened." Still surprised by the past five years of relative peace, the Indian businessman offers a two-word explanation: Nelson Mandela.

On May 10, 1994, the new president of South Africa told his nation: "The time for the healing of the wounds has come. The moment to bridge the chasms that divide us has come." This, he pledged, would be his mission. It is a measure of Mandela's success that as he prepares to step down next month, South Africans take for granted the stability that his healing and bridging have brought. In the 12 months preceding the 1994 elections, 4,400 people died in political violence, and voters counted this—along with unemployment—as their most urgent concern. Today, the issue does not even register among their top 10 worries.

How Did Mandela Do It?

Master of the symbolic gesture, Mandela charmed his enemies into submission. From the moment he read an Afrikaans poem in his first speech to Parliament, he made it clear that his South Africa had no victor and no vanquished. He dined with his jailers and flattered his adversaries. But the same forgiving leadership that saved the country from civil war proved feeble when South Africa needed swift and firm action against a triple epidemic of AIDS, crime, and unemployment. Thabo Mbeki, who now serves as deputy president and is a shoo-in to succeed Mandela after parliamentary elections on June 2 [1999], will inherit a largely unified nation. But he also must grapple with death, violence, and despair. As South Africans evaluate Mandela's accomplishments, they weigh these two opposing legacies. For most, the balance still holds Mandela very high. "You can't get everything in one person," argues Tony Leon, leader of the opposition Democratic Party. "Mandela will go down in history as the great reconciler."

It is impossible to appreciate the scale of the reconciliation without acknowledging the depths and dangers of the old schisms. "We were ready for the war," recalls Constand Viljoen, a retired Army general who in 1994 led the right-wing Afrikaner Volksfront. "We could have raised 50,000 troops." Post-apartheid South Africa under a less accommodating leader, he says, might have resembled Northern Ireland, or even Bosnia. Before the 1994 elections, fearful citizens cleared the store shelves of baked beans and canned meat, candles and bottled gas.

South Africans, trying to explain how this threat dissipated so quickly, point to some amazingly simple acts by Mandela. In 1995, he entered an all-white town to shake hands and take tea with Betsie Verwoerd, the 94-year-old widow of the architect of apartheid, Hendrik Verwoerd. Mandela also cheered on the national rugby team, a largely Afrikaner squad that previously had elicited boos from black South Africans. When he took the field in a rugby uniform after South Africa won the 1995 World Cup, the virtually all-white crowd chanted, "Nelson! Nelson!" The president also humored Afrikaners, such as General Viljoen, who demanded a volkstaat, a homeland of their own. Even though many whites ridicule the idea, Mandela has never ruled it out. "He created a way for the Afrikaner community to participate in the New South Africa," says Viljoen, who now pursues influence constitutionally, as leader of the Freedom Front party.

Not all the threats to the new democracy came from the white right. Before the 1994 elections, Mandela's African National Congress and the Zulu-dominated Inkatha Freedom Party were virtually at war in the province of Natal, a conflict that had taken 10,000 lives. Just last week, the government uncovered a 7-ton cache of grenades, land mines, and other weapons hidden by IFP militants five years ago. Today, the killings have almost stopped, partly because of Mandela's efforts to stroke the delicate ego of Mangosuthu Buthelezi, the IFP leader. Buthelezi was invited into the cabinet as minister of home affairs. And Mandela designated his rival to serve as acting president whenever the nation's two top leaders (Mandela and Mbeki) were out of the country.

BUT MANDELA IS NOT PERFECT

If forgiveness and reconciliation seemed to come naturally to Mandela, running the country did not. He rarely involved himself in the details of governance. And he appeared to value loyalty more than competence as he allowed veterans of the antiapartheid struggle to flounder in key posts. "One of the weaknesses of the Mandela presidency is his reluctance to fire people when they do not perform," says Sipho S. Maseko, a political scientist at the University of the Western Cape.

Where AIDS is concerned, that weakness may cost lives. Since Mandela took the oath of office, the HIV infection rate among pregnant women seeking care at public clinics has rocketed from 7 percent to more than 23 percent. Education efforts have centered on splashy events, such as a $4 million AIDS musical that closed after a few performances. Ignorance remains rife.

A "Deadly Brew" That Killed Thousands

Although many viewed South Africa's transition from apartheid to democracy under the stewardship of F.W. de Klerk and Nelson Mandela as "miraculous," the transition was in fact attended by massive amounts of violence. In this excerpt, various journalists and scholars attempt to untangle the underlying causes for this "deadly brew"—the shocking waves of unrest and murder that racked South Africa during the run-up to the first democratic elections in 1994.

By the beginning of 1991 battles to the death were being fought in many parts of South Africa. In Natal and in the industrial heartland of the Transvaal, in particular, villages and township streets had become battlefields, inhabitants were being shot, hacked and burnt to death by the scores, homes and possessions were being burnt, and thousands of people had been displaced by the turmoil.

While political parties blamed their rivals, directly or indirectly, for the 'undeclared war', analysts tried to make sense of the carnage. . . .

Violence had been a feature of the South African way of life for a long time. And the killing did not stop when President FW de Klerk's reforms (including the unbanning of the liberation movements) were announced on 2 February 1990—it increased. The next month, 458 people died in what was categorised as political violence. Before that the figure had never risen above 200 a month. What should have been the start of an era of peace turned instead into what Reuters journalist Rich Mkhondo described as 'A time for weeping'.

Explanations for the rise in the bloodshed abounded. Adam and Moodley wrote: '[The political violence] is variously attributed to (1) De Klerk's double agenda and unreformed police; (2) a "third force" of right-wing elements in the security establishment, bent on derailing the government's negotiation

Crime is also unabated. Some 25 vehicles are hijacked each day in the Johannesburg-Pretoria region alone. More than 1,000 police officers have been murdered since 1994. The Mail & Guardian newspaper, in an annual grading of ministers, has repeatedly given E's and F's to the officials in charge of corrections and security. Yet they have not been called to task. And as part of his 80th-birthday celebration last year, Mandela set free 9,000 convicts who were nearing their release dates. "That can never be a birthday present to

> agenda; (3) the Inkatha/ANC rivalry, engineered by an ambitious [Chief Mangosuthu] Buthelezi who fears being sidelined rather than treated as an equal third party; (4) the ANC's campaign of armed struggle, ungovernability, and revolutionary intolerance; (5) ingrained tribalism, unleashed by the lessening of white repression that resulted in "black-on-black" violence; (6) the legacy of apartheid in general, migrantcy, hostel conditions, and high unemployment among a generation of "lost youth". . . .'
> There was no shortage of initiatives to try to halt the violence. In January 1991, ANC leader Nelson Mandela and IFP leader Chief Mangosuthu Buthelezi held a peace summit, calling on supporters to 'cease all attacks against one another with immediate effect'. The violence intensified. They met again on Good Friday—but the violence continued. . . .
> Deaths attributed to political violence climbed from 2,706 in 1991 to 3,347 in 1992 and 3,706 in 1993 (an average of more than ten a day). In the darkest month, July 1993, a staggering 547 people lost their lives—nearly 18 for every day of the month.
> 'The minute one steps back from our culture of violence, its causes as numerous as its injuries, one notices again the enormous shadow cast by the most fundamental social and economic problems,' wrote Mkhondo of Reuters. 'Millions of blacks are caught in a spiral of landlessness, homelessness, unemployment, and poverty. Add to that a clash between modern political structures and traditional tribal ones. Mix in a struggle for hegemony in the region between major political players. Stir in the security forces in all their guises. . . . Add faceless, apparently trained killers such as the "third force", etc. Sprinkle all that with ancient and recent political or social grudges and you get a deadly brew.'
> Christopher Saunders and Colin Bundy, *Reader's Digest Illustrated History of South Africa*. Cape Town, South Africa: Reader's Digest, 1994.

the nation," protests Mduduzi Mashiyane, a crime specialist with the Institute for Democracy in South Africa.

Criminality is fueled by the masses of unemployed. Since 1994, employers have shed 500,000 jobs, even as the economy grew. At least one third of black South Africans are jobless, and the unemployment rate rises by 2 to 3 points each year. Part of the problem may be the ANC's loyalty to an ally in the fight against apartheid: the union movement. But not all of the government's policies have pandered to the left. Under the firm leadership of Finance Minister Trevor Manuel, the budget deficit—calculated as a percentage of GDP—has been cut in half. The capital flight and disinvestment that marked the final years of apartheid have been replaced by five straight years of net capital inflows totaling more than $12 billion. As South African wines and fruit went from politically incorrect to flavor of the month, those exports have doubled to $822 million. And tourists have flocked to see the new South Africa; their numbers tripled from 1.7 million in 1991 to 5.4 million last year [1998].

How Will Thabo Mbeki Fare?

Can a mere mortal like Mbeki succeed in the areas where the great Mandela failed? Having spent many years in exile, mainly in London, Mbeki is expected to have a less sentimental attachment to allies from the struggle. He already has announced that government executives will be held to measured standards of performance. "Mbeki is capable of cracking the whip," says Mashiyane, the crime analyst.

Indeed, South Africans appear quite relaxed about the end of Mandela's rule—in contrast to the early days of his presidency, when the stock market plummeted on the slightest rumor of his ill health. Mandela began preparing his nation for the Mbeki era years ago, staunchly refusing to consider another term. On a continent where only three other elected presidents have voluntarily relinquished power, the greatest gesture by the master of gestures may be his long wave goodbye.

Mandela and the AIDS Crisis in South Africa

The Economist

In present-day South Africa, AIDS has become a widespread epidemic that is ravaging communities throughout the country. In some areas, infection rates are estimated to be between 20 and 30 percent, and hundreds of thousands of children have been left orphaned. Unfortunately, President Thabo Mbeki has failed to address the crisis to anyone's satisfaction: He refuses to openly discuss the problem, he has not provided government subsidized medications, and most infamously, he has publicly denied that the human immunodeficiency virus (HIV) causes AIDS.

Outraged by Mbeki's incompetent handling of this dire situation, Nelson Mandela, who retired five years ago from his office as State President, has been pressuring his successor to deal with the AIDS situation. Mandela has fought to bring the disease out of the shadows and into the public spotlight, discussing the AIDS tragedies in his own family and urging people to get tested.

The following excerpt from the British magazine *The Economist* discusses the public tensions that have arisen between Mandela and Mbeki, as the former leader refuses to watch the youth of his country die while little is being done in the form of public education and medical care.

Thabo Mbeki has great ambitions for the future of his country. But his fiercest critic is not to be shaken off.

In January 2002, when the African National Congress (ANC) celebrated its 90th anniversary, Thabo Mbeki, South Africa's president, made a long speech. To general astonish-

"In Mandela's Shadow: Thabo Mbeki and Nelson Mandela Argue It Out in South Africa," *The Economist*, vol. 365, December 14, 2002. Copyright © 2002 by The Economist Newspaper Group, Ltd., www.economist.com. All rights reserved. Reproduced by permission.

ment, he made no mention of the ANC's most famous figure, Nelson Mandela. The feeling is mutual. When Mr. Mbeki entered parliament at the state opening in February, all stood to respectful attention except Mr. Mandela, who sat stock-still in his chair despite gentle tugs from his wife.

THE TWO LEADERS

At 84, Mr. Mandela has lost none of his charisma. On his visits to dusty townships, people stand for hours waiting for him and scream with joy when he appears. In parliament, MPs leap to their feet, sway, dance and sing in adoration. At dinners and private discussions, even close friends flutter with affection and respect. As he takes an armchair at a lunch in Johannesburg a roomful of businessmen, lawyers and family friends sink to their knees and form an attentive circle at his feet. He calls Queen Elizabeth by her first name ("well, she calls me Nelson"), and goes hand-in-hand with Bill Clinton, beaming for the cameras.

Mr. Mbeki, by contrast, can be painfully shy. He admits he is an awkward showman, fondest of his own company. He has solitary interests: reading, the Internet, computer chess, landscape photography, poetry. On presidential tours, known as *imbizos*, he is stiff and formal. With journalists he is often impatient, bristling at ignorant questions. Mr. Mandela is widely known by an affectionate nickname, Madiba. Mr. Mbeki has none.

It is an open secret that another man, Cyril Ramaphosa, was Mr. Mandela's first choice as his successor. But Mr. Ramaphosa was out-manoeuvred in the early 1990s, and by 1999 Mr. Mbeki was president. Were it not for Mr. Mandela, he would be riding high and virtually unopposed. At the ANC's five-yearly conference, held next week in the vineyard town of Stellenbosch, Mr. Mbeki will be picked again as party leader; his close allies are almost certain to romp to all the high party positions; and victory is more or less assured at the general election in 2004.

His party dominates politics, holding two-thirds of the seats in parliament against a divided and feeble opposition. And his country is becoming more and more of a presence in the continent. Mr. Mbeki presides over the African Union, Africa's putative answer to the EU, and is also the brains behind the New Partnership for Africa's Development (Nepad), an ambitious plan to attract more capital investment. Last year (at Mr. Mandela's request) he sent his deputy-president, Jacob Zuma, and a battalion of soldiers to help keep the peace in Burundi, and he has offered 1,500 more soldiers as UN peacekeepers for eastern Congo. Under Mr. Mandela, South Africa shed its isolation in Africa; under Mr. Mbeki, it is actively engaged.

CAUSES FOR COMPLAINT

Yet all is not well within Mr. Mbeki's administration, not least because Mr. Mandela has let it be widely known that he is unhappy with it. The old man, tata, as Mr. Mbeki sometimes calls him dismissively, has started to meddle.

Some of his recent unhappiness stems from local politics. In the ANC's heartland of the Eastern Cape, where Mr. Mbeki and Mr. Mandela were both born, the ANC provincial government is in such disarray that Mr. Mbeki has had to send people from national government to sort it out. This has caused enormous discontent within the party. In KwaZulu-Natal, a truce between the ANC and the Zulu nationalist Inkatha Freedom Party, brokered under Mr. Mandela but largely negotiated by Mr. Mbeki, is collapsing as the two parties fight for local control.

Yet most of the animosity comes from Mr. Mbeki's handling of South Africa's AIDS crisis, which Mr. Mandela believes has been badly bungled. The disease has already killed hundreds of thousands of South Africans and is set to claim the lives of at least 4.5m more, over 11% of the population. Already, 300,000 households are headed by orphaned children. Unsurprisingly, a recent survey showed that 96% of South Africans consider the disease to be a "very big" problem for the country.

THE AIDS CRISIS

AIDS is already striking hard at the professions, notably teachers and nurses. Some analysts worry that the disease has weakened the capacity of the army (with an infection rate of well over 23%) and the police. Life expectancy is slumping as child mortality rises. Ill-health is also entrenching poverty: for a middle-income country, surprisingly large numbers of people report being short of food.

A year ago, Mr. Mandela warned that leaders and their wives must do more to fight AIDS. That was an explicit reference to Mr. Mbeki's inactivity, though also an admission of his own negligence as president between 1994 and 1999. All year Mr. Mandela has raised the profile of AIDS, drawing a stark contrast with Mr. Mbeki's wriggles and denials.

The national government and some provinces have done a lot to boost primary health care, train nurses, fund education-and-prevention campaigns and give out more free condoms. The government also helps to fund research into a vaccine and has opened 18 pilot sites to test the effectiveness of anti-retroviral drugs, which are commonly used in rich countries to keep those infected with HIV healthy. But the president himself has often frustrated these efforts.

Mr. Mbeki questions figures that show the epidemic has taken hold in South Africa. He argues that anti-AIDS drugs may be more dangerous than AIDS itself. He refuses to single out AIDS as a special threat, preferring to talk of general "diseases of poverty", and will rarely speak about it publicly. Peter Piot, the head of UNAIDS, was once brought secretly to meet Mr. Mbeki in Cape Town, in an effort to persuade him that the human immunodeficiency virus was the cause of AIDS. The two men sat late into the night drinking whisky and fruitlessly arguing the point.

A Dangerous Silence

Mr. Mbeki also refuses to encourage people to know their HIV status and to lessen stigma around the disease. He will not take a public AIDS test, and has only once been pictured holding an infected child. Taking their lead from the president, no members of his government and very few MPs, civil servants, or public figures of any sort admit the obvious when their colleagues die of the disease.

Mr. Mbeki himself seems personally affronted by the attention given to AIDS. He resents any prejudice against Africans as diseased, in part because apartheid scientists tried to create and spread viruses that would kill only black Africans. In the early 1990s the then ruling National Party even alleged that ANC leaders returning from exile in other parts of Africa (such as Mr. Mbeki himself) were bringing AIDS into the country.

Appalled by Mr. Mbeki's obtuseness on the subject, Mr. Mandela has been trying to force him to do more about it. He openly backs the Treatment Action Campaign (TAC), one of the most aggressive and effective opposition movements in the country. Earlier this year the TAC sued the government in the Constitutional Court and forced it to set up a national programme to give anti-AIDS drugs to infected pregnant women. The group's leader, Zackie Achmat, who himself has AIDS, refuses to use anti-retroviral drugs until the government makes them widely available. Madiba has visited and hugged Mr. Achmat, and promised to lobby the president on his behalf. Last week the two men again appeared together, to launch a privately-funded plan to get anti-AIDS drugs to thousands more of the poor.

Madiba Speaks Out

In September [2002] at Orange Farm, a township just south of Johannesburg, Mr. Mandela launched a particularly sharp attack. He demanded general provision of anti-retroviral drugs by the government, pushing aside worries about cost, toxicity and capitalist imperialism. Then he ordered two of his grandchildren to join him on stage, wagged his fingers at them, and told the crowd:

> I have 29 grandchildren and six great-grandchildren. They are very naughty. They tell me I have lost power and influence, that I am a has-been. They tell me to sit down. That I must stop pretending I am still the president. Now, you have heard all these important people here today, you have heard what they say about me. So, now you must stop telling me to sit down!

That message was aimed at Mr. Mbeki.

Earlier this month, Mr. Mandela launched an independent report on AIDS that concluded: "We must manage this disease or it will manage us." After perfunctory praise for government research, he said again that too little is being done, officially, to fight AIDS and the stigma that surrounds it. "I have often said to the government there is a perception that we don't care that thousands are dying of this disease. If you look at the pages of the Sowetan, at the death notices, it is clear that our young people are dying."

While many private companies—among them Anglo-American, Coca-Cola and De Beers—have decided that it is cost-effective to provide free anti-AIDS drugs to infected workers, the government is reluctant to make similar promises to other South Africans. Mr. Mandela wants such drugs to be universally available, and ordinary South Africans agree. A recent survey of nearly 10,000 people revealed that over 95% want the government to provide anti-AIDS drugs now.

NOT MADIBA ALONE

Mr. Mbeki often refuses phone calls from his predecessor. When he does, Mr. Mandela is told that he misunderstands the complexity of AIDS. The old man has been asked by senior ANC leaders to stop undermining the government, and to tell the press that the only problem with official AIDS policy is one of communication.

Will his interventions in fact have any effect? Possibly, since he is not a lone voice. Many heads of state and former presidents have privately tried to persuade Mr. Mbeki to do more on AIDS, if only for the sake of his own reputation. Mr. Clinton, who was beside Mr. Mandela at Orange Farm, confided his view of the president's position on AIDS: "In his own mind, he thinks he has moved a long way." The challenge now is to persuade him to do as much as leaders in poorer African countries.

In Nigeria, said Mr. Clinton, politicians talk openly about the disease. "It has kept its [infection] rate low because there was no organised, systematic and official denial of the problem there. In South Africa I see systemic obstacles still, to doing what has worked elsewhere. Leaving people to their own devices is just not good enough." In particular, Mr. Clinton criticises the failure to make mass use of anti-retrovirals, drugs that are already widely used in Brazil and India.

In September, Mr. Piot protested that the World Summit on Sustainable Development, held that month in Johannesburg, paid almost no attention to AIDS. Delegates conceded that the disease was given a low priority to avoid embarrassing the host. Mr. Piot and Carol Bellamy, the head of UNICEF, have both complained that Mr. Mbeki's Nepad plan for African recovery makes no substantial mention of the fight against AIDS.

Mr. Mbeki now seems to be slightly shifting his position, if only to persuade Madiba, Bishop Desmond Tutu and others to stop "backseat driving". In April the government agreed to set out a plan for provincial governments to give nevirapine, an anti-retroviral drug, to infected pregnant women and rape victims. Mr. Mbeki's chief spokesman, Joel Netshitenzhe, even suggested that factories might be built to produce generic anti-AIDS drugs. And the government has been talking to firms and health activists about a national treatment plan for the disease.

In the past few months Mr. Mbeki has kept silent on the subject, while trying to cultivate a more friendly persona (he has taken up golf so that he can bond with George Bush, who is expected to pay a visit next month). But South Africa's president will not be pushed into a position he opposes, especially not by westerners, the media, the UN or activists.

Ultimately, then, the most effective pressure will come from within his own party. Next week's ANC meeting in Stellenbosch is a chance for members to push Mr. Mbeki to act decisively. And one member, the only world-famous one, will go on pushing hardest of all, no matter how often his calls are not returned.

Appendix of Documents

Document 1: No Easy Walk to Freedom

By 1953 Mandela had been banned by the South African government for the second time and was forbidden from attending any public meetings. The following excerpt, from his presidential address to the Transvaal branch of the ANC, was read for him on September 21, 1953. In this speech, Mandela notes sadly that after the landmark Defiance Campaign of 1952, in which thousands of civilians went to jail for refusing to comply with apartheid laws, the government's reaction was not clemency, but increased aggression.

Since 1912 and year after year thereafter, in their homes and local areas, in provincial and national gatherings, on trains and buses, in the factories and on the farms, in cities, villages, shanty towns, schools and prisons, the African people have discussed the shameful misdeeds of those who rule the country. Year after year, they have raised their voices in condemnation of the grinding poverty of the people, the low wages, the acute shortage of land, the inhuman exploitation and the whole policy of white domination. But instead of more freedom repression began to grow in volume and intensity and it seemed that all their sacrifices would end up in smoke and dust. Today the entire country knows that their labours were not in vain for a new spirit and new ideas have gripped our people. Today the people speak the language of action: there is a mighty awakening among the men and women of our country and the year 1952 stands out as the year of this upsurge of national consciousness.

In June 1952, the African National Congress [ANC] and the South African Indian Congress [SAIC], bearing in mind their responsibility as the representatives of the downtrodden and oppressed people of South Africa, took the plunge and launched the Campaign for the Defiance of the Unjust Laws. Starting off in Port Elizabeth in the early hours of June 26 and with only thirty-three defiers in action and then in Johannesburg in the afternoon of the same day with one hundred and six defiers, it spread throughout the country like wild fire. Factory and office workers, doctors, lawyers, teachers, students and the clergy; Africans, Coloureds, Indians and Europeans, old and young, all rallied to the national call and defied the pass laws and the curfew and the railway apartheid regulations. At the end of the year, more than 8,000 people of all races had defied. The Campaign called for immediate and heavy sacrifices. Workers lost their jobs, chiefs and teachers were expelled from the service, doctors, lawyers and businessmen gave up their practices and businesses and elected to go to jail. . . .

Today we meet under totally different conditions. By the end of July last year, the Campaign had reached a stage where it had to be suppressed by the Government or it would impose its own policies on the country.

The government launched its reactionary offensive and struck at us. Between July last year and August this year forty-seven leading members from both Congresses in Johannesburg, Port Elizabeth and Kimberley were arrested, tried and convicted for launching the Defiance Campaign and given suspended sentences ranging from three months to two years on condition that they did not again participate in the defiance of the unjust laws. In November last year, a proclamation was passed which prohibited meetings of more than ten Africans and made it an offence for any person to call upon an African to defy. Contravention of this proclamation carried a penalty of three years or of a fine of three hundred pounds. In March this year the Government passed the so-called Public Safety Act which empowered it to declare a state of emergency and to create conditions which would permit of the most ruthless and pitiless methods of suppressing our movement. Almost simultaneously, the Criminal Laws Amendment Act was passed which provided heavy penalties for those convicted of Defiance offences. This Act also made provision for the whipping of defiers including women. . . .

The intensification of repressions and the extensive use of the bans is designed to immobilise every active worker and to check the national liberation movement. But gone forever are the days when harsh and wicked laws provided the oppressors with years of peace and quiet. The racial policies of the Government have pricked the conscience of all men of good will and have aroused their deepest indignation. The feelings of the oppressed people have never been more bitter. If the ruling circles seek to maintain their position by such inhuman methods then a clash between the forces of freedom and those of reaction is certain. The grave plight of the people compels them to resist to the death the stinking policies of the gangsters that rule our country.

But in spite of all the difficulties outlined above, we have won important victories. The general political level of the people has been considerably raised and they are now more conscious of their strength. Action has become the language of the day. . . .

Our immediate task is to consolidate these victories, to preserve our organisations and to muster our forces for the resumption of the offensive. To achieve this important task the National Executive of the ANC in consultation with the National Action Committee of the ANC and the SAIC formulated a plan of action popularly known as the "M" Plan and the highest importance is [given] to it by the National Executives. Instructions were given to all provinces to implement the "M" Plan without delay.

The underlying principle of this plan is the understanding that it is no longer possible to wage our struggle mainly on the old methods of public meetings and printed circulars. The aim is:

1. to consolidate the Congress machinery;
2. to enable the transmission of important decisions taken on a national level to every member of the organisation without calling public meetings, issuing press statements and printing circulars;
3. to build up in the local branches themselves local Congresses which will effectively represent the strength and will of the people;
4. to extend and strengthen the ties between Congress and the people and to consolidate Congress leadership.

This plan is being implemented in many branches not only in the Transvaal but also in the other provinces and is producing excellent results. . . .

You can see that there is no easy walk to freedom anywhere, and many of us will have to pass through the valley of the shadow (of death) again and again before we reach the mountain tops of our desires.

Dangers and difficulties have not deterred us in the past, they will not frighten us now. But we must be prepared for them like men in business who do not waste energy in vain talk and idle action. The way of preparation (for action) lies in our rooting out all impurity and indiscipline from our organisation and making it the bright and shining instrument that will cleave its way to (Africa's) freedom.

Nelson Mandela, "No Easy Walk to Freedom," Presidential Address to the ANC (Transvaal branch), September 21, 1953.

DOCUMENT 2: THE FREEDOM CHARTER

The following document, which ultimately provided the basis for the constitution of the new South Africa in 1994, was written by Mandela and the ANC leadership and ratified at the Congress of the People in Kliptown on June 26, 1955. The congress was a multiracial, multicultural meeting of three thousand representatives from political parties across South Africa. The Freedom Charter clearly states the basic rights and liberties of all South Africans under the law, while announcing the ANC's aim to equalize the disproportionate levels of wealth so that all are provided with housing, jobs, and education.

WE, THE PEOPLE OF SOUTH AFRICA, DECLARE FOR ALL OUR COUNTRY AND THE WORLD TO KNOW:

That South Africa belongs to all who live in it, black and white, and that no government can justly claim authority unless it is based on the will of the people;

That our people have been robbed of their birthright to land, liberty and peace by a form of government founded on injustice and inequality;

That our country will never be prosperous or free until all our people live in brotherhood, enjoying equal rights and opportunities;

That only a democratic state, based on the will of the people, can secure to all their birthright without distinction of colour, race, sex or belief;

And therefore, we the people of South Africa, black and white, together equals, countrymen and brothers, adopt this Freedom Charter. And we pledge ourselves to strive together, sparing nothing of our strength and courage, until the democratic changes here set out have been won.

THE PEOPLE SHALL GOVERN!

Every man and woman shall have the right to vote for and stand as a candidate for all bodies which make laws;

All the people shall be entitled to take part in the administration of the country;

The rights of the people shall be the same, regardless of race, colour or sex;

All bodies of minority rule, advisory boards, councils and authorities shall be replaced by democratic organs of self-government.

ALL NATIONAL GROUPS SHALL HAVE EQUAL RIGHTS!

There shall be equal status in the bodies of state, in the courts, and in the schools for all national groups and races;

All national groups shall be protected by law against insults to their race and national pride;

All people shall have equal rights to use their own language and to develop their own folk culture and customs;

The preaching and practice of national, race or colour discrimination and contempt shall be a punishable crime;

All apartheid laws and practices shall be set aside.

THE PEOPLE SHALL SHARE IN THE COUNTRY'S WEALTH!

The national wealth of our country, the heritage of all South Africans, shall be restored to the people;

The mineral wealth beneath the soil, the banks and monopoly industry shall be transferred to the ownership of the people as a whole;

All other industries and trades shall be controlled to assist the well-being of the people;

All people shall have equal rights to trade where they choose, to manufacture and to enter all trades, crafts and professions.

THE LAND SHALL BE SHARED AMONG THOSE WHO WORK IT!

Restriction of land ownership on a racial basis shall end, and all the land be redivided amongst those who work it, to banish famine and land hunger;

The state shall help the peasants with implements, seed, tractors and dams to save the soil and assist the tillers;

Freedom of movement shall be guaranteed to all who work the land;

All shall have the right to occupy land wherever they choose;

People shall not be robbed of their cattle, and forced labour and farm prisons shall be abolished.

ALL SHALL BE EQUAL BEFORE THE LAW!

No one shall be imprisoned, deported or restricted without fair trial;

No one shall be condemned by the older of any government official;

The courts shall be representative of all the people;

Imprisonment shall be only for serious crimes against the people, and shall aim at re-education, not only vengeance;

The police force and army shall be open to all on an equal basis and shall be the helpers and protectors of the people;

All laws which discriminate on the grounds of race, colour or belief shall be repealed.

ALL SHALL ENJOY HUMAN RIGHTS!

The law shall guarantee to all their right to speak, to organize, to meet together, to publish, to preach, to worship and to educate their children;

The privacy of the house from police raids shall be protected by law;

All shall be free to travel without restriction from countryside to town, from province to province, and from South Africa abroad;

Pass laws, permits and all other laws restricting these freedoms shall be abolished.

THERE SHALL BE WORK AND SECURITY!

All who work shall be free to form trade unions, to elect their officers and to make wage agreements with their employers;

The state shall recognize the right and duty of all to work, and to draw full unemployment benefits;

Men and women of all races shall receive equal pay for equal work;

There shall be a forty-hour working week, a national minimum wage, paid annual leave, and sick leave for all workers, and maternity leave on full pay for all working mothers;

Miners, domestic workers, farm workers and civil servants shall have the same rights as all others who work;

Child labour, compound labour, the tot system and contract labour shall be abolished.

THE DOORS OF LEARNING AND CULTURE SHALL BE OPENED!

The government shall discover, develop and encourage national talent for the enhancement of our cultural life;

All the cultural treasures of mankind shall be open to all, by free exchange of books, ideas and contact with other lands;

The aim of education shall be to teach the youth to love their people and their culture, to honour human brotherhood, liberty and peace;

Education shall be free, compulsory, universal and equal for all children;

Higher education and technical training shall be opened to all by means of state allowances and scholarships awarded on the basis of merit;

Adult illiteracy shall be ended by a mass state education plan;

Teachers shall have all the rights of other citizens;

The colour bar in cultural life, in sport and in education shall be abolished.

THERE SHALL BE HOUSES, SECURITY AND COMFORT!

All people shall have the right to live where they choose, to be decently housed, and to bring up their families in comfort and security;

Unused housing space to be made available to the people;

Rent and prices shall be lowered, food plentiful and no one shall go hungry;

A preventive health scheme shall be run by the state;

Free medical care and hospitalization shall be provided for all, with special care for mothers and young children;

Slums shall be demolished and new suburbs built where all shall have transport, roads, lighting, playing fields, creches and social centres;

The aged, the orphans, the disabled and the sick shall be cared for by the state;

Rest, leisure and recreation shall be the right of all;

Fenced locations and ghettos shall be abolished and laws which break up families shall be repealed.

THERE SHALL BE PEACE AND FRIENDSHIP!

South Africa shall be a fully independent state, which respects the rights and sovereignty of all nations;

South Africa shall strive to maintain world peace and the settlement of all international disputes by negotiation, not war;

Peace and friendship amongst all our people shall be secured by upholding the equal rights, opportunities and status of all;

The people of the protectorates, Basutoland, Bechuanaland and Swaziland, shall be recognized, and shall be free to decide for themselves their own future;

The right of all the peoples of Africa to independence and self-government shall be recognized, and shall be the basis of close co-operation;

LET ALL WHO LOVE THEIR PEOPLE AND THEIR COUNTRY NOW SAY, AS WE SAY HERE:

'These freedoms we will fight for, side by side, throughout our lives, until we have won our liberty.'

John Pampallis, *Foundations of the New South Africa*. London: Zed, 1991.

Document 3: The Struggle Is My Life

After the ANC had been banned, the organization's leadership decided to move operations to beyond the borders of South Africa. In mid-1960, Oliver Tambo was sent to London to start the ANC office there, and others relocated operations to Lusaka, Zambia. Mandela, however, publicly declared his intention to remain in South Africa and to continue his work underground. In the following statement, released from within South Africa but published by the ANC in London on June 26, 1961, Mandela announced that he would not abandon the liberation struggle, nor would he willingly give himself up to the authorities. (June 16, 1961, marked the ninth anniversary of the start of the 1952 Defiance Campaign.)

Today is 26 June, a day known throughout the length and breadth of our country as Freedom Day. On this memorable day, nine years ago, eight thousand five hundred of our dedicated freedom fighters struck a mighty blow against the repressive colour policies of the government. Their matchless courage won them the praise and affection of millions of people here and abroad. Since then we have had many stirring campaigns on this date and it has been observed by hundreds of thousands of our people as a day of dedication. It is fit and proper that on this historic day I should speak to you and announce fresh plans for the opening of the second phase in the fight against the Verwoerd republic, and for a National Convention.

You will remember that the Pietermaritzburg Resolutions warned that if the government did not call a National Convention before the end of May, 1961, Africans, Coloureds, Indians and European democrats would be asked not to collaborate with the republic or any government based on force. On several occasions since then the National Action Council explained that the last strike marked the beginning of a relentless mass struggle for the defeat of the Nationalist government, and for a sovereign multi-racial convention. We stressed that the strike would be followed by other forms of mass pressure to force the race maniacs who govern our beloved country to make way for a democratic government of the people, by the people and for the people. A full-scale and countrywide campaign of non-co-operation with the government will be launched immediately. The precise form of the contemplated action, its scope and dimensions and duration will be announced to you at the appropriate time.

At the present moment it is sufficient to say that we plan to make government impossible. Those who are voteless cannot be expected to continue paying taxes to a government which is not responsible to them. People who live in poverty and starvation cannot be expected to pay exorbitant house rents to the government and local authorities. We furnish the sinews of agriculture and industry. We produce the work of the gold mines, the diamonds and the coal, of the farms and industry, in return for miserable wages. Why should we continue enriching those who steal the products of our sweat and blood? Those who exploit us and refuse us the right to organise trade unions? Those who side with the government when we stage peaceful demonstrations to assert our claims and aspirations? How can Africans serve on School Boards and Committees which are part of Bantu Education, a sinister scheme of the Nationalist government to deprive the African people of real education in return for tribal education? Can Africans be expected to be content with serving on Advisory Boards and Bantu Authorities when the demand all over the continent of Africa is for national independence and self-government? . . . Non-collaboration is a dynamic weapon. We must refuse. We must use it to send this government to the grave. It must be used vigorously and without delay. The entire resources of the Black people must be mobilised to withdraw all cooperation with the Nationalist government. Various forms of industrial and economic action will be employed to undermine the already tottering economy of the country. We will call upon the international bodies to expel South Africa and upon nations of the world to sever economic and diplomatic relations with the country.

I am informed that a warrant for my arrest has been issued, and that the police are looking for me. The National Action Council has given full and serious consideration to this question, and has sought the advice of many trusted friends and bodies and they have advised me not to surrender myself. I have accepted this advice, and will not give myself up to a government I do not recognise. Any serious politician will realise that under present-day conditions in this country, to seek for cheap martyrdom by handing myself to the police is naive and criminal. We have an important programme before us and it is important to carry it out very seriously and without delay.

I have chosen this latter course, which is more difficult and which entails more risk and hardship than sitting in gaol. I have had to separate myself from my dear wife and children, from my mother and sisters, to live as an outlaw in my own land. I have had to close my business, to abandon my profession, and live in poverty and misery, as many of my people are doing. I will continue to act as the spokesman of the National Action Council during the phase that is unfolding and in the tough struggles that lie ahead. I shall fight the government side by side with you, inch by inch, and mile by mile, until victory is won. What are you going to do? Will you come along with us, or are you going to co-operate with the government in its efforts to suppress the claims and aspirations of your own people? Or are you going to remain silent and neutral in a matter of life and death to my people, to our people? For my own part I have made my choice. I will not leave South Africa, nor will I surrender. Only through hardship, sacrifice and militant action can freedom be won. The struggle is my life. I will continue fighting for freedom until the end of my days.

Nelson Mandela, *Nelson Mandela: The Struggle Is My Life*. London: International Defence and Aid Fund for Southern Africa, 1990.

Document 4: Umkonto we Sizwe

In December 1961 the splinter group of the ANC led by Nelson Mandela, Umkonto we Sizwe (MK), announced its decision to resort to armed violence against the apartheid government. This decision, taken painfully and after many years of nonviolent struggle, emerged in reaction to the government's increased aggression against (and mass murder of) protesters and activists. However, MK stressed it was targeting only government installations such as power stations and communications networks, rather than individuals, in an effort to bring the government to the negotiating table.

Units of Umkonto We Sizwe today carried out planned attacks against Government installations, particularly those connected with the policy of apartheid and race discrimination.

Umkonto We Sizwe is a new, independent body, formed by Africans. It includes in its ranks South Africans of all races. It is not connected in any way with a so-called "Committee for National Liberation" whose existence has been announced in the press. Umkonto We Sizwe will carry on the struggle for freedom and democracy by new methods, which are necessary to complement the actions of the established national liberation organizations. Umkonto We Sizwe fully supports the national liberation movement, and our members, jointly and individually, place themselves under the overall political guidance of that movement.

It is, however, well known that the main national liberation organizations in this country have consistently followed a policy of non-violence. They have conducted themselves peaceably at all times, regardless of Government attacks and persecutions upon them, and despite all Government-inspired attempts to provoke them to violence. They have done so because the people prefer peaceful methods of change to achieve their aspirations without the suffering and bitterness of civil war. But the people's patience is not endless.

The time comes in the life of any nation when there remain only two choices: submit or fight. That time has now come to South Africa. We shall not submit and we have no choice but to hit back by all means within our power in defense of our people, our future and our freedom.

The Government has interpreted the peacefulness of the movement as weakness; the people's non-violent policies have been taken as a green light for Government violence. Refusal to resort to force has been interpreted by the Government as an invitation to use armed force against the people without any fear of reprisals. The methods of Umkonto We Sizwe mark a break with that past.

We are striking out along a new road for the liberation of the people of this country. The Government policy of force, repression and violence will no longer be met with non-violent resistance only! The choice is not ours; it has been made by the Nationalist Government which has rejected every peaceable demand by the people for rights and freedom and answered every such demand with force and yet more force! . . .

Umkonto We Sizwe will be at the front line of the people's defense. It will be the fighting arm of the people against the Government and its policies of race oppression. It will be the striking force of the people for liberty, for rights and for their final liberation! Let the Government, its supporters who put it into power, and those whose passive toleration of reaction keeps it in power, take note of where the Nationalist Government is leading the country!

We of Umkonto We Sizwe have always sought—as the liberation movement has sought—to achieve liberation, without bloodshed and civil clash. We do so still. We hope—even at this late hour—that our first actions will awaken everyone to a realization of the disastrous situation to which the Nationalist policy is leading. We hope that we will bring the Government and its supporters to their senses before it is too late, so that both Government and its policies can be changed before matters reach the desperate stage of civil war. We believe our actions to be a blow against the Nationalist preparations for civil war and military rule.

In these actions, we are working in the best interests of all the people of this country—black, brown, and white—whose future happiness and well-being cannot be attained without the overthrow of the Nationalist Government, the abolition of white supremacy and the winning of liberty, democracy and full national rights and equality for all the people of this country.

David Mermelstein, ed., *The Anti-Apartheid Reader: The Struggle Against White Racist Rule in South Africa.* New York: Grove Press, 1987.

DOCUMENT 5: BLACK MAN IN A WHITE COURT

After the establishment of Umkonto we Sizwe (MK), Mandela worked undercover in South Africa for several months, before being smuggled outside the country. Once abroad, he traveled widely in Africa and Europe, rallying funds and support for MK and gaining military training expertise. Upon returning, Mandela drove to Durban disguised as a chauffeur in order to update Chief Albert Luthuli, the ANC president, about his trip, and it was soon after leaving Durban, on August 5, 1962, that Mandela was captured by the South African police. At his trial in November of that year for illegally leaving the country, Mandela took the stand in his own defense, arguing that the judicial system in which he was being tried was part of an inherently unjust system.

I want to apply for Your Worship's recusal from this case. I challenge the right of this Court to hear my case on two grounds.

Firstly, I challenge it because I fear that I will not be given a fair and proper trial. Secondly, I consider myself neither legally nor morally bound to obey laws made by a Parliament in which I have no representation.

In a political trial such as this one, which involves a clash of the aspirations of the African people and those of whites, the country's courts, as presently constituted, cannot be impartial and fair.

In such cases, whites are interested parties. To have a white judicial officer presiding, however high his esteem, and however strong his sense of fairness and justice, is to make whites judges in their own case.

It is improper and against the elementary principles of justice to entrust whites with cases involving the denial by them of basic human rights to the African people.

What sort of justice is this that enables the aggrieved to sit in judgement over those against whom they have laid a charge?

A judiciary controlled entirely by whites and enforcing laws enacted by a white Parliament in which Africans have no representation—laws which in most cases are passed in the face of unanimous opposition from Africans—. . . cannot be regarded as an impartial tribunal in a political trial where an African stands as an accused.

The Universal Declaration of Human Rights provides that all men are equal before the law, and are entitled without any discrimination to equal protection of the law. . . .

In its proper meaning equality before the law means the right to participate in the making of the laws by which one is governed, a constitution which guarantees democratic rights to all sections of the population, the right to approach the court for protection or relief in the case of the violation of rights guaranteed in the constitution, and the right to take part in the administration of justice as judges, magistrates, attorneys-general, law advisers and similar positions.

In the absence of these safeguards the phrase 'equality before the law', in so far as it is intended to apply to us, is meaningless and misleading. All the rights and privileges to which I have referred are monopolized by whites, and we enjoy none of them.

The white man makes all the laws, he drags us before his courts and accuses us, and he sits in judgement over us. . . .

Why is it that no African in the history of this country has ever had the honour of being tried by his own kith and kin, by his own flesh and blood?

I will tell Your Worship why: the real purpose of this rigid colour-bar is to ensure that the justice dispensed by the courts should conform to the policy of the country, however much that policy might be in conflict with the norms of justice accepted in judiciaries throughout the civilized world.

I feel oppressed by the atmosphere of white domination that lurks all around in this courtroom. Somehow this atmosphere calls to mind the inhuman injustices caused to my people outside this courtroom by this same white domination. . . .

I raise the question, how can I be expected to believe that this same racial discrimination which has been the cause of so much injustice and suffering right through the years should now operate here to give me a fair and open trial? Is there no danger that an African accused may regard the courts not as impartial tribunals, dispensing justice without fear or favour, but as instruments used by the white man to punish those amongst us who clamour for deliverance from the fiery furnace of white rule. I have grave fears that this system of justice may enable the guilty to drag the innocent before the courts. It enables the unjust to prosecute and demand vengeance against the just. It may tend to lower the standards of fairness and justice applied in the country's courts by white judicial officers to black litigants. This is the first ground for this application: that I will not receive a fair and proper trial.

The second ground of my objection is that I consider myself neither morally nor legally obliged to obey laws made by a Parliament in which I am not represented.

Nelson Mandela, *Nelson Mandela: I Am Prepared to Die.* London: International Defence and Aid Fund for Southern Africa, 1979.

DOCUMENT 6: I AM PREPARED TO DIE

By the time of the Rivonia Trial, the Umkonto we Sizwe (MK) hideout at Rivonia had been discovered by the police, and Mandela became implicated in far more serious charges than he had initially been arrested for in 1962. Knowing that he would receive the death penalty or lifelong imprisonment at best, Mandela used the opportunity of his trial defense to articulate his personal history, his political beliefs and how he had reached the decision to found MK. The speech, which lasted over five hours and firmly established Mandela as an international leader, was widely published in newspapers and books all over the world (except for South Africa), and became one of the central documents of African liberation.

Some of the things so far told to the Court are true and some are untrue. I do not, however, deny that I planned sabotage. I did not plan it in a spirit of recklessness, nor because I have any love of violence. I planned it as a result of a calm and sober assessment of the political situation that had arisen after many years of tyranny, exploitation and oppression of my people by the Whites.

I admit immediately that I was one of the persons who helped to form Umkhonto We Sizwe, and that I played a prominent role in its affairs until I was arrested in August 1962....

But the violence which we chose to adopt was not terrorism. We who formed Umkhonto were all members of the African National Congress, and had behind us the ANC tradition of non-violence and negotiation as a means of solving political disputes. We believed that South Africa belonged to all the people who lived in it, and not to one group, be it Black or White. We did not want an inter-racial war, and tried to avoid it to the last minute....

It must not be forgotten that by this time violence had, in fact, become a feature of the South African political scene. There had been violence in 1957 when the women of Zeerust were ordered to carry passes; there was violence in 1958 with the enforcement of cattle culling in Sekhukhuniland; there was violence in 1959 when the people of Cato Manor protested against pass raids; there was violence in 1960 when the Government attempted to impose Bantu Authorities in Pondoland. Thirty-nine Africans died in these disturbances. In 1961 there had been riots in Warmbaths, and all this time the Transkei had been a seething mass of unrest. Each disturbance pointed clearly to the inevitable growth among Africans of the belief that violence was the only way out—it showed that a Government which uses force to maintain its rule teaches the oppressed to use force to oppose it. Already small groups had arisen in the urban areas and were spontaneously making plans for violent forms of political struggle. There now arose a danger that these groups would adopt terrorism against Africans, as well as Whites, if not properly directed. . . .

After a long and anxious assessment of the South African situation, I and some colleagues came to the conclusion that as violence in this country was inevitable, it would be unrealistic and wrong for African leaders to continue preaching peace and non-violence at a time when the Government met our peaceful demands with force. . . .

Africans want to be paid a living wage. They want to perform work which they are capable of doing, and not work which the Government declares them to be capable of. Africans want to be allowed to live where they obtain work, and not be endorsed out of an area because they were not born there. Africans want to be allowed to own land in places where they work, and not to be obliged to live in rented houses which they can never call their own. We want to be part of the general population, and not confined to living in our own ghettoes. African men want to have their wives and children to live with them where they work, and not be forced into an unnatural existence in men's hostels. African women want to be with their men folk and not be left permanently widowed in the Reserves . . . we want to be allowed to travel in our own country and to seek work where we want to and not where the Labour Bureau tells us to. We want a just share in the whole of South Africa; we want security and a stake in society. Above all, we want equal political rights, because without them our disabilities will be permanent. I know this sounds revolutionary to the Whites in this country, because the majority of voters will be Africans. This makes the White man fear democracy. . . .

It is not true that the enfranchisement of all will result in racial domination. . . . The ANC has spent half a century fighting against racialism. When it triumphs it will not change that policy. This then is what the ANC is fighting for . . . it is a struggle of the African people, inspired by their own suffering and their own experience. It is a struggle for the right to live.

During my lifetime I have dedicated myself to this struggle of the African people. I have fought against White domination, and I have fought against Black domination. I have cherished the ideal of a democratic and free society in which all persons live together in harmony and with equal opportunities. It is an ideal which I hope to live for and to achieve. But if needs be, it is an ideal for which I am prepared to die.

Mary Benson, ed., *The Sun Will Rise: Statements from the Dock by Southern African Prisoners.* London: International Defence and Aid Fund for Southern Africa, 1979.

DOCUMENT 7: LETTER TO WINNIE

Mandela was sentenced to life imprisonment in 1964, and throughout the late 1960s and 1970s it was impossible for him to communicate with his supporters or with the ANC. He was denied access to news, and the few letters each year he was allowed to write or send to his family were read by prison guards and heavily censored. In a letter of October 26, 1976, he writes to his wife, Winnie, comparing his situation to the dry Karoo desert.

To Winnie:

I have been fairly successful in putting on a mask behind which I have pined for the family, alone, never rushing for the post when it comes until somebody calls out my name. I also never linger after visits although sometimes the urge to do so becomes quite terrible. I am struggling to suppress my emotions as I write this letter.

I have received only one letter since you were detained, that one dated 22 August. I do not know anything about family affairs, such as payment of rent, telephone bills, care of children and their expenses, whether you will get a job when released. As long as I don't hear from you, I will remain worried and dry like a desert.

I recall the Karoo I crossed on several occasions. I saw the desert again in Botswana on my way to and from Africa—endless pits of sand and not a drop of water. I have not had a letter from you. I feel dry like a desert.

Letters from you and the family are like the arrival of summer rains and spring that liven my life and make it enjoyable.

Whenever I write you, I feel that inside physical warmth, that makes me forget all my problems. I become full of love.

Fatima Meer, *Higher than Hope: 'Rolihlahla We Love You.'* Johannesburg: Skotaville, 1988.

DOCUMENT 8: A CALL TO THE PEOPLE

On the fourth anniversary of the 1976 Soweto Uprising, when the police notoriously opened fire on protesting black schoolchildren (and the twenty-fifth anniversary of the June 1955 Freedom Charter), Mandela managed to smuggle a statement out of Robben Island.

Published by the ANC abroad, Mandela's message is not only one of remembrance, but also of hope for the continuing struggle against apartheid.

The gun has played an important part in our history. The resistance of the black man to white colonial intrusion was crushed by the gun. Our struggle to liberate ourselves from white domination is held in check by force of arms. From conquest to the present, the story is the same. . . .

Apartheid is the rule of the gun and the hangman. The Hippo [armored car], the rifle, and the gallows are its true symbols. These remain the easiest resort, the ever ready solution of the race-man rulers of South Africa.

In the midst of the present crisis, while our people count the dead and nurse the injured, they ask themselves: What lies ahead? From our rulers, we can expect nothing. They are the ones who give orders to the soldier crouching over his rifle, theirs is the spirit that moves the finger that caresses the trigger. Vague promises, tinkerings with the machinery of apartheid, constitution juggling, massive arrests and detentions, side by side with renewed overtures aimed at weakening and forestalling the unity of us blacks and dividing the forces of change—these are the fixed paths along which they will move. For they are neither capable nor willing to heed the verdict of the masses of our people.

The verdict is loud and clear: Apartheid has failed. Our people remain unequivocal in its rejection. The young and the old, parent and child, all reject it. At the forefront of the 1976–1977 wave of unrest, were our students and youth. They come from the universities, high schools and even primary schools. They are a generation whose whole education has been under the diabolical design of the racists to poison the minds and brainwash our children into docile subjects of apartheid rule. But after more than 20 years of Bantu Education, the circle is closed and nothing demonstrates the utter bankruptcy of apartheid as the revolt of our youth. The evils, the cruelty and the inhumanity of apartheid have been there from its inception. And blacks, Africans, Coloured and Indians, have opposed it all along the line. . . .

We face an enemy that is deep-rooted, an enemy entrenched and determined not to yield. Our march to freedom is long and difficult. But both within and beyond our borders the prospects of victory grow bright. The first condition for victory is black unity. Every effort to divide the blacks, to woo and pit one black group against another, must be vigorously repulsed. Our people—African, Indian, Coloured and democratic whites—must be united into a single massive and solid wall of resistance, of united mass action. . . .

We who are confined within the grey walls of the Pretoria regime's prisons reach out to our people. With you we count those who have perished by means of the gun and the hangman's rope.

We salute all of you—the living, the injured and the dead, for you have dared to rise up against the tyrant's might. Even as we bow at their graves we remember this: The dead live on as martyrs in our hearts and minds, a reproach to our disunity and the host of shortcomings that accompany the oppressed, a spur to our efforts to close ranks, and a reminder that the freedom of our people is yet to be won. We face the future with confidence. For the guns that serve apartheid cannot render it unconquerable. Those who live by the gun shall perish by the gun.

Between the anvil of united action and the hammer of the armed struggle we shall crush apartheid and white minority racist rule.

Mary Benson, *Nelson Mandela.* London: PANAF, 1980.

DOCUMENT 9: I CANNOT SELL MY BIRTHRIGHT TO BE FREE

During the early 1980s, President P.W. Botha repeatedly offered Mandela his freedom on one or another condition: such as that the ANC relinquish the armed struggle or that Mandela accept the so-called independence of the homelands. But the South African government refused to make any concessions of their own, such as unbanning the ANC and the PAC, repealing any apartheid laws, or renouncing their own violent policies. In 1985 Mandela managed to smuggle out a statement in response to Botha's offer of conditional release. His daughter Zindzi Mandela read the statement at a mass rally in Jabulani Stadium in Soweto on February 10, 1985.

I am a member of the African National Congress. I have always been a member of the African National Congress and I will remain a member of the African National Congress until the day I die. Oliver Tambo is much more than a brother to me. He is my greatest friend and comrade for nearly fifty years. If there is any one amongst you who cherishes my freedom, Oliver Tambo cherishes it more, and I know that he would give his life to see me free. There is no difference between his views and mine. I am surprised at the conditions that the government wants to impose on me. I am not a violent man. My colleagues and I wrote in 1952 to Malan asking for a round-table conference to find a solution to the problems of our country, but that was ignored. When Strijdom was in power, we made the same offer. Again it was ignored. When Verwoerd was in power, we asked for a national convention for all the people in South Africa to decide on their future. This, too, was in vain.

It was only then, when all other forms of resistance were no longer open to us, that we turned to armed struggle. Let Botha show that he is different than Malan, Strijdom, and Verwoerd. Let him renounce violence. Let him say that he will dismantle apartheid. Let him unban the people's organization, the African National Congress. Let him free all who have been imprisoned, banished, or exiled for their opposition to apartheid. Let him guarantee free political activity so that people may decide who will govern them.

I cherish my own freedom dearly, but I care even more for your freedom. Too many have died since I went to prison. Too many have suffered for the love of freedom. I owe it to their widows, to their orphans, to their mothers, and to their fathers who have grieved and wept for them. Not only I have suffered during these long, lonely wasted years. I am not less life loving than you are. But I cannot sell my birthright, nor am I prepared to sell the birthright of the people to be free. I am in prison as the representative of the people and of your organization, the African National Congress, which was banned.

What freedom am I being offered while the organization of the people remains banned? What freedom am I being offered when I may be arrested on a pass offense? What freedom am I being offered to live my life as a family with my dear wife who remains in banishment in Brandfort? What freedom am I being offered when I must ask for permission to live in an urban area? What freedom am I being offered when I need a stamp in my pass to seek work? What freedom am I being offered when my very South African citizenship is not respected?

Only free men can negotiate. Prisoners cannot enter into contracts. . . .

I cannot and will not give any undertaking at a time when I and you, the people, are not free.

Your freedom and mine cannot be separated. I will return.

Sheridan Johns and R. Hunt Davis Jr., eds., *Mandela, Tambo, and the African National Congress: The Struggle Against Apartheid, 1948–1990*. New York: Oxford University Press, 1991.

DOCUMENT 10: LETTER TO PRESIDENT P.W. BOTHA

The following is excerpted from a statement that Mandela wrote prior to meeting with President P.W. Botha in July 1985. Mandela stresses the need for the ANC and the ruling National Party (NP) to meet to discuss the future of South Africa. By July 1989 South Africa had been racked by decades of repression and violence that had reached its worst levels in the mid-to-late 1980s. This violence, in addition to the plummeting currency that had massively devalued due to international sanctions, finally began to reverse the NP's obstinate refusal to enter into discussions with the ANC. This letter was published in late January 1990, just before Mandela's release from prison.

The deepening political crisis in our country has been a matter of grave concern to me for quite some time, and I now consider it necessary in the national interest for the African National Congress and the government to meet urgently to negotiate an effective political settlement. . . .

Majority rule and internal peace are like the two sides of a single coin, and white South Africa simply has to accept that there will never be peace and stability in this country until the principle is fully applied.

It is precisely because of its denial that the government has become the enemy of practically every black man. It is that denial that has sparked off the current civil strife. . . .

A meeting between the government and the ANC will be the first major step towards lasting peace in the country, better relations with our neighbor states, admission to the Organization of African Unity, readmission to the United Nations and other world bodies, to international markets and improved international relations generally.

An accord with the ANC, and the introduction of a nonracial society, is the only way in which our rich and beautiful country will be saved from the stigma which repels the world.

Two central issues will have to be addressed at such a meeting: firstly, the demand for majority rule in a unitary state; secondly, the concern of white South Africa over this demand, as well as the insistence of whites on structural guarantees that majority rule will not mean domination of the white minority by blacks.

The most crucial task which will face the government and the ANC will be to reconcile these two positions. Such reconciliation will be achieved only if both parties are willing to compromise. The organization will determine precisely how negotiations should be conducted. It may well be that this should be done at least in two stages—the first where the organization and the government will work out together the preconditions for a proper climate for negotiations. Up to now both parties have been broadcasting their conditions for negotiations without putting them directly to each other.

The second stage would be the actual negotiations themselves when the climate is ripe for doing so. Any other approach would entail the danger of an irresolvable stalemate.

Lastly, I must point out that the move I have taken provides you with the opportunity to overcome the current deadlock and to normalize the country's political situation. I hope you will seize it without delay. I believe that the overwhelming majority of South Africans, black and white, hope to see the ANC and the government working closely together to lay the foundations for a new era in our country, in which racial discrimination and prejudice, coercion and confrontation, death and destruction, will be forgotten.

Greg McCartan, ed., *Nelson Mandela: Speeches 1990.* New York: Pathfinder, 1990.

DOCUMENT 11: NOW IS THE TIME TO INTENSIFY THE STRUGGLE

On Sunday, February 11, 1990, Nelson Mandela was finally released after twenty-seven years in prison. That afternoon, he and Winnie traveled to Cape Town, where Mandela addressed enormous crowds in front of City Hall. The address, which was televised and broadcast throughout South Africa and the rest of the world, was Mandela's first public speech since the 1960s. Yet by concluding with his own words from his 1964 trial, he indicated that he and his views had remained steadfast since that time.

Today, I wish to report to you that my talks with the government have been aimed at normalizing the political situation in the country. We have not as yet begun discussing the basic demands of the struggle. I wish to stress that I myself had at no time entered into negotiations about the future of our country, except to insist on a meeting between the ANC and the government.

Mr. de Klerk has gone further than any other Nationalist president in taking real steps to normalize the situation. However, there are further steps as outlined in the Harare Declaration that have to be met before negotiations on the basic demands of our people can begin....

Negotiations on the dismantling of apartheid will have to address the overwhelming demand of our people for a democratic, nonracial, and unitary South Africa. There must be an end to white monopoly on political power and a fundamental restructuring of our political and economic systems to ensure that the inequalities of apartheid are addressed and our society thoroughly democratized.

It must be added that Mr. de Klerk himself is a man of integrity who is acutely aware of the dangers of a public figure not honoring his undertakings. But as an organization, we base our policy and strategy on the harsh reality we are faced with, and this reality is that we are still suffering under the policy of the Nationalist government.

Our struggle has reached a decisive moment. We call on our people to seize this moment so that the process towards democracy is rapid and uninterrupted. We have waited too long for our freedom. We can no longer wait. Now is the time to intensify the struggle on all fronts.

To relax our efforts now would be a mistake which generations to come will not be able to forgive. The sight of freedom looming on the horizon should encourage us to redouble our efforts. It is only through disciplined mass action that our victory can be assured.

We call on our white compatriots to join us in the shaping of a new South Africa. The freedom movement is the political home for you too.

We call on the international community to continue the campaign to isolate the apartheid regime. To lift sanctions now would be to run the risk of aborting the process towards the complete eradication of apartheid.

Our march to freedom is irreversible. We must not allow fear to stand in our way....

In conclusion, I wish to go to my own words during my trial in 1964. They are as true today as they were then. I quote:

"I have fought against white domination, and I have fought against black domination. I have cherished the idea of a democratic and free society in which all persons live together in harmony and with equal opportunities. It is an ideal which I hope to live for and to achieve. But if needs be, it is an ideal for which I am prepared to die."

Steve Clark, ed., *Nelson Mandela Speaks: Forging a Democratic, Nonracial South Africa.* New York: Pathfinder, 1993.

DOCUMENT 12: MANDELA VOTES

In the following excerpt from his autobiography, Long Walk to Freedom, *Mandela recounts the day he voted in South Africa's first multiracial free elections in April 1994. This event represented the culmination of Mandela's life-long struggle against apartheid.*

I voted on April 27, the second of the four days of voting, and I chose to vote in Natal to show the people in that divided province that there was no danger in going to the polling stations. I voted at Ohlange High School in Inanda, a green and hilly township just north of Durban, for it was there that John Dube, the first president of the ANC, was buried. This African patriot had helped found the organization in 1912, and casting my vote near his grave site brought history full circle, for the mission he began eighty-two years before was about to be achieved.

As I stood over his grave, on a rise above the small school below, I thought not of the present but of the past. When I walked to the voting station, my mind dwelt on the heroes who had fallen so that I might be where I was that day, the men and women who had made the ultimate sacrifice for a cause that was now finally succeeding. I thought of Oliver Tambo, and Chris Hani, and Chief Luthuli, and Bram Fischer. I thought of our great African heroes, who had sacrificed so that millions of South Africans could be voting on that very day; I thought of Josiah Gumede, G.M. Naicker, Dr. Abdullah Abdurahman, Lilian Ngoyi, Helen Joseph, Yusuf Dadoo, Moses Kotane. I did not go into that voting station alone on April 27; I was casting my vote with all of them.

Before I entered the polling station, an irreverent member of the press called out, "Mr. Mandela, who are you voting for?" I laughed. "You know," I said, "I have been agonizing over that choice all morning." I marked an X in the box next to the letters ANC and then slipped my folded ballot paper into a simple wooden box; I had cast the first vote of my life.

Nelson Mandela, *Long Walk to Freedom: The Autobiography of Nelson Mandela.* Boston: Little, Brown, 1994.

DOCUMENT 13: FIRST PRESIDENTIAL ADDRESS

The ANC won the April 1994 elections with an overwhelming majority, and Nelson Mandela was sworn in as the president of South Africa on May 10, 1994. In his first official address to the nation as president, Mandela affirmed his commitment to the causes of freedom for all, justice, peace, and dignity. He described the new South Africa as, finally, a "rainbow nation at peace with itself and the world."

Today, all of us do, by our presence here, and by our celebrations in other parts of our country and the world, confer glory and hope to newborn liberty.

Out of the experience of an extraordinary human disaster that lasted too long, must be born a society of which all humanity will be proud.

Our daily deeds as ordinary South Africans must produce an actual South African reality that will reinforce humanity's belief in justice, strengthen its confidence in the nobility of the human soul and sustain all our hopes for a glorious life for all.

All this we owe both to ourselves and to the peoples of the world who are so well represented here today.

To my compatriots, I have no hesitation in saying that each one of us is as intimately attached to the soil of this beautiful country as are the famous jacaranda trees of Pretoria and the mimosa trees of the bushveld.

Each time one of us touches the soil of this land, we feel a sense of personal renewal. The national mood changes as the seasons change.

We are moved by a sense of joy and exhilaration when the grass turns green and the flowers bloom.

That spiritual and physical oneness we all share with this common homeland explains the depth of the pain we all carried in our hearts as we saw our country tear itself apart in a terrible conflict, and as we saw it spurned, outlawed and isolated by the peoples of the world, precisely because it has become the universal base of the pernicious ideology and practice of racism and racial oppression.

We, the people of South Africa, feel fulfilled that humanity has taken us back into its bosom, that we, who were outlaws not so long ago, have today been given the rare privilege to be host to the nations of the world on our own soil.

We thank all our distinguished international guests for having come to take possession with the people of our country of what is, after all, a common victory for justice, for peace, for human dignity.

We trust that you will continue to stand by us as we tackle the challenges of building peace, prosperity, non-sexism, non-racialism and democracy.

We deeply appreciate the role that the masses of our people and their political mass democratic, religious, women, youth, business, traditional and other leaders have played to bring about this conclusion. Not least among them is my Second Deputy President, the Honourable F.W. de Klerk. . . .

We have, at last, achieved our political emancipation. We pledge ourselves to liberate all our people from the continuing bondage of poverty, deprivation, suffering, gender and other discrimination.

We succeeded to take our last steps to freedom in conditions of relative peace. We commit ourselves to the construction of a complete, just and lasting peace.

We have triumphed in the effort to implant hope in the breasts of the millions of our people. We enter into a covenant that we shall build the society in which all South Africans, both black and white, will be able to walk tall, without any fear in their hearts, assured of their inalienable right to human dignity—a rainbow nation at peace with itself and the world.

As a token of its commitment to the renewal of our country, the new Interim Government of National Unity will, as a matter of urgency, address the issue of amnesty for various categories of our people who are currently serving terms of imprisonment.

We dedicate this day to all the heroes and heroines in this country and the rest of the world who sacrificed in many ways and surrendered their lives so that we could be free.

Their dreams have become reality. Freedom is their reward.

We are both humbled and elevated by the honour and privilege that you, the people of South Africa, have bestowed on us, as the first President of a united, democratic, non-racial and non-sexist government. . . .

Never, never and never again shall it be that this beautiful land will again experience the oppression of one by another and suffer the indignity of being the skunk of the world.

Let freedom reign.

The sun shall never set on so glorious a human achievement!

God bless Africa!

Nelson Mandela, Inaugural Address, May 10, 1994.

Discussion Questions

Chapter 1

1. How does Martin Meredith describe Nelson Mandela's father? Characterize the relationship between the younger and older Mandelas. In what ways did the young Mandela resemble his father? Cite evidence from the text to support your answers.
2. According to Martin Meredith, what were the various facets of Mandela's education? What role did oral history play in Thembu society in general, and in Mandela's life specifically? Did the different facets of Mandela's education contradict each other? If so, in what ways?
3. According to Virginia Curtin Knight, what did Mandela learn from Jongintaba that he later applied to his own conception of African democracy?
4. According to Fatima Meer, why was Mandela in Johannesburg and how did he manage to remain there? In his subsequent letters about this time, what aspects of Mandela's early days in the metropolis did he recall most fondly?

Chapter 2

1. Why was 1948 such a critical year in South African history? Citing examples from the text, list and explain three of the new laws passed after 1948. How did this new legislation affect ANC policy and what specific changes did it elicit?
2. Stephen M. Davis argues that the ANC changed after World War II. Why does he suggest the organization shifted in this way? In what ways was the ANC transformed? What role did Mandela play in these changes?
3. According to Anthony R. DeLuca, what were Mandela's various responses to the increased repression of black South Africans that occurred after the Nationalist Party came to power in 1948? What were Mandela's initial strategies during the late 1940s and early 1950s? How had his

tactics shifted by the mid-1950s? How did the Sharpeville Massacre affect Mandela and the ANC's policies?

CHAPTER 3

1. According to Mandela's account of the Rivonia Trial, what were the state's key pieces of evidence? How did Mandela respond to the state's charges? Why did he choose this strategy and what did he hope to accomplish? What arguments of the defense did the state accept? Cite two examples from the text.
2. Referring to Mandela's piece on the Rivonia Trial, what was the sentence of Mandela and the others accused at the trial? How did Justice de Wet reach this decision and why? How did Prime Minister Verwoerd respond to the sentencing decision?
3. According to Joel Joffe, what were the advantages and disadvantages of Mandela taking the stand? What did Mandela decide to do? What specific factors influenced his decision?
4. According to prisoner Mac Maharaj, conditions on Robben Island changed in certain ways over the years. What brought about these changes?
5. What impression does Mac Maharaj give of Mandela? Compare and contrast Maharaj's views with those of Eddie Daniels and James Gregory. How do their different perspectives shape their respective impressions? Do you feel that one of the characterizations is most accurate? Why?
6. According to fellow prisoner Eddie Daniels, how did Mandela's leadership role continue on Robben Island? Cite examples from the text of various instances when he was called upon to lead other prisoners. What was Daniels's attitude toward Mandela's assumption of this role?
7. What did prison warder James Gregory believe about Nelson Mandela and the other political prisoners prior to his arrival at Robben Island? What were the reasons for his views? Using examples from the passage, explain how Gregory's views came to change after his first encounters with the prisoners. What were his reactions to the prisoners?

CHAPTER 4

1. Journalist René du Preez writes about the long-awaited day of Mandela's release from prison. How did South Africans react to this event? How did Mandela react to all the attention directed at him? What was his first greeting to the people?

2. According to Don Boroughs, why was reconciliation such an important ideal in South Africa in 1994? What actions did Mandela himself perform in order to ensure that he was setting a strong personal example of the spirit of reconciliation? Cite examples from the text.
3. Does the author of the *Economist* article feel that Mandela has registered concern with some of President Thabo Mbeki's actions and policies? If so, use the text to elaborate on what some of these problems may be. Compare and contrast Nelson Mandela and Thabo Mbeki's responses to the AIDS crisis in South Africa.

Chronology

1912

The South African Natives National Congress (SANNC), the forerunner of the African National Congress (ANC), is founded.

1913

The Natives Land Act divides land ownership into separate areas for blacks and whites, and restricts African land ownership to 13 percent of the country.

1918

On July 18, Nelson Mandela is born at Qunu, near Umtata. His father, Henry Mgadla Mandela, is chief councillor to Thembuland's acting paramount chief, David Dalindyebo.

1923

The Native (Urban) Areas Act segregates cities by race; the Industrial Conciliation Act excludes African migrant workers from trade unions.

1930–1937

Mandela's father dies and Nelson moves to Mqekezwini, where he becomes the ward of his father's relative Chief Jongintaba and attends the local school. He then moves to Healdtown Methodist Boarding School, from which he graduates in 1937.

1938

Mandela and his cousin Jongintaba enroll in a bachelor's degree program at Fort Hare University in Alice.

1939

Jan Smuts is reelected prime minister and South Africa enters World War II on the Allied side.

1940

Mandela is expelled from Fort Hare for participating in a student strike. Alfred Xuma becomes ANC president.

1941–1943

Mandela arrives in Johannesburg, meets Walter Sisulu, enrolls in legal studies at the University of the Witwatersrand. He works as an articled clerk and joins the ANC.

1944

Mandela forms the ANC Youth League (ANCYL) with Anton Lembede, A.P. Mda, Oliver Tambo, and Walter Sisulu. Mandela marries Eveline, Sisulu's cousin.

1946

The African Mineworkers' Strike takes place.

1947

Mandela is elected secretary of the ANC Youth League; Oliver Tambo becomes its vice president.

1948

On May 26, D.F. Malan's Nationalist Party (NP) wins the national elections by a close margin, ushering in nearly five decades of NP rule and the official implementation of the apartheid system.

1949

Mandela and Tambo are elected to the executive of the ANC; Tambo becomes ANC secretary.

1950

Major apartheid legislation is passed: The Population Registration Act classifies all South Africans by race, the Group Areas Act zones people to live in certain areas by race, and the Immorality Amendment Act and Suppression of Communism Act restricts social and political freedoms.

1951

Mandela is elected ANCYL president.

1952

Mandela is elected ANC Transvaal president, deputy national president, and national volunteer-in-chief of the 1952 Defiance Campaign. He travels the country organizing resistance to discriminatory legislation, is subsequently arrested and briefly imprisoned, and later in the year is banned along with fifty-one others. The Defiance Campaign ends.

1953

Mandela and Tambo open the first black law practice in the country in the city of Johannesburg.

1954-1955
Mandela formulates the M-Plan, dividing the ANC into smaller units that will operate from underground.

1955
On June 26, the Freedom Charter is adopted at Kliptown at the Congress of the People; Congress of South Africa Trade Unions (COSATU) is formed. Nelson and Eveline separate. Nelson meets Winnie.

1956-1961
Nelson Mandela is one of 156 activists charged with high treason during the "Treason Trial," but he is ultimately acquitted.

1960
On March 30, police kill 69 anti-pass law demonstrators and injure 180 in the Sharpeville Massacre. A state of emergency is declared; African and Coloured representation in Parliament (by whites) is ended; the ANC and PAC are banned and go underground. Mandela is detained until 1961 when he goes underground to lead a campaign for a new national convention.

1961
Mandela and others found Umkhonto we Sizwe (Spear of the Nation, MK), the paramilitary wing of the ANC, to sabotage government property and economic infrastructure. South Africa becomes a republic and leaves the British Commonwealth. The UN General Assembly imposes sanctions against South Africa.

1962
Mandela leaves the country for military training in Algeria and to arrange training for other MK members. On his return he is arrested for leaving South Africa illegally and for inciting others to strike. He conducts his own defense and is convicted and sentenced to a five-year jail term in November.

1964
While serving his sentence, Mandela is charged again, retried in the Rivonia Trial, and sentenced to life imprisonment on June 12, along with Walter Sisulu and others.

1967
Oliver Tambo becomes acting president-general of the ANC; the Terrorist Act is passed, allowing the government to hold people in indefinite detention without trial.

1975

Chief Mangasotho Buthalezi forms Inkatha Freedom Party (IFP).

1976

On June 16, black schoolchildren protest the imposition of Afrikaans as the language of instruction at schools, and police open fire on them during the famous Soweto Uprising. Dozens of children are shot, and in the violence that ensues over the next few days, hundreds of people are killed.

1980

MK sabotages a Sasol oil refinery.

1982

MK attacks Koeberg nuclear power station.

1984–1986

Police troops move into the black townships to quell growing resistance.

1985

The Mixed Marriages Act is repealed. In September, the Reagan administration imposes sanctions on South Africa and the currency begins its downward slide in the wake of mass foreign disinvestment. Mandela rejects President P.W. Botha's offers of freedom if he renounces violence.

1986

On May 19, the South Africa Defense Force attacks ANC bases in ground and air strikes in Zimbabwe, Botswana, and Zambia. On June 12, a state of emergency is imposed on the entire country, giving the government's security forces wide-ranging powers and banning all coverage of political violence. On June 25, government passes limited reforms, including an end to the pass system.

1989

F.W. de Klerk succeeds P.W. Botha as the leader of the Nationalist Party and then as president. On July 5, Mandela meets with P.W. Botha and later in the year with de Klerk. Mandela and his delegation agree to the suspension of armed struggle. The state of emergency is lifted (except in Kwazulu-Natal, where it is lifted only in 1990). Sisulu and others are released from prison.

1990

The ANC, PAC, and Communist Party are unbanned (free to

convene and operate). Mandela is released from prison. Talks between the South African government and the ANC begin.

1991

The Convention for a Democratic South Africa (CODESA) meets to draft a new constitution. Mandela is elected national president of the ANC. Several apartheid laws are repealed, including the Group Areas Act, Land Acts, Population Registration, and Separate Amenities Acts.

1992

The ongoing Inkatha-ANC violence worsened. Inkatha refuses to attend the CODESA meeting. In a whites-only referendum, a two-thirds majority endorses continuing government negotiations with the ANC and all political parties.

1993

Negotiations resume between all twenty-six political parties in South Africa. A transitional constitution is adopted. Mandela and de Klerk jointly receive the Nobel Peace Prize.

1994

On April 27, the first nonracial, democratic elections in South Africa take place. The Government of National Unity is formed, headed by Mandela, who is sworn in as president on May 10. Foreign governments lift sanctions. South Africa rejoins the Commonwealth.

1999

In June, Nelson Mandela's presidential term ends and he retires from public life.

FOR FURTHER RESEARCH

BOOKS ON NELSON MANDELA

Mary Benson, *Nelson Mandela: The Man and the Movement*. New York: W.W. Norton, 1994.

Steve Clark, ed., *Nelson Mandela Speaks: Forging a Democratic, Nonracial South Africa*. New York: Pathfinder, 1993.

Brian Frost, *Struggling to Forgive: Nelson Mandela and South Africa's Search for Reconciliation*. London: HarperCollins, 1998.

Sheridan Johns and R. Hunt Davis Jr., eds., *Mandela, Tambo, and the African National Congress: The Struggle Against Apartheid, 1948–1990*. Oxford: Oxford University Press, 1991.

Nelson Mandela, *Long Walk to Freedom: The Autobiography of Nelson Mandela*. Boston: Little, Brown, 1994.

———, *Nelson Mandela: The Struggle Is My Life*. London: International Defence and Aid Fund for Southern Africa, 1990.

Winnie Mandela, *Part of My Soul Went with Him*. New York: Norton, 1984.

Fatima Meer, *Higher than Hope: 'Rolihlahla We Love You': Nelson Mandela's Biography on his 70th Birthday*. Johannesburg: Skotaville, 1988.

Martin Meredith, *Nelson Mandela: A Biography*. London: Hamish Hamilton, 1997.

Anthony Sampson, *Mandela: The Authorized Biography*. London: HarperCollins, 1999.

Jurgen Schadeburg, ed., *Nelson Mandela and the Rise of the ANC*. Johannesburg: Jonathan Ball, 1990.

Books on Apartheid and Post-Apartheid South Africa

William Beinart, *Twentieth-Century South Africa*. Oxford: Oxford University Press, 1994.

T.R.H. Davenport, *South Africa: A Modern History*. 4th ed. Toronto: University of Toronto Press, 1991.

Rian Malan, *My Traitor's Heart: A South African Exile Returns to Face His Country, His Tribe, and His Conscience*. New York: Grove, 1990.

David Mermelstein, ed., *The Anti-Apartheid Reader: The Struggle Against White Racist Rule in South Africa*. New York: Grove, 1987.

John Pampallis, *Foundations of the New South Africa*. London: Zed, 1991.

Allister Sparks, *The Mind of South Africa*. New York: Knopf, 1990.

Leonard M. Thompson, *A History of South Africa*. New Haven, CT: Yale University Press, 1996.

Nigel Worden, *The Making of Modern South Africa: Conquest, Segregation, and Apartheid*. Oxford: Blackwell, 1994.

Websites

The African National Congress Website, www.anc.org. The ANC's website is extensive but easy to navigate. By following links, one can access everything from a history of the organization to current issues facing South Africa. Specific links lead to pages covering the life and work of Nelson Mandela. A brief biography, images, and select speeches are available.

Frontline "Intimate Portrait": The Long Walk of Nelson Mandela, www.pbs.org. The PBS series *Frontline* provides this biographical site devoted to Nelson Mandela. The site is broken up into sections detailing different aspects of Mandela's life. Link take visitors to collections of news reports, biographical excerpts, interview transcripts, film clips, and more pages related to the section topic. This site is extremely well documented and provides many diverse perspectives.

South Africa Online Travel Guide, www.southafricatravel.net. This web page is part of a tourist information site on South Africa. It contains a short history of apartheid.

Other links connect to information on South African geography, history, and people. The compact, easy-to-use site gives a good overall picture of South African history and culture.

UN Historical Images of Apartheid in South Africa, www.un.org. A small page of the United Nations website contains a brief history of apartheid as well as a valuable series of photographs from the period.

INDEX

Abolition of Passes and
  Consolidation of Documents Act
  (1952), 56
Act of Union (1910), 55
Addis Ababa (Ethiopia), 79–80
African National Congress (ANC),
  17–18, 116
  accused of planning armed
    invasion of South Africa, 91
  competition with Pan-African
    Congress, 76
  Congress of People and, 73
  early years of, 13–16, 64
  Freedom Charter of, 45, 61, 67, 74
  leaders of, 63, 87, 120, 122, 150
    banning of, 71
    in jail, 79, 110–15, 117, 124,
      126–27
    central issues for, 116, 118–19,
      123
    prison warden's impressions
      of, 130–34
    release from prison and, 136–40
  multicultural alliance sought by,
    55, 60, 70
  90th anniversary of, 147–48
  Operation Mayibuye not approved
    by, 92, 95
  postapartheid and, 11, 21–22, 141,
    153
  Programme of Action and, 57
  revival of, 47–48, 49
  rivalry with Inkatha Freedom
    Party, 143, 145, 149
  Rivonia Trial and, 105–108
  Treason Trial and, 77
  underground activities of, 16, 66,
    72, 79, 91
  see also Umkhonto we Sizwe;
    Youth League
African nationalism, 58, 76
African Resistance Movement
  (ARM), 122, 124
African Union, 148

Afrikaner Volksfront, 143
AIDS epidemic, in South Africa,
  142, 144, 147
  effects of, 149
  President Mbeki's reaction to, 150,
    152, 153
  Mandela's intervention and, 151
Alexander, Neville, 93
Alexandra (township), 38, 40–43
Algeria, 80
anti-retroviral drugs, 151, 152
apartheid, 46, 48, 68, 73
  compared to Nazism, 69
  creation of homelands under, 74
  declared crime against humanity
    by UN, 53
  end of, 141
  fears of civil war and, 142–43
  international condemnation of, 21
  as rationalized system of white
    supremacy, 45, 51
  resistance to, 15–16, 58–61, 71–72
  suppression of, 57
  violent protest included in,
    17–18
  restrictive laws of, 52–54, 57, 65,
    73
    blacks disenfranchised by, 55
    economic exploitation of blacks
      under, 56
    movement and speech rights
      affected by, 71
*Apartheid's Rebels: Inside South
  Africa's Hidden War* (Stephen M.
  Davis), 63

Bantu Authorities Act (1951), 55
Bantu Education Act (1953), 56, 73
"Basic Policy of Congress Youth
  League" (document), 51
Bellamy, Carol, 152
Benson, Mary, 17, 38, 76, 81
Bernstein, Rusty, 91–92, 96, 99, 100,
  104–105

arrested at Rivonia, 20, 89
  as member of Communist Party, 95
Berrange, Vernon, 89
Bizos, George, 89, 93
Boers, 18
Boroughs, Don, 141
Botha, P.W., 21, 116
boycotts, 49, 51, 69–71
Brandfort (South Africa), 81, 85
Brezhnev, Leonid, 98
Burundi, 149
Bush, George W., 153
Buthelezi, Mangosuthu, 143, 145

Cape Colony (South Africa), 28
Cape Town (South Africa), 137–40, 150
Castro, Fidel, 78
censorship, 73
Chaskalson, Arthur, 89, 95
children, 53, 149
Christianity, 26, 28, 32, 36
  missionary education and, 28, 32–33
  mother a convert to, 25, 35
CIA (Central Intelligence Agency), 87
circumcision, 37
Clarkesbury Boarding School, 34, 37
Clinton, Bill, 148, 152
Cold War, 57–58
colonial rule, 25
  continued Western acceptance of, 58
  Mfengu adaptation to, 28
  missionary culture of, 32–33
  role of hereditary chiefs under, 29, 31
  Xhosa resistance to, 30
Communist Party, 15, 58, 95, 105, 108
  general strike called by, 69
  outlawed by Suppression of Communism Act, 55
Communists, 66–67, 77
  changing attitude toward, 70
Congo, 149
Congress Alliance, 66
Congress of Democrats (COD), 60–61, 67, 89
Congress of the People, 60–61, 67, 73–74
Congress Youth League. *See* Youth League
Constitutional Court, 150
crime, 145, 146
Criminal Law Amendment Act (1953), 57

Daniels, Eddie, 121
Davis, R. Hunt, Jr., 45
Davis, Stephen M., 14, 63
death sentence, 89, 96, 98
Defiance Campaign (1952), 15–16, 57, 60, 72
  ANC's popularity increased by, 65–66
  collaboration in, 70
  purpose of, 59
  recruitment of volunteers for, 71
de Klerk, F.W., 12, 21–22, 136, 137, 144
DeLuca, Anthony R., 68
Democratic Party, 142
Department of Prisons, 88
de Wet, Quartus, 91, 94, 95–96, 106, 107, 109
  appointed judge, 90
  sentence passed by, 97
diamonds, 48
Drum (magazine), 93, 137–38
du Preez, René, 136
Durban, 18, 87

East London (South Africa), 37, 38
Economist (magazine), 147
economy, 18, 48–49, 56, 146
  apartheid crackdown on ANC and, 59, 60
  call for nationalization of resources and, 61, 67, 73
  blacks exploited in, under apartheid, 56, 62, 72–75
education, 28, 53, 55, 61
  apartheid and, 56–57, 60, 65, 73, 120
  black African access to, 50
  missionary roots of, 32
  in prison, 114
Egypt, 80
Elizabeth II (queen of England), 148
England, 80, 98, 110
Ethiopia, 80, 88
Europe, 58, 80
Extension of University Education Act (1959), 57

Fischer, Bram, 89–91, 94–96, 99
  argues case for defense at Rivonia Trial, 104–107
  pessimism of, 93
Freedom Charter (1955), 13, 45, 61, 73–75
  endorsed as ANC's political platform, 67
Freedom Day, 70
Freedom Front Party, 143

Gadla Henry Mphakanyiswa

Index

(father), 24–28, 34, 35, 40
Gandhi, Mao, Mandela and Gorbachev: Studies in Personality, Power and Politics (DeLuca), 68
Gandhi, Mohandas, 15, 69, 70
Garvey, Marcus, 76
gold, 48
Goldberg, Dennis, 89, 104, 105
Graham, Bob, 126
Great Place, 28–29, 33, 35
Great Trek, 18
Gregory, James, 126
Group Areas Act (1950), 15, 53, 65, 69

Hanson, Harold, 94, 97
Healdtown (South Africa), 34, 37, 41
health care, 150
Hitler, Adolf, 69, 75
homelands, 47, 54, 72, 74
homelessness, 49, 145

Immorality Act, 15, 52, 69
imperialism, 58, 62
Indians, 65, 70, 77, 78
Industrial Conciliation Act (1924), 56
Inkatha Freedom Party (IFP), 143, 145, 149
Institute for Democracy in South Africa, 146
International Defense and Aid Fund for South Africa (IDAF), 110
Ismail, Wazil, 141–42

Joffe, Joel, 89, 99
Johannesburg (South Africa), 39, 79, 82, 85, 151
  arrival in, 13, 38, 40
  Congress of the People in, 67
  increase in black population of, 48
  letters from, 41–42
  townships and, 40, 53–54
  Umkhonto strikes in, 18
Johns, Sheridan, 45
Jongintaba Dalindyebo, 32, 35–41

Kantor, James, 89, 92, 104, 105
Kathrada, Ahmed, 20, 92, 105, 121, 129–30
  arrested for sabotage, 89
  defense team hesitant to question, 100
  found guilty on one count, 96
  as member of Communist Party, 95
King, Martin Luther, Jr., 80
Knight, Virginia Curtin, 34

labor policy, 74

labor unions, 49, 97–98
  see also workers' strikes
Let My People Go (Luthuli), 123
Liberal Party, 75, 97, 121
Liberation (journal), 60, 61, 62, 74
Liliesleaf Farm, 20, 79, 88
  police raid of, 89
Lincoln, Abraham, 79
Long Walk to Freedom (book), 35, 37
Luthuli, Albert, 87, 92, 123

Madiba clan, 27, 28, 34
Maharaj, Satyandranath "Mac," 10, 110, 116, 130
Mail & Guardian (newspaper), 145
Makana (Xhosa leader), 30, 31
Malan, D.F., 45, 51, 52, 68, 116
Mandela, Eveline (first wife), 39, 43
Mandela, Nelson Rolihlahla, 87
  in Addis Ababa, 79–80
  appearance of, at All-In African Conference, 78
  armed struggle a last resort for, 17–18
  arrest of, 77
  attitude of
    toward communism, 70, 108
    toward Freedom Charter, 73
  banning of, 57, 59, 71–72
  as "Black Pimpernel," 78–79
  character of, 72, 117–20, 122, 124–25
  childhood of, 24–29
  on competition between ANC and PAC, 76
  continuing celebrity of, 148
  coordination of Defiance Campaign volunteers and, 59, 66, 71
  criticism of Mbeki's approach to AIDS crisis and, 149–53
  education of, 28, 34, 37
    at Christian schools, 32–33, 36
    at Fort Hare, 38, 50
    as part of Thembu royal family, 29–31, 35
  forgiveness and reconciliation of, 11–12, 141, 143
  Gandhi an inspiration for, 15
  marriage of, 84–85
  need for peace emphasized by, 11, 13
  as president of South Africa, 144–46
  on purpose of ANC, 14, 58, 59–60, 108–109
  release of, 136–40
  Treason Trial and, 16
  work as lawyer and, 81–83

writings of, 61–62, 74, 79
Mandela, Thembi (son), 10
Mandela, Winnie Nomzano (wife), 75–76, 81, 88–89, 136, 138–39
 on first meeting, 81–83
 on marriage, 84–85
 police harassment of, 11
Mandela, Zenani (daughter), 10
Mandela, Zindzi (daughter), 10, 76
 letters to, 40–42, 116
Manuel, Trevor, 146
Maqoma (Xhosa leader), 30, 31
Mbeki, Govan, 95, 96, 105, 146
 capture of, in police raid on Liliesleaf, 89
 Operation Mayibuye and, 92
Mbeki, Thabo, 142, 146, 147, 148
 AIDS crisis and, 147, 149–53
Meer, Fatima, 39
Meredith, Martin, 24
Mfengu (refugee Christians), 27, 28
Mhlaba, Raymond, 89, 92, 96, 100, 129
 leading figure in ANC and MK in Eastern Cape, 95
migration, of Africans to urban areas, 48–49
military training, 80, 88, 107
mine workers, 41, 56, 62
missionaries, 28, 32–33, 36, 37
Mkhondo, Rich, 144, 145
Mlangeni, Andrew, 88, 89, 105, 129
Moodley, Adam, 144–45
Moroka, J.S., 69
Motsoaledi, Elias, 89, 105
M-Plan, 16, 63, 66–67, 72
Mqhekezweni, 24, 28, 29, 32, 35
Mvezo (village), 24, 26, 34, 42

Nasser, Gamal Abdel, 80
Natal, 15, 144
National Action Council of South Africa, 17
National Day of Protest (June 26, 1950), 70
National Party, 49, 141, 150
 Afrikaner dominated, 14, 65
 apartheid agenda of, 46–47, 52
 opposition to, 57
 restrictive laws and, 16
 1948 electoral victory of, 45, 48, 51, 53, 68
 pro-Nazi, 64
 role of Dutch Reformed Church in racist agenda of, 69
Native Labor (Settlement of Disputes) Act (1924), 56
Native Laws Amendment Act (1952), 53
Natives Land Act (1913), 54

Natives' Representatives Council, 55
Natives Resettlement (Western Areas) Act (1954), 53
Native Trust and Land Act (1936), 54
Nehru, Jawaharlal, 72, 73
"New Menace in Africa, A" (article), 58
New Partnership for Africa's Development, 148, 152
Ngubengcuka (great-grandfather), 32
Nigeria, 152
Ninety-Day Detention Law, 89
Nkedama, Nosekeni (mother), 25, 28, 35
Nobel Peace Prize, 12, 21–22, 123
"No Easy Walk to Freedom" (speech), 72
nonviolence, 14–16, 19, 20, 70
 as part of political protest, 17, 69

Operation Mayibuye, 92, 95, 100, 106, 107
 discovered in police raid, 89
 not carried out, 94
Orange Farm, 151, 152

Paarl (South Africa), 136, 138
Pan-Africanist Congress (PAC), 45, 88, 122, 126, 136
 based on "Africans only" policy, 58
 founding of, 76
 outlawed under Suppression of Communism Act, 77
Paton, Alan, 97
Piot, Peter, 150, 152
police, 11, 97, 144, 149
 brutality of, 123
 empowered to suppress opposition to apartheid, 57
 informants in ANC and, 66, 87
 raid on Liliesleaf by, 88, 89
Pollsmoor Prison, 121, 126
Population and Registration Act, 15, 52, 69
Port Elizabeth (South Africa), 18, 30, 137
poverty, 49, 54, 60, 77, 149
 for blacks, caused by apartheid policies, 72–73, 74, 75
 linked to violence, 145
Pretoria Local (prison), 88, 91, 98
Pretoria University, 104
Prevention of Illegal Squatting Act (1951), 54
Programme of Action, 51, 57, 69
Prohibition of Mixed Marriages Act (1949), 52, 69

Promotion of Bantu Self-
  Government Act (1959), 46–47
Public Safety Act (1953), 46, 57

Qunu (village), 26–28, 34–35

racism. *See* apartheid; white
  supremacy
Rand Daily Mail (newspaper), 53,
  94
Reservation of Separate Amenities
  Act (1953), 54
resettlement policies, 53, 72
  mass evictions and, 54
Rivonia Trial, 19–21, 88, 90–93, 137
  aftermath of, 98
  case for defense in, 105–106
  lives of accused at stake in, 100
  Mandela's role in, 94, 102–104,
    107–109
  sentencing in, 97
  verdict of, 96
  volume of evidence in, 99
  witnesses in, 95, 101
Robben Island, 29, 87, 127, 130, 139
  changes among ANC prisoners
    on, 117–18
  Mandela imprisoned on, 10, 20,
    137
    daily routine and, 112–15,
      131–32
    living conditions and, 110–11,
      128–29
    other prisoners' impressions
      and, 119–20, 121–25
    refusal of conditional release
      and, 116
    warden's impression of, 126
  nighttime at, 133
  shrine for political prisoner on,
    123
  warden's reflection about, 134
  Xhosa leaders on, 24, 30–31

Sabotage Act, 88, 90, 93
satyagraha, 15, 17
Sauer, Paul, 47
segregation, 14, 54, 55, 57, 74
  before apartheid, 50, 52
  in education, 56–57
  forced resettlement and, 53–54
  by Group Areas Act, 15, 65, 69
  in jail, 104
Sharpeville massacre, 47, 76–77
Shaw, William, 32
Sisulu, Walter, 10, 15, 129, 133
  changes in ANC policies and, 14,
    63
  imprisonment on Robben Island
    and, 20, 117, 121, 126, 130

Mandela's first contact with, 38,
    39, 43
  Rivonia Trial and, 95
  Treason Trial and, 89, 91, 93, 96,
    105
Smuts, Jan, 64
Sobukwe, Robert, 76
Sophiatown, 40, 72
South Africa, 59
  changes in society of, 50
  Christianity in, 36
  demonstrations throughout, 97–98
  described as "rainbow nation," 22
  end of apartheid in, 110
  international attention focused on,
    47, 93, 97, 98
  as part of global movement
    against imperialism, 58
  plutonium supplied to U.S. by, 87
  postapartheid and, 141–45, 149
  turning points in history of, 68,
    73–74
  urbanization of, 48–49
  white supremacist legal structure
    of, 60
South Africa Amendment Act
  (1956), 55
"South Africa Goes on Trial"
  (*Drum*), 93
South African Colored People's
  Organization (SACPO), 60–61, 67
South African Congress of Trade
  Unions (SACTU), 60–61, 67
South African Indian Congress
  (SAIC), 58, 67, 69, 70
  ANC's Defiance Campaign
    supported by, 57
  Freedom Charter endorsed by,
    60–61
  two-year protest against
    repressive laws organized by, 15
South Africans
  black, 12, 17, 20, 51, 65, 78
    oppression suffered by, 60
    role of, in politics, 46–48, 49
    suffering of, 72–73
      publicized by Mandela, 61–62,
        77, 108–109
    voting rights of, 55
  white, 11, 14, 18, 20, 60
    electoral monopoly of, 55
    fears of violence after Mandela's
      release and, 142–43
    Mandela's philosophy of
      tolerance toward, 13, 21
    reaction to 1961 strike and,
      16–17
    workers' rights and, 56
Soviet Union, 70
Soweto (South Africa), 53–54, 116

Spear of the Nation. *See* Umkhonto we Sizwe
squatter movements, 49, 54
State Aided Institutions Act (1957), 54
Stevenson, Adlai, 98
Steyn, Rory, 12
superstition, 42
Suppression of Communism Act (1950), 46, 65, 69, 71, 77
  prestige of Communist Party increased by, 55

Tambo, Oliver, 50, 53, 81–82, 136
  friend and colleague of Mandela, 72
  reluctance to collaborate with Communists and, 66
Thembuland, 24, 27, 28, 35
  Christian missionaries in, 32
  part of Transkeian territories, 31
  part of Union of South Africa, 25
Thembu people, 26
  subclan of Xhosa, 24, 34
  ties to royal family of, 28, 35
Totiwe, Albertina, 43
tourism, 146
Transkeian territories, 10, 31, 34, 35, 38
  missionaries active in, 32, 37
Transvaal, 15, 144
  ANC conference in, 72
Treason Trial, 16–17, 67, 75–77, 83, 85, 93
tribalism, 145
Tsukudu, Adelaide, 81–82
Tutu, Desmond, 21, 123, 152

Umkhonto we Sizwe (MK, "Spear of the Nation"), 94, 104, 123
  acknowledgement of need for violent protest by, 19–20
  desire to avoid hurting individuals and, 79
  when no other methods were available, 105
  goals of, 17–18
  Liliesleaf Farm and, 87, 89
  Operation Mayibuye and, 92, 106
  recognized head of, 119
unemployment, 145, 146
UNICEF (United Nations Children's Fund), 152
Union of South Africa, 25, 47
United Democratic Front (UDF), 137, 138
United Nations (UN), 53, 58, 77, 93, 98
United Party, 17, 90
United States, 14, 58, 87, 98
  imperialism of, 62
University College at Fort Hare, 34, 41, 50, 68
  Mandela suspended from, 39
  training ground for African elite, 38
University of Cape Town, 139
University of South Africa, 50
University of Witwatersrand, 43
urbanization, 48–49
U.S. News & World Report (magazine), 141

Verwoerd, Betsie, 143
Verwoerd, Hendrik H.F., 16–17, 73, 98, 116, 130
Victor Verster Prison, 126, 136, 137
Viljoen, Constand, 142–43
violence, 11, 64, 80, 144–45
  ANC/MK adoption of, 10
  in absence of any other choice, 13, 19, 78–79
  offer to abandon, if negotiation rights granted, 20
  targeting government installations rather than people, 12, 17–18
  need for organized use of, 119
  postapartheid, 141, 142–43
voting rights, 55, 75

Weekly Mail (newspaper), 121
white supremacy, 45, 50, 51, 60–61, 64
  Bantu Education Act and, 73
Wolpe, Harold, 88, 89
women, 36, 56, 152
  active in freedom movement, 75
  call for equal pay, 61
workers' strikes, 16–17, 49, 51, 64, 69, 78
World War II, 14, 48, 49, 64

Xhosaland, 27, 28
Xhosa people, 24, 29–31, 34, 37
  Christian missionaries and, 32–33
Xuma, Alfred Bitini, 48, 49, 50, 64–65, 69

Youth League (ANCYL), 47, 50, 65
  coup against Xuma organized by, 69
  founded in 1944, 13
  goals of, 51
Yutar, Percy, 90–91, 101, 106–107
  failure of, to understand the accused, 103–104

Zulus, 79, 132, 143

WAKE TECHNICAL COMMUNITY COLLEGE

3 3063 00150839 8

Wake Tech. Libraries
9101 Fayetteville Road
Raleigh, North Carolina 27603-5696

WN DATE DUE

GAYLORD · PRINTED IN U.S.A.

OCT '09